3

PRAISE FOR SUSAN DUNLAP AND HER "FEISTILY ATTRACTIVE"* PROTAGONIST, BERKELEY HOMICIDE COP JILL SMITH

"Susan Dunlap is the leading proponent of gutsy, nontraditional women who nimbly tread in he-man territory."
—*The Washington Times*

"TOO CLOSE TO THE EDGE is the third Jill Smith mystery written by Dunlap, who has been called 'one of the Great Hopes of the policewoman procedural novel.' With her latest book, Dunlap has more than lived up to that hope."
—*The Sacramento Union*

"Jill Smith is a welcome addition to the ranks of fictional cops—a skilled investigator who is equally at home undercover on the colorful streets of Berkeley and in uniform in her squad car."
—Marcia Muller, author of *There's Nothing to Be Afraid Of*

"TOO CLOSE TO THE EDGE is a very good work, effectively plotted and with an impressive feel for the people and the milieu."
—*Jury Box*

D0956638

TOO CLOSE TO THE EDGE

A Jill Smith Mystery by

Susan Dunlap

A DELL BOOK

Published by
Dell Publishing
a division of
Bantam Doubleday Dell Publishing Group, Inc.
666 Fifth Avenue
New York, New York 10103

A special thanks for their invaluable help in answering my questions to
the Berkeley Police Department, and to Vince Alire.

For information address: St. Martin's Press, New York, New York.

The trademark Dell ® is registered in the U.S. Patent and Trademark
Office.

ISBN: 0-440-20356-2

Reprinted by arrangement with St. Martin's Press

Printed in the United States of America
Published simultaneously in Canada

July 1989

10 9 8 7 6 5 4

RAD

For Jennie Arndt

pan (frying/sauce)
popcorn
butter
~~mayonaise~~
basquick
corn meal
cat fud
litter

CHAPTER 1

In Berkeley, California, nothing is too inconsequential to be the center of controversy. No restaurant extends its hours without a committee of neighbors investigating its delivery schedule, its garbage standard, its compliance with noise ordinances. The chopping down of a shade tree can give birth to a neighborhood committee. Plans to add a bedroom that would block a neighbor's view can create a crusade. People in Berkeley love their city and its liberal heritage, and they are prepared to defend it against all comers—and against each other. The battles are fierce, attenuated, bitter, and, deep down, enjoyed by all.

So, it came as no surprise when the new city council's plan to deal with the problem of people living in vehicles on the streets was met with anger. For as long as I could remember, it wasn't unexpected to find purple or green converted school buses parked permanently on industrial streets, or pickup trucks with six-foot-high wooden shells and bubble skylights in front of stucco duplexes, or ancient Plymouth wagons with makeshift curtains squatting at the curbs in West Berkeley. The occupants of those vehicles had come to town as transients, on the way to the town where things would work out, where someone would give them a job, where someone would trust them to rent a house with no first and last month's rent and no deposit. Maybe the tolerant atmosphere of Berkeley reassured them. Maybe they were encouraged by the number of people who worked part-time, trading security for daylight hours so they could do what they wanted. Maybe they just ran out of gas or hope. Whatever the reason, some of those vehicles had been parked on the streets for years. When neighbors complained, the owners pumped up the tires and got a push or a tow two blocks east or north. Most Berkeleyans had lived on the edge at one time or another, or had a friend who did, or maybe a daughter or a son. There was a lot of sympathy for the impoverished bus people, and no small measure of envy of their freedom. The arrangement could have gone on for years, if the vehicle dwellers hadn't come, almost as if by centrifugal force, closer and closer together, until the taxpayers in that small area whose curbs they inhabited took their complaints to the new city council.

Had they been the city council of Phoenix, or Charleston, or almost anywhere else, they could have forced the bus people to move on. But not here. Berkeleyans endorsed the right to live in cars and buses, as long as those vehicles were not parked by their driveways. The issue of the bus people had become a well-wedged thorn in the municipal side.

With one swift move, the city council yanked it out. They ordered the police to tow all such vehicles off the streets to an unused lot near the city dump. The lot, christened Rainbow Village, was half the size of a city block, with no trees, no grass, no paved road, no electricity hookups, and no plumbing. But the bus people were used to living without easy access to running water and plumbing. What they had now was legitimacy.

All in all, it seemed a stroke of genius. Until the uproar started.

Residents of the poor neighborhoods, from which the buses and cars had been removed, complained that the city should have allotted the funds involved to upgrading their blocks rather than nurturing transients. Developers grumbled that the site of Rainbow Village offered a view of the inlet and, across it, the entire city of Berkeley. Although it was next to the dump, it was still immensely valuable bayfront property. The dump, they pointed out, was temporary—until its dead branches, threadbare sofas, and mounds of household garbage grew high enough to create a hummock of "land" at the end of the marina.

Berkeleyans with less direct monetary concerns feared that the accommodation of transients would become a tacit invitation to ne'er-do-wells nationwide. And the Rainbow Villagers themselves soon divided into factions—those in favor of open access to their controversial acreage, and those determined to keep newcomers from overcrowding the lot.

Within a year of its creation, Rainbow Village was the scene of a double murder. The victims were "Deadheads," young transients who floated between Grateful Dead concerts. That case was unusual; in Homicide-Felony Assault, most of our calls were assaults.

And today's was no exception. I wasn't surprised at the call; I'd been to the village on assaults often enough. It was only the hour that amazed me. It was eight in the morning. I was barely awake myself. And for Rainbow Village, this was the middle of the night.

I turned right, off the bumpy extension of University Avenue that led from Berkeley proper out to this peninsula. To my left was the boat marina where masts of sailboats thrust up toward the fog-laden sky. The salty smell of the bay mixed with the aroma of bacon from the Marriott Inn kitchen next to it. To my right was an empty lot, empty for the moment. It, and most of the shore front, had been bones of contention between the Santa Fe Railroad, the owner, and the city of Berkeley. In a few months builders would start breaking ground for a cluster of small shops oriented to the sports-minded consumer who could be expected to take advantage of the park land the city had managed to salvage.

The Berkeley marina was shaped like the profile of a face, with an exaggeratingly protruding brow, deeply sunken eyes, a long bulbous nose, and chins that melted into neck with no lines of demarcation. The docks were nestled in the eye socket, the sports complex and open land would be on the chins. I drove on, north toward the end of the nostril where Rainbow Village sat.

Fog blew in across San Francisco Bay, but Rainbow Village was sheltered by the landscaped hillside that had been the city dump—the bulb of the nose. A paved path and the hedge beside it marked the ridge overlooking the village. Even the inlet, between the nose and the body proper of the city, was calm.

Rainbow Village itself looked like an abandoned car lot. A hurricane fence surrounded the half-acre of decrepit vehicles, some rusted, some decorated with psychedelic colors their owners must have saved from the sixties, and some just deflated with time. The residents were asleep in the cabs of their pickups or the lofts of their buses. There had been all-night parties here, with music loud enough to wake guests at the Marriott Inn. Perhaps the villagers had learned to sleep through these celebrations, or perhaps they had trained themselves to take advantage of the normally quiet hours of morning. Not one of them was up listening to Brad Butz yelling at Paul Murakawa, the beat officer.

Whatever the assault had been, it was over now. And from the look of Brad Butz, flailing an arm as he yelled, his only serious injury had been rumpled self-esteem. This was the type of incident normally handled by the beat officer. Murakawa had been on beat over a year. What prompted him to call for a detective was Brad Butz, the contractor for one of the buildings planned here, his City Hall connections, and his history of complaining about the police.

Butz was an odd mixture. His hair stood out around his high forehead like a dark, wiry halo. He looked to be a bit shy of forty, ten years older than I. He was taller than average, but not much. His body had been developed through hard work; it was thick with muscles that blended into each other rather than the carefully delineated mounds that grew in health clubs. But there was a delicacy to his facial features—china-blue eyes, a short, chiseled nose, and a rosy flush to his cheeks that reminded me of a porcelain doll my grandmother once had. His body was as ill-suited to his face as his blustery stance was to the easily bruised feelings that so frequently caused him to call for us or about us.

Now those eyes narrowed, trying to place me. This thin, dark-haired woman with the "lines of command" just beginning to be visible around her eyes. Was she Murakawa's superior, they asked.

"Detective Smith, Homicide-Felony Assault." I flipped my shield open. "What's the problem here?"

"Some guy came at me, with my own sign pole. Look at this!" Butz pointed to his hair.

"He's got a swelling by the left coronal suture." Murakawa had applied to physical therapy school. "Refused medical attention."

"You should see a doctor, Mr. Butz, for your own protection." And ours, I might have added. "And, the D.A. will have to have a medical report to take this to court."

"Look, I can't waste time in court. I've got a building to put up here. I'm supposed to break ground in two weeks. I need space for equipment. And I need a police department competent enough to keep it safe. Now I can't even leave my sign on the site without it being torn down. Someone yanked out the new one yesterday. Fourth one! Those signs cost money, you know. So I'm out here, before these bums are awake. I figure, you know, maybe last night they got to passing the bottle, or the needle, and they forgot about my sign. So I start looking around. And this maniac comes out of nowhere, waving my sign post, screaming like a banshee, and threatening to shove me into the water."

I glanced questioningly at Murakawa.

He nodded. He'd already made notes on Butz's accusation.

"Mr. Butz," I said, "what do you think brought on this attack?"

"He's crazy, that's what. Isn't that obvious?"

"Even crazy people need something to touch them off, whether it seems reasonable to us or not."

"Leave off the amateur shrink number, huh? I used to work for the welfare department in New York. I can run that number better than you can."

Murakawa started to speak, but I held up my hand. Brad Butz was hardly the first complainant who thought he could hide the inadequacy of his evidence behind a barrage of accusations, even a Bronx-accented barrage. Using the same tone with which my grandmother had scolded me, I said, "If you expect us to be able to find your assailant, you're going to have to recall this incident calmly. Yelling isn't going to help."

It had the same result as Grandma's tone had with me. He too bit back the urge to stamp his foot and yell all the louder. Instead, he grumbled, "The guy's one of these derelicts here in Rainbow Village. He was screaming about me taking their land."

"To store your equipment?"

"Yeah. Look, I tried to reason with these people. I told them Marina Vista isn't going to be your ordinary high-rise. It's decent housing for people with disabilities, people who need some place with access, people who will appreciate a view. The city council risked a lot to let these transients stay here. The city could have lost hundreds of thousands in federal money. But do you think these people care?"

I glanced back at Murakawa. He was taking it all down.

Butz followed my glance. To Murakawa, he growled, "Hit me with my own pole. God knows where the sign is."

"Who, Mr. Butz?" I asked.

"What?"

"Who hit you? We can't put out a warrant till we have a name."

Butz glared at the dust-covered vehicles. "I can't give you a name."

"Describe him, Mr. Butz," Murakawa said.

"About average. Not heavy, but fast. He looked like a madman."

"What color hair?"

"Hair? I don't know."

"You don't know!"

"It was under a blue wool cap, okay? Look, he just looked like a lunatic—a male, Caucasian lunatic, to put it in your terms."

I sighed. "Mr. Butz, we're trying to get a report of your assault. You're not helping much."

He glared at Murakawa, then at me. "Why don't you ask those bums in there? Believe me, every one of them knows." Clearly, Butz's years with the New York City welfare department hadn't made him a bleeding heart.

"We'll deal with them. But now we're asking you," I said. I had intended to maintain a matter-of-fact tone, but I could hear the edge to my voice.

Apparently Brad Butz heard it, too. He took a half step back. "Okay," he said, "he may have been blond. I think I saw some long blond hairs flying around. He came at me like some crazed Viking. Look, you don't stop to take notes when a maniac is telling you he'll hold your head under the water until your lungs fill like wine sacks."

"Blond," I repeated. "Now as to height. You're, what, Mr. Butz, about five ten or eleven?"

He flushed, redder than Grandma's doll had ever been. "You're asking because he was smaller than me, aren't you? You think I should have taken the jerk on, right? What kind of department are you running here?"

"Mr. Butz, I'm asking you how tall you are. That's all. Look, it's not even eight-thirty in the morning. I haven't had a cup of coffee yet. You probably haven't either, right?"

He gave a grudging nod.

"Then let's finish this report as quickly as we can. We've all got things to do." I tried to catch his eyes, to cement the agreement, but he shook his head.

"Forget it," he snapped.

"You don't want to press charges?"

"Didn't you hear me? Just forget the whole thing." He turned and stalked toward a blue pickup truck, his halo of brown hair quivering with each step. "If you want to find him," he yelled, "look for a pickup with a hot tub on the back. Jerk thinks he's a Casanova. He's looking for some fool-woman's driveway to park it in. Plans to park himself in her bed. You just look for a truck with a red tub on it."

As he pulled off, Murakawa muttered, "Lousy posture, too. He's going to have a kyphosis in another ten years."

"Serves him right," I said. "Quote him as much as you can when you write this up. By the time we get back to the station, he'll be in City Hall bitching about us. And, Murakawa, round up the guy with the red hot tub."

CHAPTER 2

By the end of shift I had gone out on three more assaults, real felony-assaults, two with guns and one with a thirty-two-ounce can of mango pulp. I had dictated all three, along with my report on the Brad Butz incident, in the latter restraining my urge to comment that only in a city with Berkeley's commitment to the underdog could a man with so little work experience, imagination, or tact as Brad Butz be awarded a major contract. As for Butz's alleged assailant and his red hot tub, neither had been found. Perhaps the woman of his dreams had a more secluded driveway than most.

Normally, I would have headed for the Albany pool to swim off the day's tensions with Seth Howard, my office mate and closest friend. But Howard had disappeared at the end of shift. He'd been gone a lot lately. And there'd been a note in my IN box from Connie Pereira: "Jill, I'll be on stake-out at The Latte." She didn't ask me to join her. She didn't have to. We'd both endured the tedium of stake-outs, planted on small, hard chairs hour after hour, never being able to look openly at the target, never daring to let up the tense rhythm of: glance at, glance away, look down, breathe. Hours were spent staring at a book (without reading a word) and reminding yourself to turn the page every few minutes, to move the coffee cup around the table, not to take too big a sip and risk getting too full to run or letting the cup fall empty. And if a civilian friend spotted you and stopped to chat, the ante went up as you tried to carry on a normal conversation without breaking into the rhythm of surveillance. The only real respite was offered by another cop.

But friendship wasn't the only reason I was willing to postpone my laps in the pool. The Latte was a sidewalk café on Telegraph Avenue, my old beat. One of the few things I regretted when I was promoted to Homicide was leaving the Avenue.

When I had had the Telegraph beat, I had congratulated myself on how easily I fitted into the long-hair-and-frayed-jeans atmosphere of the area. Telegraph Avenue deadended at the University campus. There, in the early sixties, the Free Speech Movement had inaugurated the era of protests that changed the nation. The Avenue was still the spiritual center of the Berkeley counterculture, but in recent years the head shops had been replaced by computer stores, used clothing shops by designer outlets, and marginal health food restaurants that sold tan food had given way to chocolate chip cookie and pizza chains. But the bookstores remained —Cody's for new, Shakespeare's for used, Moe's for both, and Shambala for virtually anything ever printed about eastern religion or the occult. It didn't take much to draw me back there. And the added hook that Connie Pereira had used was her lack of explanation. She was a beat officer, but Telegraph wasn't her beat. What was she staking out that was important enough to call her off her own beat?

I parked three blocks away from The Latte. At five o'clock Monday afternoon, Telegraph Avenue swarmed with students from the University of California, hurrying in the chill of an April evening. The sun that had given the illusion of spring this afternoon was ready to set now, and when it sunk down behind the Pacific, it would leave no protection from the damp mists of night. I pulled my tweed jacket tighter around me, wishing I had had a sweater instead of just a cotton turtleneck under it. Street artists were just beginning to pack up their hand-tooled belts and tuck away their tarot cards. Former students eyed the remaining sidewalk displays, fingering tie-dyed T-shirts and picture jasper rings, as if this touch of the past could transport them back from civil service jobs or those endless hours in brokerage firms soothing fearful investors, back from lives suddenly so ordinary. As I strolled past Shambala, a turbaned Sikh wandered in, but the Moonies, the Rajneeshis, the Hari Krishnas who had once been as prevalent as marijuana along the Avenue were a rare sight now. A block beyond, men and women in heavy power wheelchairs drove into the Center for Independent Living to look for a new attendant, an apartment with a ramp, or a job.

Standing in a doorway across the street was Herman Ott. With his pale skin, thin blond hair, khaki pants, and yellow sweater that covered a burgeoning belly, he looked more like a canary standing on the bottom of his cage than a private detective. I picked up my pace. Herman Ott was the last person I wanted to run into. I owed him two hundred dollars. I had put in a demand from the discretionary fund three weeks ago. It hadn't come through. Ott had called me twice. If he didn't get his money soon, I'd never get another word out of him. I glanced across the street. But he hadn't moved. He might want to nag me, but he didn't want to be seen with me, not here. I hurried on to The Latte.

Leaning forward on the edge of a frisbee-sized table, Connie Pereira looked like one of the junior executives back for a cup of nostalgia. Her short blond hair was curled just a bit too carefully, her sweatshirt, down vest, and jeans had been cleaned too recently, and her book, *Strategies in the Commodities Market,* marked her as the investment maven that she was. I slid into a chair opposite her, shielded from the street by a large and well-secured potted fig tree. "So what are you after?"

She sighed. "Running shoes."

"Wouldn't shopping . . ."

"Spare me. I've heard every joke there is about this assignment. I've been here all week." She glanced around. The evening fog had begun blowing in, carrying with it the spicy tomato aroma from the take-out pizza place across the street and fetors of sweat-laden dust from the poncho of one of the drug casualties who had spent his day leaning against the wall begging for spare change. Connie shivered under the sweatshirt that must have been ample half an hour ago. The rest of the tables were empty. "There's a running shoe thief," she said. "He's been snatching shoes from yoga classes and temples where the devotees leave them outside. It's a perfect opportunity. The devotees line their shoes up on bookshelves just like a display in a store. All the thief has to do is look them over and choose what he wants. And what he wants, Jill, are the newest and most expensive running shoes."

"How many have been stolen?"

"Twelve pairs."

"Is that all? For twelve pairs the department is authorizing a stake-out? It'd be cheaper to buy the victims new shoes."

A motorcyclist cut across the one-way street and rolled to a stop, facing the curb. An ancient pickup truck screeched to a halt inches behind him. As the cyclist dismounted and dragged his bike onto the sidewalk, the pickup's driver, a youngish man with sandy dreadlocks halfway down his back, yelled, "Whatsamatter, you got your brains up your ass?" The cyclist flipped him the bird. On the sidewalk in front of us, students in down jackets hurried from classes, too caught up in their own discussions to notice the interchange across the street.

Connie shook her head. "Do you know anything about running shoes?"

"No more than I have to."

"Well, they are not cheap. Expensive describes some, and certainly the computerized ones. With them a runner can stagger home, dripping sweat from his cross-town miles, pull out a disk from the sole of his shoe, stick it in his computer, and be told where his weight fell during every one of those miles. For a shoe like that, it's several hundred dollars."

"Shin splints don't come cheap, huh?"

"Jill, you're not taking this seriously. Christ, no one all week's taken it seriously. I sit here every afternoon freezing my tits off and one of you guys comes to laugh."

Now I *was* laughing. "Maybe you could get a disk to sit on, so you'd know where your weight had settled."

Before Pereira could respond, the waiter came, and I ordered a decaf latte.

"The victims," Connie said, "are even more outraged than I am. I'm just glad it hasn't made the papers yet. Can you imagine?"

I nodded. The victims would complain that the flat feet of the police were not plodding fast enough. But community groups in the less affluent, less white neighborhoods west of San Pablo Avenue would be furious that a beat officer was sipping coffee in a café when she ought to be tracking down drug dealers and shooing prostitutes off University Avenue.

It was an issue made for Berkeley, one that would pit the

health-conscious against the race-conscious, the yuppies against the poor, the athletic against the laid-back. It would provide a field day for every newspaper columnist in the Bay Area. It had the potential to be Dan Rather's cute closing story.

"So where's your site?" I asked.

"Shake A Leg." She nodded toward the dance studio across the street. In front of it, three women in their mid-thirties stood, their dance shoes in bright plastic bags, their potentially imperiled running shoes still on their feet. The bookshelves that served as the temporary home for the foot-gear of those inside were full. One woman lifted a foot shoulder high on the wall and leaned toward it.

"Stretching the hamstring," Pereira said wearily. "They're obsessed with hamstrings. Watch now—she'll shift her leg to the side, see? Stretching adductors. Adductor muscles are always second."

One of the stretcher's companions bent her knee, grabbed her foot behind her and pulled. Pereira nodded. "Quadriceps. Not so popular as hamstrings or adductors, but nothing to overlook in the leggy world of fitness."

"You know, Connie, Murakawa would probably pay you for this assignment. He'd love to tell you what will happen to every one of those hamstrings in twenty years."

For the first time Pereira smiled. She glanced at the dance studio and back to me. "I appreciate your coming, Jill. You could be home now settled peacefully into your chaise lounge with a beer."

"Not peacefully."

She shifted her head so she could see the studio out of the side of her eye.

"Mr. Kepple, my landlord, and his hobby," I said to her unspoken question. "He's retired now. Peaceful moments are gone forever."

She looked directly toward me. "What are you going to do?"

"I don't know. I'm putting off dealing with it."

She nodded abruptly. Not dealing with a problem, even temporarily, infuriated Pereira. She had grown up in a household of non-dealers, a father who didn't deal with getting to work soon enough or sober enough to hold a job, a mother who shrugged her shoulders at the family's poverty, and two brothers who, from Connie's complaints, never dealt with anything at all. Only her fury had gotten Connie through. Over the years she'd learned to control that fury, but I could tell she was in no mood for the saga of Mr. Kepple, his irritating hobby, and my failure to set things right.

"How long have you been here?" I asked.

"Today? Two hours. You want to know what notices are on that kiosk?"

I glanced down the street at a four-foot-diameter cylinder that was well-thatched with advertisements. When I had this beat I'd seen people posting their own notices telling of Tabla lessons from an Indian master, or term-paper typing done cheap. Now posting notices was a business in itself. New ones covered the old every few days, and more than one fight had been sparked when a budding entrepreneur saw his notice going under.

The breeze had picked up in the few minutes I'd been here. It flicked Pereira's blond hair into her eyes and pressed the sleeve of her sweatshirt around her arm.

In front of us, a dark-haired man began to fold his display of Peruvian sweaters and shawls. Two men in plaid shirts stopped to grab a final look at a brown and white alpaca sweater. The shorter man stepped back and held the sweater up. His companion shook his head. But the potential buyer was not to be dissuaded so easily.

The loud whir of a heavy wheelchair stopped abruptly; the chair rolled to a halt beside the buyer. The chair's occupant was an elfin woman with russet-colored hair cut so short in front that it was almost straight. But the tight waves in back hung down to her shoulders. Against the pallor of her skin her eyes shone dark and angry; her full brows tightened and her sharp cheekbones seemed starker against the tight set of her jaw. She was wearing a thick blue cotton sweater, but still she shivered.

"Liz Goldenstern," I muttered to Pereira. Pereira raised an eyebrow in question. I held up a hand. Later, I could tell her that Liz Goldenstern had spearheaded the campaign to force every new business on the Avenue to comply with wheelchair access regulations. More than one shopkeeper complained loud and long when he realized he would have to give up rack space to create wider aisles. And Liz's crusade to move the street artists back a foot closer to the curb hadn't won her friends either.

I leaned back behind the fig tree. When I was on beat here, I'd handled enough of the demonstrations Liz ran. Liz had raised hackles, even among her supporters. She had little sympathy for excuses, and from a person with a disability she often seemed to expect greater persistence than was reasonable. I had never seen Liz leave a picket line— regardless of rain, cold, or wind—or cancel one scheduled during a rare heat spell or the Super Bowl. I had once run into her picketing outside a head shop in a downpour. Three weeks later, suffering from a cold and barely able to breathe, she was back picketing the same store, berating a man with two four-pronged canes who had deserted the line, and giving him a wink when he trudged back in.

Now the taller man moved the alpaca sweater an arm's length away and pondered it.

Clearly Liz Goldenstern had had enough. "How about choosing the right look *out* of the pathway," she demanded.

The sweater-holder spun around, his mouth pulled back in anger. It didn't take a great mind to guess what his next word was likely to be. He glanced down at Liz, hesitated, then moved aside. "No need to be a bitch about it," he snapped as she passed.

She backed up the chair. "You're not doing me a favor, you know. This is a sidewalk, not a waiting room."

"Look, lady, I moved."

"Big fucking deal."

"You people expect the world to make way for you. Just because you screwed up your life doesn't mean the world has to look out for you."

Behind them the sweater seller methodically packed his wools. Altercations on the Avenue were standard fare of the day. The shoppers who stopped to watch kept their distance as they stood, shifting from foot to foot, around the edges of the display table. Uncomfortably, they eyed the access to the street, then looked back at the combatants. A woman in a wheelchair being hassled by a guy about to lay out seventy-five dollars for a sweater seemed a natural for the underdog-conscious of Berkeley. But despite her flaccid legs and those hands that were moved from the shoulder, Liz Goldenstern was no underdog. Had an onlooker the temerity to ask her if she needed help, she would have responded, "Bullshit!"

Even the sweater-buyer seemed to be having second thoughts. He clutched the llama-pattern to his chest. "Listen lady, I . . ."

"Just move, huh?"

He hesitated, searching for a face-saving exit line.

"Hey, come back here, you," a barefoot man across the street yelled. Midway down the block a thin figure in a cap ran, skirting strollers, cutting between tables of jewelry onto the street. Dangling from one hand were a pair of silver and brown running shoes.

CHAPTER 3

As the shoe thief rounded the corner Pereira leapt over the café railing. "Get out of the way! I'm a police officer."

Taken by surprise, Liz Goldenstern backed her chair into Pereira's path. Pereira veered away toward the wall. Her hand hit Liz's arm. Liz jolted hard to the right.

"Go on," I yelled to Pereira. I jumped the railing, grabbed Liz's slight body, and pulled her upright. "You okay?"

"What do you think?" she snapped.

Across the street Pereira was running full out. I couldn't see the thief at all.

"I don't *know* how you are," I said to Liz. "That's why I'm asking. I can get medical help."

She moved her head experimentally. "And how many hours would that take?"

The onlookers inched closer, their former wariness fading. A confrontation between a wheelchair activist and a cop was perfect for an evening's diversion, and Liz was among the best at catching the crowd. There was an appealing delicacy to her face, somewhat like Brad Butz's. But while Butz's skin had the density of porcelain, looking at Liz was like gazing through a steamy window at the fire inside. And her eyes were where the steam escaped. They were never still. They flashed with anger, gleamed with satisfaction. The day we'd had cappuccino, I had seen them glisten, as Liz talked about a time before the accident when she had run a fishing boat for the Capellis, one of the biggest family-run fishing operations in the East Bay. One of the few women in the trade, she had also been one of even fewer women captains. It was a fog-thick February night on San

Francisco Bay that she'd told me about when, gambling on rumors that the herring were running off Sausalito, she had steered without lights or radio between the fleet boats and yanked net upon net of herring up over the side of her boat until it rode so low in the water that the rip tide could have scuttled it. "In thirty-six hours the limit was gone. We had a bottle of champagne for breakfast and slept the rest of the day. And we made five thousand dollars." As she talked I could see her braced on the stern of her boat, muscles tensed, eyes glowing as they were now. More than once, I had seen men stop dead in the middle of the sidewalk and stare at those eyes. Then their gazes would fall to her chair, and Liz's eyes would narrow in contempt. "They like their cripples to look normal," she'd muttered angrily then. "Like the lion with the burr in its paw. They think they could pull it out and have their own lion, grateful forever. If it were my face that was paralyzed . . ."

But it wasn't. And Liz knew how to use what she had. If she chose to make the most of this confrontation with me, I didn't have any illusions who would end up playing the bad guy. "I'm asking you if you've been injured," I said.

"I don't know yet. Maybe I won't know for days."

"If you're not sure, you should see a doctor now."

"Look, I don't need you to tell me about my body. I've seen more doctors than you'll go near in your lifetime. I can't drop everything and camp out in emergency for hours so some intern can say mine is an unusual case and he can't tell me if anything new is broken or shifted out of place without seeing every x-ray I've ever had taken, and he can't get ahold of those for days."

Shoppers, street sellers, and students crowded in behind Liz. The two men she'd been arguing with had vanished. I moved closer to her and lowered my voice. "I'll take you. They work faster for the police."

She raised hers in response. "Let me make it simple. No matter how long I wait, the doctors in emergency aren't going to take the chance of committing themselves on a 'complicated case' like mine. They figure if they're wrong I'll sue." A shade of a smile flickered at her mouth. "And I would." She shifted her shoulders to one side, then thrust them back to the other. "And I'll tell you another thing," she said, "I don't like this cowboy attitude in the police. Whatever it is you're doing here, you've got no business running over people. With you guys on the loose, a block of the Avenue is like the gantlet."

"Okay." The onlookers moved in.

Berkeley Detective Harasses Paraplegic. I didn't need that on the news. I said, "If I can't take you to a doctor, what is it I can do for you?"

"Nothing. Just get out of the way." She shifted her arm forward so her fingers encircled the drive lever, clasped it, and using her whole arm pushed it forward. The chair didn't move. She pushed again, but clearly the battery was dead.

"Well, that's all I need! I have to be at a meeting at seven; I don't have time to sit here and watch the traffic roll by."

"I'll call wheelchair repair." I said, glad to be able to take some positive action. The city of Berkeley has a sort of AAA for wheelchairs.

"Forget it. By the time they come for me and let me sit around while they diagnose the break, it'll be too late. It's not like dropping your car at the garage; there are no loaners with power chairs." She lowered her chin and breathed in short, thick breaths. "And if they're backed up, too bad. Every chair's an emergency. Someone's stuck without it." She dipped her chin and breathed again.

The onlookers had crowded closer. Behind them the traffic on Telegraph had slowed as passengers leaned out their windows for a better look.

"Get back," I shouted at the growing crowd. "Give her some air." I glared at the nearest, a middle-aged man with a bag under his arm. He edged back into the thick of the group.

Liz strained for each breath. In spite of the chill wind, a fine film of sweat coated her forehead and the inner edges of her cheeks. Sitting in the stilled power chair, she looked like the late-night, make-up-removed, ashen version of the peppery woman of ten minutes ago. Even her eyes were lifeless. She hunched forward, and I could hear the labored pull of her lungs. Then her breaths became softer, more regular. She hooked her upper arm around the back post of the chair and pulled her shoulders back.

"Clear off," I snapped at the crowd. "I'm a police officer." This time I chose an Avenue regular as the object of my glare, a guy who had reason to move when a cop told him to. I held my gaze until he and two friends turned and ambled off. The crowd wasn't hostile, not yet, but despite the three departees it was growing. If it got much larger it could ignite by spontaneous combustion regardless of what Liz Goldenstern or I did. And calling for a back-up could fan the flames.

To Liz, I said, "Where do you live?"

"Dana." Her voice was barely more than a whisper. "Why?"

"I'll give you a push."

She hooked her arm more firmly around the post. As I stepped behind her I could see the side of her face; she looked almost like she was grinning. "Strong lady," she said, more clearly.

It took me a moment to grasp the full import of her assessment. When I pushed the chair, I understood what she meant. It didn't move. But I didn't have a choice, I had to get her, and me, out of here now. I bent lower and put my back into it. It inched forward, cumbersomely, like a car with its brakes on. I had forgotten that the chair itself would weigh over a hundred pounds without Liz Goldenstern in it.

Behind us footsteps thudded on the sidewalk. I didn't turn to see how much of the crowd was following.

"Christ, I hate being pushed, like a sack of dog food in a Safeway cart," she muttered as I engineered the chair down the slant of the lowered curb to the street.

"I'm not crazy about this, myself," I said.

"Look, I didn't ask you to do me a favor."

"I know that. Half of Telegraph Avenue knows. Pushing you home is just the easiest way to deal with things. But it doesn't make your chair any lighter."

"And it was built so as not to make me a burden." There was a smile at her mouth.

I laughed. I'd known about Liz Goldenstern too long to take her outbursts personally.

As I turned the corner onto Dwight, a sandy-haired man in a Cal sweatshirt ran out of the crowd and alongside the chair. He thrust his yellow pad toward Liz's right arm like a greeting. "I'm a reporter for the *Daily Cal,*" he said, with unhidden pride. The *Daily Californian* was the university newspaper, but its readership spread beyond the campus, across the city. Nearly twenty-five thousand people picked it up every day. "You're Liz Goldenstern, right?"

"Right."

The crowd moved around the sides of the chair. I quickened our pace.

"Cops knocked you out of your chair, right?" the reporter demanded, his pad opened for business.

Liz's jaw tightened. I could almost see her weighing the options. Momentarily, I was tempted to move forward into her view, but I didn't kid myself that that would make a difference. If she planned to make use of this situation, I would just be part of the backdrop. Finally, she said, "Not now. I'm tired."

"It's news now."

"Not now," Liz repeated.

"If you wait, it'll be too late," he said, a mixture of rage and disappointment reddening his freckled face.

"If I change my mind I'll let you know. You can leave me your card."

With a sigh, he stuck the yellow pad under his arm, pulled his wallet from a rear pocket and extricated a card. Replacing the wallet, he started to speak, then changed his mind. He looked down at Liz's fingers, braced around the control lever. His own fingers tightened on the card. He glanced at me, questioningly—wouldn't I take it? Ignoring him, I stopped the chair.

The crowd had thinned to ten or twelve. They kept their distance now.

Shifting her shoulder, Liz raised her arm. She separated her first and second fingers. "Give it to me," she said, in a tone she might have used with a well-meaning child.

He swallowed audibly and thrust the card between the fingers, hard into the webbing. I could see Liz's jaw tighten with the pain as she forced herself to grasp it.

But the student reporter was too unnerved to notice. "Jason Hillerby," he said, then headed hurriedly, gratefully, up the sidewalk behind me.

I watched him go, then waited until the others began to amble off before I shoved the chair forward. I had seen Liz angry many times. But her forgiveness of this adolescent awkwardness was something I hadn't witnessed before. I wondered if this, too, were part of her public performance.

"Use the driveway here," she said. We were on Dana now. "This is my block. Dammit, look at this! The airhead who lives there"—she pointed to a Victorian on the corner —"locks his bike to the sign post and leaves it halfway across the sidewalk." I glanced from the protruding rear wheel—out just far enough to make it impossible for the chair to pass—to Liz. In the tight set of her jaw, I could see the toll her restraint had taken. Her pain, at least, was no performance. The bicycle owner was lucky to be elsewhere.

"Does it every time," Liz grumbled, as I pushed the chair down a driveway. "I don't know how many times I've told him, explained what the problem is, but do you think he can keep it in his head for a week? He's always sorry when I complain. He doesn't do it intentionally; he just doesn't think. But what difference does that make? I could keep on him, but, you know, you just get tired. I'm tired of having to spend two hours getting up and dressed in the morning. I'm tired of having to arrange my time so I can have the catheter in or out, so I don't get infected, so the infection doesn't shoot up into my kidneys, so I don't die."

She didn't look around. I wasn't sure she could turn that far. But now she kept her gaze ahead, and I had the impression that this admission, so unexpected and uncharacteristic of the public Liz Goldenstern, of even the Liz with whom I'd had cappuccino, was my thanks for the push. And I knew her well enough not to reply.

"Over there." Now her voice was crisp. "The white stucco triplex."

I pushed the chair across the street to the redwood ramp that sloped up to an alcove and two doors, one to an internal stairway and the other to the first floor flat. A thirty-foot California fan palm stood in the yard, its wind-rustled fronds making finger puppet shadows on the white stucco building. Alongside the ramp, a wisteria twined, and yellow, red, and violet freesias swayed in the window box. The building was typical of the Bay Area. Its white stucco had a vacation look about it, but the dark wood trim of the triptych windows in both flats gave it a more serious presence. At the top of the ramp the candy-sweet smell of the freesias met us. When Liz's windows were opened it would fill the apartment.

As Liz reached for her key, a dark-haired boy of eighteen or nineteen loped across the lawn. The day pack on his back bounced with each step. "You going in?" he called to Liz.

"The officer is helping me. I'm okay."

The boy stopped, stared from her to me. His soft hair settled against the sides of his head. He spun quickly and raced back the way he'd come.

Liz turned the key.

I shoved the chair forward and, once inside the living room, turned it toward the back.

"No," she said. "Just leave it by the phone. I have to run my messages."

"You want me to turn the machine on?" I asked. Immediately I was sorry.

Liz hesitated. "Thanks."

I looked down at Liz. Her ashen face was drawn. There was no ember of the normal fire in her eyes. I had seen her after hours of picketing in the damp cold, but I had never seen her look this deflated. And I had never heard her let another person do something she could manage herself. "Can I get you anything? Maybe a brandy?"

Her eyes half-closed; her first two fingers pressed hard together. "Thanks, but no." For the first time she met my gaze. "Sometimes I think it would be nice to have someone around again, someone I could count on to do things I need. Of course, the problem with malleable people is that what attracts you, attracts a lot of other people. You're not the only one who can manipulate them." She laughed ironically. "I just need to make a couple calls and deal with my messages."

"Okay," I said. "Good luck tonight." I pushed the playback button on the answering machine, waited until the tape announced the first caller, and walked out, shutting the door slowly. I stood for a moment, my brow clammy, sweat running from my armpits. For the first time I allowed myself to feel the swirling in my stomach. What would Liz Goldenstern say, I asked myself with forced wryness, if she knew how much just the thought of paralysis terrified me? Me, a homicide detective. My eyes closed; I gave my head a sharp shake; I flexed my fingers and pressed my toes down against the soles of my shoes, feeling a wave of guilt at the relief those movements gave me.

The sharp breeze slapped my face. I realized I had been standing on Liz Goldenstern's porch for minutes. I was just starting down the ramp when the voice on the tape said, "Liz, you were right; only they are up to date. My fee is dinner. Let me know when." There was an unusual tone to that voice, but that wasn't what caught my attention. The caller hadn't bothered with a name. He knew Liz would recognize his voice. I could understand that. I recognized it too. It was the voice of Herman Ott.

CHAPTER 4

It didn't surprise me that Liz Goldenstern knew Herman Ott. Ott was more of a fixture on the Avenue than Liz, or at least he'd been there a lot longer. I wasn't sure how long Liz had been spearheading the access campaign on Telegraph, but I had the impression when I got the Telegraph beat three years ago that she was fairly new. Herman Ott, on the other hand, had been around since the sixties. Then he had been an introverted student at Cal, the type who would now be a hacker. But in those precomputer days, there were only math, sciences, and philosophy for the adolescent Herman Otts to nest in. Ott had chosen philosophy. He had followed the well-worn path of social awareness, volunteering in the offices of the ACLU. But early on he realized that he had no more ability as part of a system, even one he believed in, than he had as a student of a system. From the ACLU he had shifted to doing leg work for an old Avenue detective whose ethics he could support. And over the years, his college classes had become fewer and fewer, and cases more. And when Ott's boss finally died (of natural causes) the Ott Detective Agency was born. Ott's office, which doubled as his home, was in a shabby building on the Avenue. He dealt with the shadiest of characters, but he didn't carry a gun, and I had never seen him in a fight or even a standoff. Over the years Herman Ott had come to know everyone on the Avenue, and everything they were up to.

As I came abreast of the Avenue, Connie Pereira hurried toward me. In the failing light, she looked like she had intended to run but couldn't muster the effort. Her blond hair stood out in recalcitrant clumps, and her face had an indistinct look—she had sweated her make-up off. "Jill! Where were you?" she demanded.

"Getting Liz Goldenstern home," I said, hoping I no longer resembled the woman who had stood shaking on Liz Goldenstern's porch. That fear of paralysis had haunted me since childhood. It was there whenever I swam. The hours of physical training the department required had given me a control of my body I hadn't dreamed of before. It made the possibility of losing it more terrifying. Swallowing, I asked, "What about your thief? Did you catch him?"

"What do you think? By the time I got going he was half a block away. I spotted him at the corner; then he cut down a driveway; and when I got to the garage there was no sign of him. I spent the next hour rooting through the neighboring yards. You wouldn't believe the garbage people leave piled up behind their houses. One man told me he redid his roof five years ago. Jill, the old shingles are still heaped next to the porch! And piles: compost, wood, scraps, cardboard! It's like the concept of empty space never occurred to these people. They've created a labyrinth back there. There are hundreds of places to hide. I know the shoe thief was hunkered down in one of those yards, watching me and laughing."

I almost said, "At least it's not your case," but once

you've devoted as much time as Pereira had to a case, its hold is permanent. I pulled my jacket tighter around me. There was no sign of the sun now. It had settled down into the pillow of fog behind San Francisco. Now it was just a matter of that fog becoming an ever deeper gray-brown until it signaled night proper.

But on the Avenue it might have been night already. The clutches of students who had rushed past our table an hour ago were gone. The street sellers had packed every ceramic toothbrush holder and cloisonné earring away. The Nepali import shops and the computer stores were closed, the latter with metal grates pulled across their windows. Even the pizza and the cookie take-out places were nearly deserted. The only spark of life was Pereira, kicking the sidewalk with each step.

"You can't dig him out that way," I said.

"It just makes me so mad. If I hadn't let myself get distracted, I would have had him."

"Maybe."

"No, definitely. I run every morning. I'm in good shape. I could have been on him before he had his fingers through the laces."

I turned toward her and stopped. "Look Connie, the fact is that he got away. Now the only choice you have is whether you're going to kick yourself about it for the rest of the night or get on with things."

"Yeah, well, it's not so easy," she said, continuing her pace.

"I know."

"I'm not going to let this case go back to Caldwell like this."

"So what are you going to do?"

Now it was Pereira's turn to stop. "I've given that a lot of thought while I was waiting for you. I could stake out Shake A Leg from now till Christmas and get nowhere. We could have someone on every one of these al fresco shoes spots and

still not catch him, or them. We're not going to get anywhere till we know what the plan is, right?"

Slowly, I nodded. I knew Pereira's need-a-favor tone.

"Most of the thefts have occurred on the Avenue. So it's
safe to assume that the plan is centered here."

I could see the request taking shape.

"And the person who will know what that is is Herman
Ott."

I sighed. "And you want me to ask him, right?"

"Jill, you're the master of dealing with Ott. No one, not
even the venerables in Details, has your record."

"I don't know how true that is; I've gotten maybe three
leads from him in the same number of years. I also don't
know what it says about me." Herman Ott viewed the police
in much the same way his clients did. He was just more
practical about it. He had survived all these years by knowing exactly how much he could withhold from us legally and
how much he was required by law to admit but could still
bargain for. He produced as little as possible, never incriminating information about his clients and nothing without
being paid. For his clients to confide in him was like whispering in the confessional. As for us, threats and cajoling
only devoured his minute store of patience. To say I was the
officer he dealt with best or, more accurately, least unpleas-
antly, was a dubious endorsement. "Anyway, Connie, the
department hasn't come through with the two hundred I
promised him last month. He's not going to tell me anything."

"You could at least give it a try."

I looked down at my watch. "You know Ott better than
that."

"What were you going to do that can't wait half an
hour?"

"I was going to do some laps." I was going to make myself swim laps.

"The pool's open till nine-thirty."

"And eat dinner."

Connie laughed. "You cán buy junk food all night."

I sighed, again. "Okay, as a personal favor I'm doing this. But I don't hold out any hopes."

"Thanks."

I nodded. I needed time to come up with an angle—Ott's scorn for the unsupported request was legendary—but nothing would still be nothing half an hour from now. I could wing it now as well as later. Ott's building was across the street. I waited until an old blue sedan passed and then crossed toward it.

The building had been constructed for offices in the early part of the century. The double staircase and the fold-down seat for the elevator operator were reminders of a day when it was a stylish place to work. But it had been many years since Telegraph Avenue had been a sought-after location for business offices. Telegraph was too student-oriented, too left-wing. Today, the most respectable business in the building was the Ott Detective Agency. Most of the "businesses" weren't businesses at all but people living in the ten-by-twelve offices who used the bathrooms down the hall. Many didn't even bother with the pretense of work.

The door of the building was between a pizza outlet and a poster shop. As I neared it, the aroma of garlic and tomato sauce replaced the smell of exhaust left by the blue sedan. Suddenly the thought of confronting Ott, with no ace in the hole—indeed, no cards whatsoever—and doing it on an empty stomach seemed even more appalling. I stepped inside the pizza place behind a student who had a pile of books so daunting that I couldn't imagine how he could balance them and a slice of pizza, much less the large Coke he was ordering. But in a minute he had placed the Coke in a paper bag, had folded the pizza in half, and was ambling out. I ordered two slices with anchovies and pepperoni.

As usual, the light was out at the entrance to Ott's building. I climbed the stairs to the second floor. The door at the top was unlocked, as always. The double stairs wound up the center of the old building, one flight on the inside, the next, split to rise on both sides of it. As I reached the third floor, the acrid smell of marijuana and the stench of dried urine almost masked the aroma of the pizza, and the liquor-thick yells of a man and woman in a room near the landing were mixed with a laugh track from their television. The hallway made a square around the stairs, with the offices on the outside and the old-fashioned bathrooms, the ones with the toilet in one room and the sink in another, on the inside. Ott's office was at the end of the hall. Through the opaque glass in the door a light was visible.

I knocked.

"Who?" he demanded in a tone unfriendly even for Ott.

"Detective Smith."

"Okay, hang on." Ott never opened the door right away. Doubtless there were times he used the minute or so to put suspicious items out of sight. But I felt sure the rest of the time he just sat at his desk and let me wait. Whatever his motivation this time, it was more than two minutes before he pulled the door open and stood by the jamb.

Herman Ott never looked good. His blond hair was thin and getting thinner. His midriff was getting rounder. And the chinos and sweaters he wore, regardless of season, were invariably tan, brown, or yellow. They were never new. I suspected Ott was like a book collector, prowling the used goods stores in his spare moments for a discarded ecru crew neck, a mustard or gold striped shirt, or saffron pants. Today's ensemble was topped with a smudged lemon tennis sweater. He glared down at the slices of pizza. "You haven't got my money, huh, Smith?"

I extended a slice. "I'm keeping on them at the department. This is to show you I haven't forgotten."

His pale brown eyes narrowed. He stared at the pizza like it was a letter bomb.

"Aren't you going to invite me in?"

"Two slices? What do you want, Smith?"

"Only one's for you. But you can eat it, no strings attached."

"Smith, I don't have time to chat, particularly with a cop who owes me."

I took a bite of my own piece. It tasted as good as it smelled. Holding the other slice out, I said, "It's getting cold, Ott."

"Two hundred bucks, Smith. You should have gotten it to me three weeks ago. I don't deal like MasterCard."

"I'm doing my best. I've written three reports justifying your two hundred dollars. It's bugging me more than it is you. Now, are you going to eat this pizza or not?"

"Okay." He reached for the proffered slice and stuffed the end in his small mouth, leaving red ellipses at the corners.

Through the adjoining door I could see the room he slept in. It looked like a nest, with heaps of clothes, blankets, and books completely obscuring the floor and any furniture that might be in there. I had never been here when it hadn't been in that shape. I was sure Ott hadn't seen the floor in the last decade.

But his office was the work place of a professional. No file was ever left out, no book was turned face down. No errant sheet of paper marred the surface of his mahogany desk. And there had never been a time when Herman Ott had had to look in two places for the fact he had deigned to give me. I wondered what metamorphosis occurred when Herman Ott crossed the threshold from his bedroom.

As he stepped back to let me in, his movements seemed tense, even for him. I glanced at his desk. It was covered with papers. This, for Herman Ott, was akin to the Pope leaving his mail on the altar. I looked more closely. Suddenly I realized why Ott was so tetchy. The papers on his desk were tax forms.

"It's good I brought you something to eat," I said, "it looks like you'll be here all night."

"Till tomorrow night. Today's the fourteenth. I'll tell you, Smith, every time I do taxes, I wonder if I should have stayed in school and gotten some job with a salary, like yours." He took a bite of the pizza. "I'm eating this, Smith," he said through a mouth of cheese and tomato sauce, "but I'm not going to tell you anything."

My own mouth was full. I nodded. I almost told him the information wasn't for me, but that wouldn't make any difference. In Ott's code, the favor was toted against the asker. Instead I picked up the thread of his complaint. "Even we cops have to pay taxes, you know."

He shoved a pepperoni-filled corner of pizza into his mouth. "Not the same. Not hardly, Smith. It's self-employment forms that kill you."

"It's only one form."

"That's what they let you believe." A piece of pepperoni slithered across his lip. He herded it back with his upper teeth.

I have something of an iron stomach, but Ott's eating habits were beginning to get to me. I was caught between a strong desire to look away and a fascination with what he would do next.

I didn't have time to decide. He crammed the remaining pizza, a full third, into his mouth. Tomato sauce ran out both sides, down his cheeks, across the cleft of his chin to the center, and down from there. He slurped, sucking back a string of cheese. Wiping his hands on his chinos, he got up and grabbed a form from his desk. "Schedule C. Look at this. See here, 'depreciation.' Well, there are things I have to depreciate. But do I do them for three years, for five years, or for ten years?"

"Doesn't it tell you?"

"It does if I get form forty-five sixty-two."

"Can't you get that from the IRS?"

"I called them. They'll send it in ten working days. Ten working days! Smith, it's a government conspiracy. How many people do you know who allot three weeks to their taxes so they can wait two of those weeks for the government to send them a form? And then when they do get that form"—he grabbed a 4562—"it refers you to a thirty-four sixty-eight, for chrissakes."

"Ott," I said slowly. "You've got a problem here. I can't help you with it."

"I didn't think . . ."

I held up my hand. "I can't, but I've got a friend who knows everything there is to know about finances. For her this would be a snap. She could get you your thirty-whatever, fill it out, and have your desk clear in half an hour."

He wiped his sleeve slowly across his chin. The tomato sauce spread around the cuff. "You're in a generous mood tonight," he said warily.

I didn't have him yet. "She's done capital gains, investment tax credits, and even overseas investments. She's the best, Ott. She'll do it fast, and it'll be right. If you do it yourself, you won't even get the forms before the deadline."

"What do you want?"

"The running shoe thief."

"I don't know who's behind that."

"Maybe, but Ott, you could find out. It would take you a lot less time to check that out than to do these forms."

He hesitated.

"And you won't get audited for that."

Still he said nothing.

"He's not your client. He's ripping off people with influence. The department's already getting heat on this. If we don't get this guy soon, the taxpayers are going to start grumbling about the Avenue. Why aren't we monitoring the regulars, where are these addicts getting their money? I don't have to spell it out for you."

The ridges above his nose deepened. He was weighing the sense of my argument against his aversion to dealing with the police. Finally he shook his head. "No."

"Ott."

"No." His face flushed orange against the residue of tomato sauce on his chin.

"Ott, listen . . ."

He stood up. "Beat it, Smith. I had a gut full of frustration already before you came."

"I've offered . . ."

He pulled open the door. "How many times do I have to tell you—No. The only reason I let you in when you haven't paid up is because I saw you pushing Liz's chair. I figured you couldn't be all bad. But I'm changing my mind. So, Smith, don't bug me till you come with money."

"You've got pizza on your chin," I said as I turned and headed out. His mention of Liz reminded me of his message on her phone machine. I was still curious about that.

The couple near the head of the stairs had quieted; the laugh track was clearer in their silence. As I started down the stairs, I smiled. Despite Herman Ott's performance, I was willing to bet when Pereira showed up tomorrow morning with the 4562 and 3468 in hand, he'd be chirping a different tune.

CHAPTER 5

It was quarter after seven when I got to the pool. I grabbed the day pack with cap, goggles, suit, and towel from the boot of the car and loped across the street. In the lobby I dialed the pay phone. When Pereira answered, I said, "Good news. Ott didn't say yes, but I made him an offer he finds very tempting. If you stop by tomorrow, he'll be even more ready for the plucking."

"What am I giving him, my body?"

"Better than that, Connie, your mind. More precisely, your expertise on taxes. He's going crazy with his Schedule C's. I told him you were the all-time expert."

"Why did you tell him that?" Connie demanded, "I don't know anything about taxes."

I stared blankly at the coin slot. "You, the financial expert of the department? I thought there was nothing you didn't know about money."

"I'm interested in investing, sure. Expert, hardly."

"Matter of opinion. But how can you say you don't know anything about taxes? Filling out tax forms must be child's play compared to making money in the commodities market."

"Maybe. But the thing is, Jill, I haven't made money in commodities. I would have made money—my plan was good—but, Patrick, my younger brother, had to pay back a guy who loaned him money to buy those government surplus rafts he got to take tourists down the Delta."

"The Delta! There are no rapids there."

She sighed. "Patrick didn't think about that when he bought his flotilla. That's why he never had the money to pay back his debt. By the time he hit me up, things were getting pretty nasty. So this has been one more year I haven't had anything but my salary to declare on my ten-forty. Jill, I don't have enough money in the bank to declare interest. Some people have assets; I have relatives."

I took a breath. I could feel my face turning the same color as Herman Ott's. "Ott doesn't know that. I told him you were the all-time expert."

"Jill . . ."

"Listen, with all your financial friends, you must have someone who can teach you about two or three forms. You've got all night to learn."

"It's not so easy." She sighed again. "Thanks for what you did. I owe you."

"Hey, wait! I just spent an hour on this. It was hard enough dealing with Ott when the discretionary fund hasn't come through. But I really put my credibility on the line here. You can't just let it drop."

I could hear Connie breathing. Behind me a couple walked in, kissed, agreed to meet inside at the pool, and kissed again. I wondered how long they planned to spend undressing. Connie said, "Ott turned down the offer, right?"

"For the moment, but—"

"So, if I don't pursue it, it'll just die."

"Unless Ott changes his mind. If he decides to give up on his taxes tonight because he can call you in the morning . . . if he finds out I've conned him on this, I'll never get another thing out of him no matter what I offer."

She sighed.

"Whether you go to see Ott tomorrow is up to you. But by eight A.M. you need to be an expert on the Schedule C, form thirty-four sixty-eight, and form forty-five sixty-two."

"Okay, okay. But for this Herman Ott better give me the thief strung up by his laces." She hung up.

Connie will come through, I assured myself. It won't take her that long to figure out the forms, if Patrick doesn't have another crisis with his inflatable armada and call on Connie to bail him out. Or if her parents don't have one of their semimonthly battles that ends with Connie rescuing the loser and devoting the night to soothing his or her psychological bruises. Or if her older brother Kiernan . . . How could intelligent, meticulous Connie Pereira have sprouted from this tribe? I'd asked her that after her father had spent a week sulking in her apartment. "Catholic school," she had replied with a sigh. In it she had learned responsibility, ambition, and daughterly guilt.

But I had done all I could now. My only choice was to worry or not. I turned and headed into the changing room. The steamy warmth and the familiar smell of chlorine—the fragrance of summer vacations—greeted me at the door.

The pale green walls never completely dried in here, and splotches of mold filled the corners. From the showers on both sides the reedy sound of water striking the tiles mixed with the relaxed voices of women showering. The picture of my father's cousin's house, of the green-walled staircase that led to his room, flashed with dull familiarity in my mind, as it did every time I came here. I felt the same dread I had every time I'd been forced to climb those stairs to the room where he lay unable to move, barely able to speak.

I pushed that childhood memory back, replacing it with the thought of Howard. Would he be in the pool? I hadn't noticed his Land Rover outside.

I stuck my clothes in a pool bag, pulled on my suit, and stepped briefly into the communal shower.

The pool was still crowded, but there was no six-foot-six redhead in either of the fast lanes. But I hadn't really expected him to be here. Knowing Howard, his sudden preoccupation meant a new lady. He wouldn't tell me about her now, not until she became old and he needed a friend to confide in. It was a system we both used, but one with which neither of us was comfortable.

I slipped in the shallow end. As I pushed off, the cool water flowed over my face and down the sides of my body. I reached, stretching my fingertips to the farthest forward point, pulling the water back, forming an S with my hand, feeling the bubbles against my chin, feeling the emptiness of my lungs, and the roll up and the breath, looking down at the pale green water, at the lines on the pool bottom, pulling, kicking, feeling the water flow over my breasts, along my sides, down the insides of my legs. I turned, pushing off harder, concentrating on the length of my strokes, the evenness of the kick. I pulled harder, feeling the water moving more swiftly under my body.

When I climbed out of the pool an hour later, my arms were leaden, my legs tingling. I stood under a spigot in the main shower, knowing that my body would smell as strongly of chlorine each time I showered for the next twenty-four hours. Brad Butz and his altercation at Rainbow Village seemed long ago. Even Herman Ott and Pereira's tax cramming seemed slightly unreal. I put on my clothes, strolled to the car, and headed for Vivoli's for a pint of Bittersweet Orange for dinner.

Five minutes later, I pulled up in front of my flat and got out. My wet hair dripped on my neck. The bag of Bittersweet Orange hung from my hand. I glanced at the window of Mr. Kepple's house, willing it to be dark. A seam of blue light from the television showed through the curtains. I could deal with him now, but I was tired. It had been a long day. After dealing with Brad Butz, Liz Goldenstern, and Herman Ott, I deserved a pleasant evening. And Mr. Kepple, his electric mower, his electric blower, his electric edger that never started on the first eight pulls would be there tomorrow or whenever I got around to making him stop mowing, blowing, or edging long enough to tell him he'd have to garden more quietly or . . . Definitely, not tonight.

I ran across the manicured lawn toward the unlit cement walkway beside the house. Installing a light there was another thing I would have to tell him about. Swinging the ice cream bag, I jumped from the driveway to the path and fell face down!

There was no walkway! He'd taken the cement out. I was lying in the dirt.

As my eyes adjusted to the dark, I could make out a stick just inches to the right of my nose—a stick with a string attached to it.

"Damn!" I pushed myself up and shook out each leg slowly. "Damn him!" I ran across the lawn, up the stairs to the front door of Mr. Kepple's house and pounded.

Through the curtain I could see the blue light from his television and hear the fast-paced background music from a chase sequence. But there was no thump of his own footsteps. I pounded again—the police knock.

I brushed the dirt off the front of my pants. Vaguely I recalled him telling me, one rain-free afternoon last week as he weeded the back lawn, that cement paths were pedestrian (a play on words that escaped him) and redwood burls made a "more aesthetically pleasing entryway to a garden." He had recounted, in detail, the aesthetic concepts espoused by his latest landscape design teacher in the community college. He had gone on about the beauty and durability of redwood. He'd explained, at length, how the new path would fit into his planned treatment of the strip of garden beside it. What he hadn't told me in that half an hour, while I was trying to balance tenantly consideration against the need to extricate myself, was that he planned to dig out the cement walkway today.

Where was he? He should be getting ready for bed. He had to be tired. He had been up at six, trimming the hedge with his electric clippers. I rapped on the door again, but I knew it would do no good. Leaving the television on was Mr. Kepple's idea of burglar-proofing. While I had been finishing up the reports on the Brad Butz incident this afternoon, Mr. Kepple doubtless had been napping, and now he was off at the junior college, entranced with windbreaks or ground covers.

I stomped down the steps, rescued my Bittersweet Orange, and walked carefully on around back.

My flat, originally the back porch of Mr. Kepple's house, ran the full forty-foot width. The interior wall had aluminum siding, one of Mr. Kepple's earlier aesthetic inspirations, and the three outer ones had jalousie windows that leaked every time it rained. Mr. Kepple had installed them himself thirty years ago, when the idea of building a porch had struck him. Then there had been a Mrs. Kepple who, doubtless, had complained about their failings as a shield from the elements. But her words must have fallen on the same deaf ear I frequently encountered. And, knowing what I did of my landlord, I felt sure he had never lighted long enough on the porch to consider its discomforts. For him the porch would have been solely a boundary to his back garden. Eventually, Mrs. Kepple (and her complaints) died, and he had eyed his jalousied boundary one day and seen the possibility of it bringing in money for fertilizer, and mulch, and a self-turning compost box with drawers that slid out individually. So, with the addition of indoor-outdoor carpet, a bath and a kitchen, Mr. Kepple had created my flat. He assured me, it would someday have a view of one of the loveliest gardens in Berkeley. I could sit with the jalousies open and see the gardenias in the spring, the lilies in summer, the holly berries at Christmas. In the warm spring afternoons I could sunbathe on his proposed deck.

But now, two years later, the deck was still in the planning stages and the back garden a patch of dirt. Each year Mr. Kepple showed me his garden plans, where the gardenia would be, the shady spot suitable for cineraria, the full sun for the roses. Weekly the sketches changed. Sometimes six packs of baby plants appeared on trays along the edges of the yard. Once or twice the plants made it into the soil, only to be yanked out days later when the master plan changed.

I pushed the door open and stalked across the ten feet of indoor-outdoor carpet to the kitchen. Briefly I considered scooping the ice cream into a dish. Who was I kidding? I grabbed a spoon from the pile of stainless in the sink, rinsed it off, and dug into the carton. I had lived in this flat since my divorce—almost two years. The jalousie windows still functioned more like screens than glass. In winter they let in the cold and the rain. And in summer, half the time I kept them closed to cut the smell of manure or the sound of the electric hedge clipper.

I had to decide what I was going to do about Mr. Kepple, and about this flat. I couldn't go on being jolted awake at dawn and putting off coming home until after dusk to avoid a forty-five minute monolog on the clay content in the soil. Mr. Kepple was an old man. His garden was his life. My disinterest was a slap in his face. And disinterest was the mildest emotion I felt about the pile of dirt outside my door. I didn't want to hurt his feelings. I just wanted to live like a normal person. But that would never happen here. I'd been through it all before. I just didn't want to face the obvious conclusion.

I took another shower to wash the dirt off my arms and the chlorine out of my hair and finished half the pint of ice cream.

It was just after ten when the dispatcher called. "Smith?"

"Yes."

"Homicide by the inlet, next to Rainbow Village."

CHAPTER 6

The night was damp with fog. My car windows were steamed on the inside, but I didn't stop to wipe them. I cleared a rectangle with the side of my hand and drove down Cedar to San Pablo Avenue, running yellow lights, picturing Brad Butz with his thick, dark hair fluttering over that bruise he had complained about this morning. Did he have more than a bruise now? Or was it his assailant who now lay dead on that unpaved road next to the dump? Or was it a Rainbow Villager? Or had the body of someone unconnected with the waterfront community been dumped there?

I crossed the freeway and took the access road beside it, turning right on Virginia Street, skirting the inlet, and driving beside the chins of the marina where the sports boutiques and playing fields would be. The road was rough and unlit. The musty smell of low tide rushed in through the window. In the middle of the inlet the half-sunken hull of a junk ship jutted black against the fog. And the headlights of the patrol car and the ambulance sent white cotton-candy cones across the water into the oblivion of the fog. The red pulsers blinked on and off, turning Rainbow Village an unnatural pink. That acre of sagging vehicles looked like a neon mirage.

I pulled up next to the patrol car. A gusty cold wind blew in from the bay, carrying with it the fresher smell of salt water. By the entrance to Rainbow Village two homemade flags flapped. Both of the patrol officers protecting the scene had their collars turned up. Behind them a crowd of maybe seventy-five people had divided itself into three groups. The nearest and by far the largest section was predominantly tourists from the Inn, dressed for a casual dinner by the bay —men in sports jackets, women with vacation skirts pressed tightly around the backs of their legs and light jackets pulled around arms they couldn't protect from the wind. A few still clutched wine glasses.

Next to them, a dozen men and three women in fishing gear stood, several hunched against the night, hands in pockets, gazing straight ahead; several others smoked. For them death was not an abstraction. It lurked in the ocean waters every time they headed out into the vast predawn blackness of the Pacific. It hid behind a freak wave, or in a storm that rose with fatal suddenness, tossing forty-foot crafts, obliterating the shore. They stood silent, fearful, waiting. This close to the docks, the dead person could be one of their own.

A knot of Rainbow Villagers clustered by the hurricane fence, as if that wall would protect them from danger or suspicion. Those villagers who had been around for a while had seen death here. And the transients knew well enough what it was to be undesirable, expendable, the obvious suspect of affront to "regular society."

The tourists divided their attention between the activity at the shoreline and the spectacle of the wary villagers.

I moved on past them toward the three men at the water's edge. The headlights threw their shadows—long, emaciated forms jerking spastically on the ripples of the water.

Murakawa, the beat officer, turned toward me. He was assigned to Morning Watch, seven A.M. to three P.M.; he had covered for a friend on Day Watch; and now it was nearly midnight, but he didn't look tired. "Drowning. No I.D."

The medics moved back and I saw the chair—the wheelchair—lying on its side.

I took a breath, then moved closer. Next to it, laid on a tarpaulin, was the body. It was Liz Goldenstern.

I turned away and swallowed hard. The nauseatingly thick ice cream welled in my throat. I swallowed again. I had seen my share of bodies, but those had belonged to strangers, not to a woman I had just pushed home.

I closed my eyes and swallowed once more, then forced myself to turn back and look down at Liz. The piercing white of the headlights struck her face, sending a dark triangle of shadow from her nose onto the forehead. Those dark eyes that had flashed with her anger and glowed in triumph when an Avenue merchant capitulated were coated with mud and brine. Her April-pale skin was colorless except for a brown oval beside her nose where the blood had settled after death. Her mouth, which I'd seen so often set determinedly, hung open. Death had so distorted her face that it looked not like Liz but a relative of hers, a relative I didn't need to care about.

But there was no flaccidity in her fingers; the skin was taut and the first two fingers were pressed together harder than I'd thought her damaged body would allow.

"Drowned," Murakawa said. "The chair was tipped; it must have catapulted her."

I stared down at her swollen face, then back at her hands.

"Couldn't have been more than a foot of water," he said.

"The bank drops off pretty sharply here. When the witness found her only her head and shoulders were submerged. Her hands were on the shore, above the water level."

I gasped, turned away, and clasped my mouth to keep from retching. I squeezed my eyes shut against the thought of Liz, but the image behind the lids was that green-walled staircase leading to the bedroom of my father's cousin, who would be lying mashed under a pile of stiff gray blankets . . . waiting for us. By my feet, the water from the inlet lapped against the shore. I tightened my throat and stood staring across the dirt, which was alternating brown and pink, to the black of the inlet, picturing Liz as her body slapped down into the water, knocking the air out of her lungs. I could see her scrambling to pull herself up with arms that wouldn't work. I could see her gasping, feel her terror as her nose and mouth filled with water.

Anyone but Liz could have pulled herself out of the water without so much as swallowing a mouthful.

"What makes you think it's homicide?" I asked Murakawa.

The glare of the headlights sharpened his cheekbones to raw edges under his eyes. As he looked down at Liz's body, he was as pale as she. And when he spoke, his voice was almost a whisper. "The belt. She wore a seat belt to hold her in. They have those on wheelchairs. If you lack tone in your gluteals, your hamstrings, and your erector spinae muscles in the back there's nothing to keep you from falling forward. The degree and effects of paralysis vary a great deal depending on where the injury occurred and how it affected the spine. There are cases . . ." He stopped abruptly.

I put a hand on his arm. "Is this your first homicide?"

"Does it show that much?"

"Of course it shows. What kind of person wouldn't be churned up seeing her like this?" I looked back down at Liz. The bay wind plucked at the dark curls that were still stuck to her face. The thick blue wool sweater that had protected her from the afternoon chill lay heavy against her breasts. It had dried just enough to give off the stench of wet wool and brackish water.

I took Murakawa's flashlight and bent down to check her face for marks, her hair and clothes for alien fibers. I pointed to a twig caught in her left sleeve. Murakawa nodded.

"The belt," he said when I stood up. "It was cut. The edges are still sharp."

I didn't need to be told that, had the belt been buckled, Liz would have fallen well short of the water. "It's not just that she's dead," I said as much to myself as to Murakawa. "Liz Goldenstern must have been some woman before the accident put her in that chair. Later, she made herself some woman, in spite of not having legs, arms, or even fingers she could use well. She was ready to take on any comer." I shook my head. "This way of killing her—it's such an insult."

"I guess that's what murder is," he said.

I shrugged.

"You want shots of the chair?" It was the I.D. Tech. He would do the photography, dust for prints, take the molds, and preserve the samples. Behind him, by the Marina Vista construction shack, the press officer conferred with Lieutenant Collins, the Night Watch Commander. Three reporters stood a few feet away, one checking a camera, the others sidling in toward the press officer.

I turned away from Liz, from "the body." To the I.D. Tech, I said, "Take the chair, the body, and the shore twenty feet in either direction. Get what prints you can from the chair and molds of all the footprints within five feet of it. And make sure you label that twig that's caught on her sleeve."

"Smith," Murakawa said, "I checked the twig. It looks like it's from the hedge up on the ridge."

"Get a sample up there," I said to the I.D. Tech.

"Right," the tech muttered.

I asked Murakawa, "Have you called for additional backup? We're going to need to talk to everyone in that crowd. I need two people to watch the rear of Rainbow Village." I looked at the acre of vehicles. There were probably thirty or more in it. "And four or five to go door to door in there. And a couple more to check at the Marriott, the docks, and the rest of the lounges down here. If there's anyone where he shouldn't be, or acting out of line, I want him held till I can get there."

"Back-ups are on the way. I'll call in and make sure they're adequate."

"Have someone go over the hedge. See if you can find the spot this twig is from. Maybe more of it broke off."

"Right."

"Where's the person who found her?"

"Over there, sitting on the box by the fence, the woman in the black cape. She says she knows why she was killed."

CHAPTER 7

"This is Aura Summerlight, a.k.a. Penelope Lynn Garrett," Murakawa said with only the slightest suggestion of a sigh as he pronounced her self-appointed name. To twenty-four-year-old Murakawa, the sixties was an ancient oddity, characterized by old-hat political action and slovenly dress. Anachronisms like Aura Summerlight baffled him. "She discovered the body."

Half the Rainbow Villagers who had been standing by the fence watching our activity at the water's edge moved off when we started toward them. The remaining ten edged in protectively to Aura Summerlight.

I glanced at the group. There was no one member who could be taken as representative of all. Two men in their early twenties wore cheap, shiny polyester pants and jackets, garments that would betray them after the first wash. Next to them was an older man, for whom the next wash was well overdue. A woman in a balding, black fur coat, with the lining hanging from both sleeves and the hem, stood next to a couple in jeans, denim jackets, and cowboy boots. Aura Summerlight sat slumped against the fence. The filtered light from the windows of a purple school bus behind the fence skimmed her limp, light-brown hair.

There was a theory in the psychic circles that contended the name you are called shapes your character because it is a symbol of you and, more prosaically, because you hear it more frequently than most words. Advocates chose to be called qualities they wished to embody. The aura of summer light was such a clear and hopeful image. It seemed to mock the very ungracefulness of this woman's slumping body. As if to balance her own blandness, she wore a fringed black Punjabi cape embroidered with huge red roses. Even slumped as she was, the thin wool didn't disguise her thick shoulders and full breasts. She had that type of narrow-hipped figure that carries its fat around the middle without losing the slimness of the ankles.

I stepped between the blue-jeaned couple and looked down at Aura Summerlight. My body blocked the sporadic red light from the patrol car pulsers. The ground on either side of her blinked red, but she remained in darkness. I said, "I know this evening has been a shock. I don't want to keep you any longer than I have to. Where can we talk?"

"Lady, she can—"

"Ms. Summerlight?" I said, cutting off the speaker, a crew-cut man in a red plaid wool jacket. He shrugged. It was obvious he had objected only for form's sake.

Aura Summerlight stood. Now I could make out her scrunched features: the short sharp nose, the tight thin mouth, the sharp cheekbones, and the dark eyes that were sunk so far in they seemed, in the dim light, to be empty hollows. "You can . . . come to my truck." She walked to the gate. The wind lifted the flags above it, snapping the cloth back against itself. It blew Aura Summerlight's hair across her mouth, but she made no move to push it away. She walked on, hurriedly, but making surprisingly little progress, as if she were on a moving sidewalk going the wrong way. Beside her, I found myself taking longer, slower steps, controlling my urge to grab her arm and run to wherever her truck was parked to find out why Liz Goldenstern had been killed.

We passed the purple school bus. "University of Life" it declared in gold letters on the side. An old Buick, one of the ones with the three holes on the sides, had settled next to it. The light from the bus windows showed the rust on the Buick's door. We passed a Ford wagon in not much better shape, two Volkswagen vans, and a pickup from the late sixties—new for this lot—with a tarp over a wide load on the back.

Another time I might have taken her to my own car, but not now, not with the lights from the nearby patrol cars and the staccato squeals from their radios to intimidate her.

"Here," she said, indicating a white Chevy pickup that looked only slightly better than average. Behind it she had created a clear plastic lean-to from the fence to two poles. A hibachi, charcoal, lighter fluid, and two buckets huddled under it. In the wind, one of the plastic sides flapped against the fence, striking the metal fitfully, creating the type of irregular noise that would drive the average person crazy. But here, no one seemed to mind.

Aura Summerlight climbed into the cab. I opened the other door and waited while she lifted paper bags, four of them, from the floor and fitted them behind the seat. I could smell the onions in one. She pulled a box of tissues across the seat toward her and shifted a cup with an immersion heater back farther onto the dashboard.

"How did you come to discover the body?" I asked.

She clutched the steering wheel, as if she were battling rush hour on the Bay Bridge, staring tensely ahead with the look of one prepared to cut off lane hoppers. I wondered if she had chosen to use the cab because it was more convenient to sit in or because she wouldn't have to face me when she talked. "You see, I was walking. I came home late. Most days I'm here by sunset; the buses don't run much at night." The words rushed out. "But, well, I don't know, I got hung up. I had things to do in town, you see. I got here late. Well, the thing is, you see, I was bummed out. A guy I worked for owes me money, fifty dollars. Fifty dollars may not seem like much to you, but I need that money, and, dammit, he owes me, and he's weaseling out. So I went by his place and I waited. I waited a long time. And when he finally came, it was dark, but I saw him at the corner, and he saw me, and he beat it, and I ran after him, but he was too fast. I lost him. I was so damned mad. I was going to go back to his place and wait some more. He had to come home. But he has money—he could go to a bar and have a few drinks. He could wait me out. So I figured I'd better come on home, but by then the buses don't run so regular, and I was hungry, and I went into one of those pizza places and bought myself a slice. I hadn't eaten anything since I left here this morning, and I was hungry. There was a line, and then I couldn't find all the change I thought I had, and it took me a while, and the little bitch behind the counter was getting all huffy as if she didn't believe I really had the dollar fifty-five cents. A dollar fifty-five cents for one slice! But I was starved. I mean, I get like panicked when I'm that hungry. I can't think straight. So I had to have it. And then by the time I got back to the bus stop, the bus had gone and I had to wait another hour." She was squeezing the steering wheel. Sweat covered her forehead. I couldn't tell whether her nervous rush of words was a normal reaction to the shocks of the day or a screen of words to shield me out.

"But you finally got here," I prompted.

"And then Marie in the bus over there was having a party. You could hear it halfway to the marina. I knew I couldn't face people. I was too bummed out. I just walked along the water. Christ, I almost fell over the wheelchair."

"And then?"

"It was awful. Her head was in the water, just her head. The water was only up around her shoulders. And she was dead."

I waited a moment; she stared straight ahead, silently. "What did you do then?"

"That was the worst thing that's ever happened to me, and there's been plenty bad in my life." She grabbed a big plastic purse and began rummaging through it.

"Ms. Summerlight, what did you do when you saw the body?"

"I knew she was dead. I've seen dead people before. When I was a kid a boy drowned in the river behind the school. It was at lunch time. One of the teachers jumped in and pulled him out, but he was dead. We all saw him. I know what dead people look like. I knew this woman was dead. So I ran up here and got Ian to call the co—the police."

Suddenly the musty closeness of the cab filled my nose and throat. "Didn't you lift her head out of the water?"

She squeezed the steering wheel tighter. "I don't remember. I must have. I just remember . . . standing in the water. I was holding her, by the shoulders. She was dead. I knew she was dead."

"Did you try artificial respiration?"

"I don't know. I don't remember . . . anything . . . but holding her. The next thing, I was here, and telling Ian. You can ask him if you don't believe me. He'll tell you."

"How did the body get back to the ground?" Murakawa had found Liz's face and shoulders in the water.

"I don't know. I told you."

If she dropped Liz back into the bay, it was no wonder she blocked that out of her mind. I said, "What time was this?"

"Time? I don't know."

"Okay." The dispatcher would have a record of the call. "Did you see anyone near the body when you were walking toward it?"

"No. I told you I wanted to be by myself."

"Anyone who looked like they were walking or running away?"

"No."

"Hiding behind something? Doing anything odd? Take your time. Try to see the area like it was before you came across the body."

She pulled her fingers off the steering wheel, arched them, then crossed her arms over the wheel. The cape hung like a red-flowered tent. "No."

I couldn't decide about her lack of emotion. Was she in shock? People lived in Rainbow Village for a number of reasons. Mental problems was one. Aura Summerlight looked like she was on the edge, psychologically. She might well not have noticed anything unusual near Liz's body. There might have been nothing to notice, or there might have been plenty she was too preoccupied to see.

"You said you know why she was killed."

She continued to gaze through the windshield. "I don't know, like God told me, but it sure makes sense. Like he said, when something bad happens down here who gets the blame? Us here in the village, that's who. You cops, you're going to be on us now, right?"

"He?" I asked, assuming she didn't mean God.

"Anything that makes us in the village look bad, makes it easier for the guy who's going to put up that high-rise, right? He's been bugging the city to get us out. See where he was tonight."

"Like who said?" I insisted. "Who told you that?"

For the first time she looked at me, her dark eyes wide. I had the sense of having broken through the face she had chosen, however consciously or unconsciously, to show me. "Ian," she said so softly I had to strain to hear.

"Who is Ian?"

"Ian Stuart. He lives here, in the pickup by the fence, the one with the hot tub on the back."

"Is he blond?"

She nodded stiffly. She was shrinking back behind her façade. I could have tried to reassure her, but I didn't have time. Murakawa could get her statement. I needed to finish with her and find Ian Stuart, the blond man with the hot tub, the "maniac" who, only this morning, had threatened to hold Brad Butz's head under water until he drowned.

"Where is his truck?"

"His truck?" She shrank back against the door. "Across by the fence. It's the one with the tarp on the back."

CHAPTER 8

The blond "maniac" Ian Stuart was not in his truck, certainly not in his drained hot tub, and nowhere else in Rainbow Village. According to two witnesses, he had stalked back inside the village after his fracas with Brad Butz that morning and harangued his neighbors long enough to disperse all but those who hoped for a ride downtown. His truck was one of the few in running order. When the intent of his audience became clear, he had stalked off. "We could have taken his truck and driven right past him into town," a white-haired man in a pea jacket had laughed. "He got the key stuck in the ignition. We all knew that. He changed the door lock. Guess he never heard of broken windows." He laughed again.

It was after three in the morning. Canvassing Rainbow Village, the cocktail lounges, the Marriott, and the marina, as well as checking through the newly landscaped park that skirted the bay, had taken hours, even with more patrol officers than the Watch Commander wanted to release. The only people we had turned up were two men in sleeping bags settled in under the junipers, and they had been rousted out enough times before to be considered regulars.

I walked back to the water's edge and stood just outside the cordon. The tide was lower. If Liz Goldenstern had landed in the same spot now she would have been alive. If she had come here later . . . I could feel myself being pulled into the "if only's" that I had seen relatives and friends of victims do so often. I'd watched them leap into those brief respites of delusion where, for a moment, the dead daughter or cousin had never driven off or the husband hadn't gone looking for the guy who owed him money. For that moment he had never left, he was still sitting on the sofa—I had seen the widow turn to touch him and stare uncomprehendingly at the empty seat beside her.

I looked out across the inlet. The junk boat seemed larger now in low tide. Beyond the freeway the muted white street lights on University, Solano, and San Pablo Avenues blended into lines, and traffic lights blinked red and amber in the early morning hours. The city looked like a giant pinball machine. I pulled my jacket tighter around my shoulders, but the damp of the bay had penetrated and I only felt wetter.

"Smith?" Murakawa's thick hair flopped over his forehead. He had that wired, purposeful look of a beat officer handling his first murder case. "I finished with the last of the witnesses."

"And?"

"It's a bust. Would you believe, no one saw the dead woman arrive here. No one saw her murdered. No one saw anything suspicious."

"That must be some kind of record. You ask any twenty people in Berkeley if they saw anything unusual, and you can count on half of them coming up with something."

"Not these folk," he said in disgust. "Of course, you've got to consider the sources, Smith. The first bunch are tourists. They think everything in Berkeley's bizarre. Nothing stands out. And in Rainbow Village, anyone who's been here over a month has seen drug busts, freak outs, and fights. To them, 'out of the ordinary' is the way things are. They wouldn't think to tell us if a flying saucer landed."

"Well, we have names and addresses. We can have another go around if we need to. Run them through files, all of them. Do Aura Summerlight and Ian Stuart first. And have someone check with the Center for Independent Living. See what Liz was involved with there besides getting her chair fixed. Find out if she's got a lawyer. Check her finances. The works."

"When do you need that?"

"The file checks now. But by eight-thirty will be okay. For C.I.L. we'll have to wait for business hours." A gust of wind slapped a clump of hair against my cheek. Irritably, I pushed it back behind my ear. Liz's body was gone. Her chair had been moved into a van, but the gouges the wheels made as it turned over still scarred the shore. To Murakawa, I said, "What could Liz Goldenstern have been doing here?"

Murakawa shook his head.

"And how did she get here?"

He glanced across the inlet to the freeway. "I wondered that too. But you know, in spite of motor neuron lesions, people with spinal cord injuries can navigate in power chairs surprisingly well. Most of us don't realize how much potential each muscle has, and how much variety there is in the effects of the injuries. After some injuries, patients have some feeling in their trunk and extremities, but no control of movement. In other cases the spinal cord is diffusely injured and some nerve tracts still function, so there's only weakness, not paralysis. With the Brown-Sequard syndrome, for instance, one side of the spinal cord is functional and the other isn't. And there's the anterior spinal artery syndrome, where only the posterior third of the cord functions. And—"

"Liz was as capable as they come," I snapped. Some time I might need to know these physiological possibilities, but now they only made the cruelty of Liz's murder seem all the greater.

Murakawa hesitated. It was his first murder; he wasn't used to overlooking the short fuses that were as much a part of investigations as paperwork. "Telegraph is two miles over the freeway. That's a long way to come in a power chair, in the cold."

"It wasn't that cold five or six hours ago, Paul."

"But Smith, people with spinal injuries don't have good circulation. They feel the cold a lot more than the rest of us."

I recalled Liz Goldenstern picketing the Caliban Café during last winter's rain. Had she had better circulation than Murakawa thought? Or for her had the iciness of the hours on the line been just one more thing to endure? Compared to those hours, the forty-five minutes it would have taken to drive to the marina in her chair would have been a snap.

Murakawa leaned toward me with excitement. "She wouldn't have had to come on University, if she didn't want to be noticed. She could have taken side streets all the way to the overpass."

I nodded slowly. "It's possible, but not likely."

"Why not?"

"There's no sidewalk on the freeway overpass. Even with a taillight of sorts on her chair, she'd have had a fifty-fifty chance of being killed." I stopped abruptly.

Murakawa finished the thought. "Whatever made her come here must have been worth taking that chance."

We both looked toward the freeway lights. "Or maybe someone brought her here to kill her," I said. The ambulance crew had agreed that the settling of the blood in her face and body made it one in a thousand she had died anywhere but where we found her.

"The killer would have needed a truck or van, some vehicle big enough to handle a power chair, something with a ramp to drive it up. Those chairs aren't light."

That I knew only too well. "We're going to have to find that vehicle and the driver."

Murakawa nodded slowly. I had never heard him complain about overwork, no matter how much time was demanded—unless he thought it was bureaucratic nonsense. And even then he had more patience than most. Maybe because he didn't see himself doing it for the next thirty years of his life. Murakawa's future lay not with dead bodies but with ones who could still be helped. "So you want us to go over every vehicle here?"

"Every one this side of the freeway. Call me if you find anything. Leave word if you don't. And you can take some comfort in the fact that you're not doing the worst of the jobs."

"Oh, yeah?"

"I'm going to Liz Goldenstern's house. If she had a friend living with her, I'm going to wake them up and tell them she's dead."

I parked in the driveway of Liz Goldenstern's triplex and walked up the redwood ramp to the two doors in front. In the early morning stillness, my footsteps resounded on the boards.

Liz hadn't said she lived with anyone. In the brief time I had been in her apartment, I had seen no sign of another tenant. There was no light now, no reason to assume anyone would be inside. But I pushed the buzzer and waited. From within the living room came the shrill demand of the buzzer. It wasn't a sound the average person could sleep through.

In the yard the fronds of a foot palm tree scraped against each other. Here, two miles from the bay, the air was drier. On Liz Goldenstern's protected entryway the night seemed almost warm. I rang the bell again, not expecting a response. None followed.

With a mixture of relief and irritation, I turned and pressed the buzzer of the upstairs unit. Perhaps there would be no next of kin to break the news to. When I started as a patrol officer I had assumed the time would come when I'd handle those scenes dispassionately, murmuring a few comforting phrases, then moving on to the necessary questions. I'd wised up over the years. Still, each time I knocked on the door of an unsuspecting relative or lover, I knew this would not be the time it didn't get to me. I pushed the buzzer again, waited, then knocked four times, loud—the police knock.

Five minutes later, I conceded no one was home there either.

I walked down the ramp, across the yard, and along the driveway. The back yard couldn't have been more than ten feet deep and twenty-five feet wide. The cement driveway had been expanded and consumed half of it so that this side of the rear cottage looked out solely on cement.

I climbed the two steps to the third unit of the main building and pressed the buzzer. There was no answer. And none at the cottage. Where were these people at four-thirty in the morning?

* * *

After telling a patrol officer, who was settled across the street, to call in and find out who these other tenants were and what we had on them, I headed back to the station. I could have run the checks myself, but they weren't first priority. For this guy, who had nothing to do but sit in a dark car for the next two and a half hours and watch an empty building, any task was a boon.

Dillingham, the Night Watch desk man, glanced up as I climbed the stairs. "Smith? I thought you'd been promoted to nine to five."

"Seven-forty-five to four-fifteen."

"So? Did you just drop by to raid our donut box again?" He grinned. He knew my reputation for junk food consumption from my stint on Night Watch. Then Dillingham had threatened me with dire intestinal consequences. "Only wine improves with age," he'd muttered, each time I'd grabbed another chocolate old fashioned on my way home. "Are you going to will your intestines to Roto Rooter, Smith?" That one he'd saved for a larger audience.

"What have you got in that box?" I asked now.

He glanced beneath the desk, wrinkling his nose. "Three plain, a couple old-fashioned, one with pink glop, two with white glop, and those colored things that look like confetti. And Smith, we still have two jellies."

I extricated a dollar. "Hand them over."

"This stuff will kill you."

"You're wrong, Dillingham. It might do you in, but I keep up my immunities. My stomach thrives on donuts the way yours does tofu."

Paper towel in hand, I walked down the hall to my office. The sugary smell of the donuts, which Dillingham had once described as "reek of bubblegum and plastic," reminded me that I had had only half a pint of ice cream for dinner. I might not have reached the level of professionalism where despair didn't faze me, but I had missed plenty of meals racing around after suspects who didn't observe the standard lunch and dinner hours. Now I ate when the chance came, regardless of the circumstances. But I had also learned, the hard way, the dangers of eating a jelly donut while walking. I plopped in my chair and stuffed a sugary edge in my mouth.

When I finished the first donut, I checked my IN box. No word from the coroner as to time of death. And no message from Murakawa at all. I dialed the coroner's office.

"Coroner's Department," a gravelly voice said.

"Matthew? How're things down there?"

"Quiet." He chuckled softly. It was an old joke. He'd been saying it as long as anyone in the department could recall.

"This is Jill Smith, in Homicide."

"I know your voice, Smith. How many times did you call me about your last body? But that's okay. There's no one else to talk to here."

"Well, a couple more hours and you can be up on the fire trail." Matthew Harrison was an avid hiker. He cherished his daylight hours. To him, the time after dark was dead time anyway. And the morgue was as good a place as any to kill it. In the quiet he could catch a catnap or two at his desk. "Is Dr. Eastman still there?"

"It's five in the morning. He went home hours ago."

"Rats. Well, what's the status on the body you brought in tonight? The name's Liz Goldenstern."

"Hang on."

I took a bite of the second donut. It didn't taste as good.

"Scheduled for the morning."

Wonderful! The pathologist's report wouldn't come back for three to five days, no matter how desperately I needed it. And the pathologist wouldn't even begin until morning. "What about time of death?"

"Won't know till morning, Smith."

"Didn't Eastman do anything?"

"He was busy. You're not our only customer, you know."

"He must have taken the body temperature."

"No record of it."

"Maybe he didn't get around to dictating. Maybe he left the notes in his office." I held my breath. There had to be some record of the entry exam. If I were forced to track down Eastman tomorrow, it could take all day. The coroner doesn't spend his time sitting by the phone.

"Hang on." It was several minutes before he said, "Smith?"

"Yes?"

"We took delivery at eleven thirty-eight. Body temp was ninety-five point four."

Body temperature drops about 1.5 degrees an hour. In the cold, Liz's could have fallen faster. "Dead two hours?"

"Give or take."

"Thanks, Matthew. For that you deserve to see a deer on your walk."

I finished the donut and got the address for Brad Butz the builder, the man who had stood to gain by any commotion near Rainbow Village. I wasn't ready to give Aura Summerlight's conclusion too much credence. But Butz had been furious with his blond maniac yesterday morning, and nothing about him suggested he was one to turn the other cheek. He was the type to spend the day stewing about his stolen sign, down a six pack, and by nine o'clock be hunting Ian Stuart, right by the spot where Liz Goldenstern had died.

Butz would hardly be pleased to have me drag him out of bed at this hour. If he hadn't already called his City Hall friends about the morning's fracas, he'd probably be on the horn as soon as I left. It was a chance I'd have to take.

CHAPTER 9

I would have assumed that the contractor for a project the size of Marina Vista would live high in the hills, in a house he had designed and built himself, with a glass wall that overlooked the bay, cathedral ceilings, or one of those kitchens filled with gadgets I couldn't guess the use for. But for Brad Butz, this southwest Berkeley address didn't surprise me. What I knew of this area was mostly from my office mate, Seth Howard. In recent months the Oakland police and the Contra Costa County sheriff, to the north, had run a startlingly successful series of drug raids in Oakland, Richmond, and the city of San Pablo. They had caught a number of the big guys. The ones they'd missed had taken the warning and moved their operations. Not all of them had landed in South Berkeley, but enough. And together with the lower echelon dealers, who figured the sheriff's success had emptied slots for them to move up to, they had created a war zone in this small area. On California Street gunmen fired from speeding cars in mid-afternoon. Residents thought twice before walking to the store. The department added extra foot patrols. And Howard and his buddies in Vice and Substance Abuse worked overtime.

At 5:30 A.M. it was still nighttime dark. Down the block a husky man headed for his car. He glanced toward the patrol car but didn't break his stride.

The house Brad Butz lived in was a single-story, twenty-five-foot square. The tiny, red cement porch had shifted away from the house, leaving an inch-wide gap between it and the door. Cracks meandered down the stucco façade. Most California houses had cracks in one or two walls—"from the house settling" people said. "From the earth mov-

ing" would have been more accurate. The Hayward Fault
ran beneath the Berkeley hills, and tributaries from it—fault
traces—some visible, some not, threaded their way under
the city, shifting and growing with each new quake, so that
a new fault map was out of date as soon as the earth moved
again. Most fissures were small, most damage manageable.
The average homeowner grumbled and repaired. But Brad
Butz's house gave new meaning to "deferred maintenance."

I rang the bell and listened to its trill inside. No footsteps
followed it. Was Butz not home, either? What was I dealing
with here, a herd of vampires who wouldn't be home till
dawn?

I rang again.

"Okay, okay. Keep your pants on," Butz grumbled from
the rear of the small dwelling. His Bronx accent was thicker
than it had been yesterday morning, as if his sinuses were
still stopped up with sleep. He stomped toward the door. I
caught a glimpse of a T-shirt and jeans in the window to my
left. Then Butz yanked open the door and stood with one
hand on it and the other on the frame.

His wiry dark hair stood out like a rumpled brown tiara
pushed far back on his head. Still flushed from sleep, his
skin looked more porcelain than it had yesterday. As he
stared at me, his blue eyes narrowed, and any resemblance
to a pleasant doll-like expression vanished.

"You're the cop, right?" he demanded.

"Detective Smith."

"Christ, it's the middle of the night. You got my vandal,
right? Well, it's about time. It shouldn't have taken the
Berkeley Police Department all day and all night. You
shoulda had him by noon. I'll tell you, lady—"

"Detective."

"De*tec*tive," he said, in mock respect, "if you hadn't
nabbed him by morning I was ready to make a few calls."

I decided to ignore the whole vandalism issue. "I'm in

Homicide. A woman was murdered last night. Can I come in?"

"Murdered? Who? How?" He flicked on the light switch and stepped back to let me into the ten-by-twelve room that occupied the left corner of the house. The walls were papered in a faded floral design; the overstuffed sofa was surrounded by mahoghany end tables with turquoise speckled lamps from the fifties. It looked like a room some-one's great-aunt had died in. And it looked like she hadn't cleaned it for months before her demise. Dustballs crowded around the feet of the coffee table—the small pine table looked like it was floating on a cloud. Or it would have been, had it not been weighed down by a pile of newspapers, three beer cans, and a pizza box that hung precariously over the edge. The room still smelled of beer and tomato sauce.

I sat on the chair, leaving him to settle on the sofa oppo-site me where I could see his reactions. "The woman was killed at the waterfront, at the Marina Vista site."

"Can you believe that? Now they're murdering people at my site!" He shook his head slowly; his wiry hair flapped like stalks of corn in the wind. Leaning forward, he pushed the pizza box back onto the table. "But why? Why at my project? Jesus, I don't have enough trouble, without them killing each other there. I've had delays up the wazoo. First off, I had a blow-up trying to get a use permit from the Building Department. Then there was the BCDC, the Bay Conservation Development Commission, carrying on about not permitting residential development on the waterfront. The laws are a lot stricter for apartments than hotels. You don't want to know how long it took dealing with them. You don't want to know about the variances from zoning I needed to get. Then there were questions about the environ-mental impact report. For that I had to get back to the guy who wrote the report to begin with, and he was in Guadala-jara for three weeks. I wanted to set a date with QuakeChek, the place that runs the computer checks on a structure's ability to ride out the big one, but everything else was so screwed up. . . . I couldn't come to terms with the electrician I wanted—*he* wasn't about to commit his men to a schedule that had been changed as many times as mine. Then the union wage went up. And now this! Jesus, it was bad enough when the city was hassling me. Now it's complete strangers. At least suicides have the decency to jump off the Golden Gate Bridge where they're supposed to. Who was this woman, anyway?"

I sat silent a moment, amazed at the totality of Butz's self-absorption. It wasn't so much that he was too literal to have any imagination—the rap on him at the station—there was no room left in his head for thoughts not centered on himself. I said, "The murdered woman was Liz Goldenstern."

His eyes snapped open. His mouth dropped. He sat staring for a full half minute. "Liz? You can't be right."

"I'm afraid so, Mr. Butz."

"But Liz, God, she's in a wheelchair. What would she be doing down there? The road isn't even paved, for Chrissakes."

I wasn't surprised he knew Liz Goldenstern. As the contractor for Marina Vista, it would have been odd had he not run across her. I was only surprised by the seeming genuineness of his dismay. I said, "I was hoping you could tell me that."

"Liz. She's dead? But how? She was speaking at the Landscape Development Subcommittee tonight. I called her at ten. She didn't answer. I figured she was still there. Those things can run half the night. Everyone wants his say, and no one wants to cut it short. Liz was way down the agenda. She knew it could run late . . . but dead!" He stared at me, still wide-eyed, with that glazed look that people have on the subways. Finally, he said, "How? How did she die?"

"She drowned."

"But she was in a chair. She didn't swim."

"She was murdered."

"In the water? Some bastard drowned her?" He grabbed one of the beer cans with his thick hands and twisted the aluminum until it cracked. His incongruously delicate eyes scrunched together in grief, or possibly fear. Staring at the can, he smashed it down on the pizza box. The table bounced; the box jolted to the right and hung precariously on the edge of the table. The mutilated beer can rolled ninety degrees; the box tipped and dropped off the table, flinging the can against the wall.

"How well did you know Liz Goldenstern?" I asked.

"She got me the Marina Vista contract."

"Liz Goldenstern?" I had only seen Liz in an adversary position. "How did she do that?"

"Marina Vista will be apartments for people with physical impairments, right?" he asked rhetorically. "The city wanted a consultant who knew what those people would need."

"Liz was that consultant?" She would be a likely choice. It was not a new policy in the establishment to draw in a leader of the demonstrators. And Berkeley was quicker than most to see the value of dissenting views and weave them into city policy. "But why did she choose you?"

He glared at me. "Why not?"

I sighed. "Look Mr. Butz, I don't know about your background, or your work experience. The only time I've seen you was yesterday morning, when you were upset." I let hang the implication that no one would hire Butz as he had presented himself then.

"Yeah, sure," he muttered, squeezing one of the remaining beer cans. If my implication had gotten through to him, it hadn't motivated him to make himself more cooperative.

So much for subtlety. "This is a murder case. While you sit here pouting, the killer is covering his tracks. If you care that Liz was murdered, then stop wasting time and answer my questions."

He hauled back with the beer can. For a moment I thought he was going to hurl it at me. Then he caught himself. He set it down gently. "Okay, okay. You want my past, huh? Well, I came here from New York. From 183rd Street and Fordham Avenue to be exact. But you could have guessed that, right?"

I nodded, wondering vaguely if that comment was another example of egocentricity or if he had picked up on the remnants of my own accent.

He didn't smile, but for the first time his glower lightened. "I came out here seven or eight years ago. I thought I'd see the country. You know what I mean? Half of Berkeley could say the same. I had been working for Social Security back there, assessing disability applications. I wasn't about to do that again. There are only so many times you can tell a guy with sciatic pain so bad he can't sit down that Social Security doesn't believe him. Social Security wants hard proof of back injuries and a lot of times there isn't any. X-rays don't show anything . . . but the guy's still in agony. If his doctor isn't willing to go to bat for him, and sometimes even if he is, it's too bad. It's a real bummer all around."

"So you left New York," I prompted.

"Got one of those you-drive cars, headed west, and lived until my money ran out. Then I did carpentry for a few years. And when the work ran out, I got General Assistance. One thing about working for Social Security, it teaches you how to deal with bureaucracies. And, actually, I was lucky. I wasn't planning on a free ride, particularly not on two hundred fifty dollars a month, which is what G.A. was paying then. But just when my first check came through, the city was starting an apprenticeship program to train its destitute, like me. Some guys trained as electricians, some women as plumbers. I had enough experience and the brains to take the test, so I became a licensed contractor."

"How did you know Liz?" I asked, steering him back to my question.

"I built her ramp."

"That doesn't sound like a contracting job."

"Hardly," he said. "It was before I was in the program, while I was working as a carpenter."

"How did you hear about the job?"

He sighed. Reluctantly, he said, "Well, I'd been seeing her landlord, the shrink, just a couple times, just to deal with the stress from that job at Social Security and the stress of being marginally employed. I just needed someone to listen a while, till I could straighten out my head."

"And Marina Vista?"

"They were looking for a contractor. Liz remembered me —a graduate of their own program. It would have been hard for them to turn me down."

I glanced around the room. The nylon curtains were flung up over the rod. There was an internal order to the room, albeit an old and shabby one. The only things that didn't fit here were Brad Butz and his food. "How long have you lived here?"

He glared at me, then down at the floor. Spotting the fallen pizza box he kicked it. "Listen lady, just because you've got a house up in the hills, don't be looking down your nose at me, calling me a slob. I didn't invite you in here."

Where did that defensiveness come from? He certainly hadn't seen any sign of slumming from me. Compared to the remodeled porch I lived in, Brad Butz's house was a mansion. Making a point to keep my voice calm, I repeated, "Mr. Butz, how long have you lived here?"

Again he hesitated. But unlike the moment when he held the beer can poised, this time his eyes were half closed in thought. He shrugged. "Well, I'll admit it, this place is a dump. The landlord's been on me for months. When I moved in here I agreed to fix the place up in lieu of rent. I was barely in when I got the call about Marina Vista. So I put off the work here. That was almost two years ago."

"Why didn't you move out?"

"I can't. It's like the company store. If I broke the lease I'd have to pay up all the back rent. Two years' rent is a lot of money. I got some cash up front for the preliminary work on the project, but most of that has gone straight out to subcontractors, and lawyers. I tried to talk Bonner out of it, he's the owner. He told me he'd take me to court. And that kind of publicity I can't afford. If I had Bonner accusing me of being a deadbeat, people would forget I was a graduate of the city apprenticeship program, and remember I was on G.A. before, so they'd figure I really was a deadbeat. There's no way I can get out of this hole until I revamp the entire house."

I nodded. "Well, at least it's small."

"You can say that again."

"Mr. Butz," I said, "I'm going to have to ask you where you were last night."

He stared. "Hey, you don't think that I killed Liz? I just told you how Liz helped me. We were in this together. When Marina Vista was done, Liz was going to manage the place. She'd already picked out her apartment. I couldn't have gotten the job without her. I couldn't have done the plans without her. She's the one who got the shrink to back up my plans to have a pool and an exercise room. She's the one who okayed the spiral ramp outside so the tenants could have some outdoor movement.

"Look, I've worked with sick people a long time. A chance to do something important like build Marina Vista is a once in a lifetime thing. You talk to anyone in a chair. Access is so hard, they have to live anywhere where there aren't steps to keep them out. They don't choose; they take what they can get and consider themselves lucky. No one thinks of them when they build high-rises with views of the city. Marina Vista is a breakthrough, for them and for me. And I owe it to Liz."

He certainly sounded concerned, committed, knowledgeable. He sounded, in fact, like he had made this protestation, or one similar, before. I waited a moment, letting the silence bracket his declaration. "In a murder investigation we ask everyone where they were," I said. Then I smiled and added, "You worked in a bureaucracy; you understand these things."

He nodded, still glowering. But it was a companionable glower. "It's hardly worth your asking. You know how the day started. It didn't get any better. I spent most of it trying to get someone reliable to lay the foundation. I wanted Bill Milligan, he's the best, but, of course, he was booked for months. The next guy I called . . . well, I'll spare you the details. I spent the afternoon trying to work out a reasonable date for completion, so I could get QuakeChek out here, and make sure I could get Green Growing Things, the only landscapers who seem to be able to guarantee anything like what's in the architect's drawings. I'll tell you if even one tree in the sketch is missing, there'll be someone raising Cain. But the way things are going there were so many possible hang-ups—like there's talk of a carpenters' strike—that I couldn't swear to any date. So, the afternoon was pretty much a waste. After that I was too pissed off to do anything useful. I got a pizza and a six pack and rented a movie. I wanted to be home anyway. Liz was supposed to call me after the meeting. She . . . God, I figured the meeting had run over and she was too bushed to bother. But, that's not it, is it? When did she die?"

"Before midnight."

We both sat silent for a moment. "Mr. Butz, this meeting. What would Liz be likely to wear to it?"

"I don't know. What do you mean?"

"She said something about not just throwing on a dress."

"I've never seen Liz in a dress."

"What about a wool jacket?"

"Maybe. Liz was particular about her appearance when she went before these committees. She was always prepared, and part of that preparation was being dressed for the part. When she was out on the line, that was one thing, but when she spoke at a committee she was dressed for success."

Her body lying in the morgue was clothed in the same jeans and sweater she'd worn this afternoon.

"Mr. Butz, can you think of anyone who would want to kill Liz?"

He shook his head slowly. "Liz has raised some dander. Ask the Telegraph merchants. But you don't kill to avoid widening your aisles. And anyway, that campaign is long gone."

"What about Marina Vista?"

"I thought of that. It was her big campaign this last year. But there's never been anyone opposed to it, except that jerk at Rainbow Village. You want Liz's killer, get on him. You've got him in your own jail, for chrissakes."

"No, we don't, Mr. Butz. We found his truck, but not him. What else can you tell me about where to find him?"

He jumped up. "What's the point of telling you anything? With police work like that I might as well rip out my own signs. No wonder helpless women get drowned."

I stood to face him. "Mr. Butz—"

"Look, I've got friends in City Hall. One call from me and they'll get action on this."

"Fine, then we're after the same thing. Call whoever you think can help, but in the meantime, tell me what you know about the blond guy at Rainbow Village."

"I already did. Yesterday."

"Uh-huh," I said, making no attempt to cover my sarcasm. "Who else would benefit from Liz's death? Who's next in line to manage Marina Vista?"

"I don't know. That never came up."

"What about the apartment she has now? With access being such a problem, that place must be quite a prize."

"It is. I did the renovation inside, and I had a free hand.

Liz's landlord told me to do whatever it took to make over the place for her."

"Isn't that pretty unusual?"

He shrugged. "The guy's a shrink. He does a lot of counseling for people with disabilities. It's probably good P.R. for him."

"And he's the shrink who consulted on Marina Vista?"

"So?"

"What's his name?"

Again Butz hesitated.

"Are you interested in helping or not?" I said, disgusted.

"Laurence Mayer," he snapped. "He lives in the cottage behind Liz."

At four-thirty in the morning he wasn't home! He would have a lot of explaining to do.

CHAPTER 10

Situated behind the palm tree, Liz Goldenstern's building looked very white, very "California." The sky too was very "California"—no hint of sun, just the backdrop shifting from the deep charcoal of night to the pale gray of morning fog. If this were an average spring day, the fog would lift by ten and the sky would be a clear blue, unbroken by clouds.

Nothing appeared to have changed here since I left an hour and a half ago. There was no sign of life, no indication that any of the tenants had returned. I walked down the driveway to the rear cottage and knocked. Now in the light I could see that the cottage had been remodeled from a two-car garage. And there was something odd about the result. It took me a moment to realize that the building was earthbound. Few Bay Area houses had basements, but underneath most there were crawl spaces three or four feet high that housed gas heaters, pipes, and frequently many boxes of old clothes, school books, and Christmas gifts too appalling to be used but too dear to be thrown out—items that would have been consigned to an attic, if these houses had had attics. But Laurence Mayer's cottage had no crawl space. His door was at ground level. There wasn't even a sill.

I knocked again. Footsteps sounded on the stairs.

The man who pulled open the door was wearing red and gray striped nylon shorts and a T-shirt that said "Bay to Breakers." His graying hair hung in curly wet clumps around a long, intelligent looking face. His body was toned in a way that Brad Butz's would never be, with the mounds of each muscle and taut tendons on his limbs sleekly defined. His was a body that could have been ten or fifteen years younger than fifty. But the lines in his face betrayed that illusion. They crowded around his eyes and across this brow, the signs of straining to penetrate more deeply, to consider more thoroughly—markers of tensions and frustrations that could not be thrown off. I wondered if the much-touted runner's euphoria ever pushed his patients' miseries from his thoughts.

"I'm Detective Smith, Homicide." I held out my badge.

Most people either don't bother looking at it or they give it a passing glance. But Laurence Mayer leaned toward it and read the inscription and repeated the number. When he had satisfied himself, he said "What can I do for you, Detective?"

"I'm sorry to disturb you so early—"

"No problem. I just got back from a run. I was just about to jump in the shower." He stood in the doorway, but unlike Brad Butz, who had planted himself defensively on his threshold, Laurence Mayer leaned one hand on the door and waited for me to explain myself. He looked like he had had a lot of experience waiting, and there was something about the pleasant crinkling around his eyes and that expectant half smile that made me feel obliged to get to the point. In reaction, I took a breath and held my silence an extra moment before saying, "Liz Goldenstern has been killed."

For a moment his expression didn't change. Then he flushed. "Liz? Are you sure? Have you checked her flat?" He squeezed his eyes shut, then breathed deeply in and out. "I'm sorry, Officer. It's such a shock for me. You'd better come in."

I walked into a sparsely furnished waiting room without windows but with doors leading from both interior walls. Opening the door at the rear he said, "This way. We could talk in the office, but my flat upstairs is more comfortable."

I followed him through a compact kitchen and up a loop of metal circular stairs to a studio that occupied the entirety of the second floor. Unlike the windowless waiting room, here we could look out on a magnolia tree in the neighboring yard, or through French doors to a small porch at the rear. A faint aroma of sandalwood incense permeated the room. Dhurrie rugs covered the hardwood floors, and for heat there was a potbelly stove next to the doors—not the most energy efficient arrangement. I wasn't surprised to see the double bed, in the other corner, unslept in.

He plucked a Walkman off the white bamboo sofa facing the French doors, placed it atop the stereo, and sat down, holding out a hand to indicate the other end of the couch for me. "How did Liz die?"

"She was drowned."

"Oh my God." Again, he closed his eyes and breathed deeply. "I'm sorry, I'm usually better controlled than this. A psychologist is supposed to control his reactions. We can't be falling apart . . . but Liz . . . well, she was much more than just a tenant. She changed my life . . ." He swallowed, and said so softly that I had to lean in toward him, "And I hers."

I waited a moment, but he didn't go on. "Was Liz Goldenstern a patient of yours after her accident?"

"No, no. When I said I changed her life, I didn't mean I helped her." Cold air blew in beneath the French doors. Under the light thatch of hair his legs shivered, but he didn't seem to notice. "I know," he said slowly, directing his gaze out the doors into the fog, "that you will respect my confidence as much as you can in a murder investigation."

I nodded.

Still staring blankly out the doors, he said, "Before the accident, I didn't treat people with disabilities. Then I led an entirely different life, a very hedonistic life, I'm afraid. I had a private practice that brought me a considerable amount of money, and even considering I have two ex-wives and three children, I still had enough left for sailing, flying, to go to Mazatlan for the hang gliding, and Aspen for skiing. I was obsessed with winning, then. My patients were runners, drag racers, pilots, swimmers; a couple played pro football. They came to me to rid themselves of those personality holdovers that made them flabby in competition. I called it Mental Cellulite. I was fascinated with what made a winner and what was necessary to free a winner from the superficial entrapments of mediocrity. It was a very specialized practice, very upper middle class, I'm afraid. But in fairness, I will say that I was helpful to my clients," he said, turning toward me. He sounded more relaxed now, discussing his successful past. He hadn't even winced when he said "Mental Cellulite."

I was on the point of prodding him, when he flushed and mumbled a few words.

"Would you repeat that?"

He swallowed. "The accident changed everything."

"Liz's accident?"

"Yes. I want you to know exactly what happened." His voice sounded as if it were being controlled by will power alone, and one moment of carelessness would allow it to break like an adolescent's.

I nodded.

"She was running to her truck—she had a truck from work. It was dusk. She was in a hurry. A car rounded the corner"—he swallowed—"going too fast." His hands pressed against his thighs. "The impact threw her against a truck. It snapped her neck." He swallowed again, staring hard out the window. "The driver was drunk."

His face was red, and the effort it took him to turn to face me was evident. "I was that driver."

Another time I might have been surprised. But after seeing Liz's body, hassling with Brad Butz, and racing around all night, it would have taken a lot more to raise a reaction in me. He didn't comment on my lack of response, but his eyes opened just a bit wider, and I don't think I was imagining a certain disappointment in them. I let a moment pass before asking, "What was your sentence for that?"

"Probation and a fine, a stiff fine. But no fine could be enough. No judge could have sentenced me to what I sentenced Liz. Years in jail, loss of my profession, all my money . . . whatever a judge took, I would still be able to walk out of the courtroom. This sounds mawkish, I know, but there's no way I can express the horror I felt. For weeks I woke up every morning thinking it had all been a nightmare. If only it . . ." He shook his head. "As soon as she could have visitors, I went to see Liz. I told her I was the one who had hit her. I told her I would spend the rest of my days doing whatever I could to make her life more comfortable. I promised her I would never drive again. I know that sounds like something out of a soap opera, but I wasn't doing it for her, but for me. The accident scarred me—I'd be a fool to say as much as it scarred her—but that one instance changed my life completely."

"How did she respond to your offer?"

"Just as I would have expected if I had known about the

psychological sequences of adjustment to the trauma of spinal injury."

I lifted an eyebrow.

"She told me to drop dead." He shrugged. "I left. But I came back the next day, and the day after that, until eventually she believed me."

"And then you redid the front apartment for her?"

"It wasn't as simple as that. I didn't own this building. At the time I was renting the lower flat. There were just two flats then. But I knew Liz would need a place like that, and she'd certainly need it more than I did. I bought the building, and gave it to her so she'd always have a place to live."

"The whole building?"

"I'm still making payments," he said. "But Liz didn't want the whole first floor. She said it would be more trouble than it was worth. So I divided it in two. At first her attendant lived in the rear flat. That way Liz had someone she could call, and she also had her privacy. She wasn't a person who wanted someone living with her."

"Her attendant doesn't live there now?"

"Oh, no. It's not the same attendant. Liz must have been through ten or twelve since then. That's not unusual. Attendant work is hard and ill-paid. And even though I pay well above the going rate, Liz was still in the position of drawing from the pool of people who are accustomed to working for minimum wage, and who frequently are willing to do that kind of work because it's a job they can quit whenever they want. It's a very unusual person who sees attendant work as a career."

"You're saying *you* paid Liz's attendant?"

"I wanted to be sure she had the best. And the rent from the back unit more than covers it. Liz insisted I make use of that, even though as the building's owner, it's legally hers. But to get back to Liz's living situation, Liz was much more independent as the months passed. She didn't need someone next door. And if she did have a problem, I'm right back here all day, and all night."

Except last night, I thought.

"I understood her difficulties. Now I don't fill my time seeing athletes. My patients are in chairs or have mental disorders. Three-quarters of the people I see are on MediCal or Social Security. I don't make near the money I did before, but I provide a much more valuable service."

I recalled Liz Goldenstern snapping at me, telling me how much she hated being pushed in her chair. "How did Liz feel about your commitment to her?"

For the first time he seemed to relax. "She asked me to be on the planning committee of Marina Vista. I'd say that was a pretty clear endorsement."

"What was your role on that committee?"

"To begin with, I found her two of the four backers—two guys I knew from the professional sports scene who were looking for a legitimate investment and looking to clean up their images." He shrugged. "I will be active on the planning committee until Marina Vista is finished. Then I'll be on the board. And it's a good thing I've been there. Over the past three years I've gained a great understanding, more than I would have wanted. I don't think I overstate it when I say I understand as well as an unimpaired person can. Let me give you an example. The contractor was planning to construct just another nice looking apartment building. Oh, he was taking wheelchair access into consideration, but he didn't give a thought to the psychological outlook of the people who would be living there. That's understandable. He's a carpenter, not a psychologist. For instance, it didn't occur to him that social contact with the other tenants is important. The average person can hop in their car and whip over to a friend's. But for someone in a power chair, that's a big undertaking. So a community room in the building is important. Many have to have meals cooked for them, so a community kitchen made sense. And people with disabilities need exercise as much, if not more than others. Exercise facilities are important. And a pool. For a number of people with disabilities, gentle calisthenics in the water is excellent conditioning. So I insisted on a pool, a pool as good as anyone else would expect. And a court for wheelchair basketball. The entirety of the first two floors will be devoted to those concerns. And then there's the outdoor ramp. It will spiral around the building. It'll be a great way for those who are ambulatory to use the muscles necessary for climbing and descending. And for the people in chairs, it'll be a pleasant ride. So," he said, with the self-assurance of one who was comfortable espousing Mental Cellulite, or the riddance of it, "I think I'm safe in saying I've made a difference in Marina Vista."

"Brad Butz just told me the pool and the exercise room were his ideas."

He smiled. "Well, he probably thinks they were."

"Were they?"

"It doesn't matter who conceived the plan. The important thing is that it will be carried through."

I glanced at my watch. Barely an hour to the Detectives' Morning Meeting. "Did Liz say anything about being afraid, or being threatened?" I asked.

He thought a moment. "No, nothing. I can't remember her ever admitting she was afraid."

"She died on the site of Marina Vista. Would you like to speculate why Liz was down there?"

There was no hesitation now. "If Brad Butz needed her help she would have gone. Liz was a sharp woman, Detective, but I'll tell you, I don't know what got into her when she chose Brad Butz as the project contractor. Oh, I don't mean that the man can't handle the rudiments of building. I'm sure he can read a blueprint as well as the next guy. But he's got no imagination. If something unexpected comes up, he panics. Lately he's had trouble with some of the Rainbow Villagers. They're not doing anything more than petty vandalism, but Butz is completely thrown by it. So, if he asked her to come with him to deal with them, I can't imagine her saying no."

Butz had said he hadn't seen Liz all evening, but, of course, suspects had been known to lie. "Any other reason?" When he didn't answer, I stood. "One more thing, Dr. Mayer, I need to know where you were last night."

Unlike Brad Butz's outraged reaction, Laurence Mayer greeted the question with the type of smile that was an answer in itself. "With a lady friend."

"I'll need her name and address."

"Of course. It is Greta Tennerud. She lives on Claremont."

"Greta Tennerud, the marathon runner?"

His smile widened. "You're thinking she's beautiful, a world class athlete, and half my age, right?"

That was exactly my reaction.

"What can I say? I'm a lucky guy."

"Is she at home now?"

"She should be training. The Bay to Breakers is next month. It's an important race for her. But I think today's one of her off days. She said she was going in to work early. So you may catch her at Racer's Edge."

"One last thing," I said, moving toward the staircase. "Who are the tenants in the other flats? And where are they?"

"Don't ask," he said, suddenly looking entirely his age. "My son and his girlfriend have the upstairs. One of his friends is downstairs. The lot of them took off for San Diego over the weekend. In need of some sun and surf, they said. Apparently, it was a greater need than a week of education. But once they're in college, what can you do?"

I shrugged and gave him my card and the usual request to call me if he remembered anything useful.

As I hurried to my car, I recalled what Connie Pereira

had said about Racer's Edge, the running shoe store on Telegraph. Nine of the twelve pairs of stolen shoes came from there.

CHAPTER 11

Five times the number of stolen shoes could have stood in the window of Racer's Edge. But it held only two cardboard figures dressed for speed. I knocked on the glass door. I was due for some luck in finding a witness where she was supposed to be.

At 7:20 A.M., Telegraph Avenue looked like an abandoned movie set. Most shopkeepers wouldn't be here for a couple hours. Students were still eating breakfast or catching a last few minutes of sleep. And for the street people who leaned against the walls watching one minute flow into the next, this time of morning was still yesterday.

I pounded again.

A tall, sleekly muscled woman with corn-blond straight hair strode toward the door. I recognized her from pictures in the papers when she won the Bay to Breakers in San Francisco two years ago. Her skin was already tan, even though the rains had been heavy and seemingly constant for the past three months. In red and gray striped nylon running shorts and a T-shirt that said "Racer's Edge," she looked as warm as I felt in my wool jacket. Her red headband wasn't even stained from sweat. "I'm Detective Smith." I held out my shield.

She shook her head. "Not another theft?" She pulled the door open. "Come talk in back, where people from the street cannot see. Even at seven-thirty in the morning, they will bang on the door if they see me." Greta's delivery had that pleasant lyric quality of Scandanavian speech. And there was just enough hesitancy in her word choice to suggest a lack of sureness with the idiom.

She strode past racks of running shorts, shiny lightweight suits, lycra pants, displays of weighted armbands, inner soles, disks offering computerized running programs, and an array of glossy books that must have contained the entirety of collected knowledge on putting one foot before the other. From the shelf beneath the cash register, she drew forth a manila envelope and plucked out a receipt. "We have to keep these copies from the charge cards. The woman who helps my bookkeeper alphabetizes them for me. But in the year I've managed this store, this is the first time I have ever looked at one after the sale. I just stuff them in an envelope for her. Here, you will want to see this. It is good for a detective to be after this craven thief." She extended the receipt.

I glanced at it but didn't take it from her. "He lost his New Balances," she went on. "He bought them only last week. Eric Parosco," she read from the attached credit card receipt. "He was very distressed. He tried on"—she glanced at the opposite wall—"half of my stock." There must have been sixty running shoes, each on an individual little shelf. "He was very particular about minimizing his pronation. But you see he didn't want a straight shoe; he liked the curve-lasted shoes. I told him they don't give the same protection from pronation, but"—she flung her hands to the side—"it is very difficult with these people. They think they know what they want. But they want five or six things that are not compatible, and they want them with green racing stripes." She laughed, showing strong straight teeth. She had pale blue eyes, but her mouth was too wide for her chiseled nose, and when she laughed it overwhelmed the upper half of her face. "Come with me to the back. I must start my training soon. Now is my time to have coffee. The caffeine will make my body burn the fat—more efficient."

She led me into the storeroom. Shoe boxes filled the walls and shelves floor to ceiling. It looked like a library of shoes. By the rear door was a scarred wooden table that held the coffee pot, a cup, and a computer. The file cabinet was next to it.

Taking a swallow from the cup, she held out her hand as an invitation for me to sit. "It is better for me to continue to stand now," she added.

The chair looked very appealing. I figured I'd better continue to stand, too. "Miss Tennerud," I said, "what I've come to ask you about is last night. Would you tell me what you were doing from, say, six o'clock till this morning?"

"Ah, that is a bit personal." She laughed in the same way Laurence Mayer had smiled. "Why is it you ask me this?"

"A woman has been killed."

"No. You don't think that I . . ."

"No. But knowing where you were might help us to assess some of the other factors."

Her pale blue eyes narrowed and that wide mouth drooped. "I will tell you what I can. I don't want trouble. I am not a citizen here. I want to cooperate. I need my green card."

I was tempted to assure her that we were not here to threaten her immigration status, but that, I decided, could wait until she had cooperated. "What were you doing at six?"

"I closed up at five-thirty. Then I totaled the receipts and closed the cash register. The bookkeeper comes in the afternoons. I have to have everything ready. When I finished it was then about six. My boyfriend was already here. He walks over here when he is through with his patients and waits in the back where he is sure none of them will see him. He has no car, you see. Sometimes if he has a late patient I go to his place and listen to his stereo until he's done. I have a key. But last night he came here. Then we went out for pasta and came back to my apartment. Do you want me to go on?"

"Who is your boyfriend?" I asked for the record.

"Larry Mayer. He is a psychologist here in Berkeley. He will tell you I was with him."

"He has, Miss Tennerud."

"Then why—"

"We need to double check."

"He is very reliable. I refer to him my customers who complain they should be running better than they are. Not just to him, though he is the best. He has counseled top-seeded runners, and tennis players—you would recognize their names—and even some of your football stars. I am not saying this just because I love him, you know," she grinned, that appealing wide-mouthed smile I had seen in the ads for Racer's Edge. "It is my job to help customers with their training questions. I tell them of the sports clinics, to see if they have a physical problem, and of the sports physiologists. You can't run seriously without a physiologist to test you and tell you how to maximize your training. I myself was running too fast in my practice. I was wasting energy, courting injury, when I could have run a whole minute slower each mile and had the same benefit. Many people think the physiologists are a great expense, but for a serious runner . . ." She shrugged. "For the beginners, I tell them of yoga classes to stretch in, and podiatrists."

"How did you meet Laurence Mayer?"

"He was at a local marathon I was running a few months ago. It was the last one I ran. Too many marathons is not good. To win the Olympics after running fewer than five marathons is common. You have to save your body for the ones that count."

"With the big purses."

She smiled. "Of course."

"But you're running the Bay to Breakers in San Francisco

next month." There was no great monetary reward for that seven-mile race. One year first prize had been two tickets to Paris and the *use* of a BMW.

"Yes, yes. It is not wise. Where I come from we don't train in winter. In Norway, you can't. But that is good. The muscles need to rest, the tears and strains have time to heal. But here we can run every day. It is not so good. I tell my boss this. But he wants a famous runner managing his store, not a 'has-been' whose last win was fourteen months ago." She shrugged. "So I train."

"Good luck."

"Thanks. I'm training well, but I can use luck, regardless of what Larry says."

"You said you met Larry at a race," I prodded. That didn't sound like the pastime of a man who had given up his obsession with winning.

"He told me he had seen me run before. He thought he could help me clear my mind. He said a mind stuffed with unproductive complexes is like a windbreak holding you back." She laughed. "I told him I do not have complexes, but he could take me to dinner."

That didn't sound like the psychologist whose life had been changed.

"But I have referred others to Larry, and he has helped me too," she added. "I have no complexes, but I am not good with the books. He sent me his bookkeeper. She comes for an hour, three days a week."

"Wouldn't it be easier to have her for three hours at a time?"

"For me, yes. But she is in a wheelchair. I think this schedule is less tiring for her. Even with the computer—"

"What is her name?" I asked, suspecting the answer.

"Liz Goldenstern."

The picture of Liz pressing two fingers together to take hold of the reporter's card flashed in my mind. It hadn't been the thumb and forefinger but the first two fingers. I wouldn't have thought Liz could operate a computer. I would have been wrong. I wondered how much I had underestimated her. "What exactly did she do?"

Greta flushed under her tan. "I have to tell you I don't know. The owners of the store told me I needed to have someone to do the books and prepare for the taxes. She did that. But what is involved, that I don't know. I don't want to know. I cannot clutter my mind with the little tasks of shopkeeping. I have my training."

"But she came three days a week?" I insisted.

"Monday, Wednesday, Friday. From four to five."

"And she was here yesterday?" She must have been going home from here when Pereira ran into her.

"Yes. Today she is off. But tomorrow she will be here if you need to talk with her."

"I'm afraid she won't," I said. "She is the woman who has been killed."

Greta gasped. Her small features scrunched in together and tears dripped from her eyes. Intermingling her sobs with great sniffles, she cried like a child. "It is so sad. Life was so hard for her. Everything was hard. I tried to make this as easy as I could. I told her to come the hours she wanted. It was fine if the woman who took care of her came here with her. She didn't come often. Only a few times she stopped to talk with Liz. But that was fine. I was paying Liz by the hour, but it was fine if she had visitors here. I told her it was fine if her son stopped to see her here. It was no problem, the attendant was there."

"Liz had a son?"

"Yes. I think he is at university. He didn't come often either. Maybe two or three times."

"What was his name?"

She shook her head. "That I don't know." Running a hand across her eyes, she glanced at her watch. I looked down at my own. Detectives' Morning Meeting would start in twenty minutes.

"What does he look like?"

"He is a student," she said in the off-hand manner used to describe sneakers.

"Tall, short, blond, brunette . . ." I prodded.

She sighed. "He was not here long, not often. But I will tell you what I can remember. He has average height. Hair some shade of brown. He could jog, but never run well. He is too wide in the hip."

"Do you mean he's fat?"

"No, not that," she exclaimed with horror. "The bones of his legs are set wide. I know these things. In school I studied not only business and sports management, but physiology. That is why I can advise runners now. But this boy, he hasn't the body for long distances." She shrugged. "Some don't."

I wondered how Liz Goldenstern had managed to keep her temper when Greta assessed the lesser mortals. I wondered *why* Liz had bothered, or if indeed she had. I said, "How did you know this boy was Liz's son?"

"Let me see. How did I? Ah yes, it was the first time he came here. He was not so confident then. He didn't walk straight through to the back like he does now. Then he stood by the cash register. He looked like he needed help. But when I asked him he said no, he didn't want to buy shoes. He needed to see the woman in the back. 'Liz?' I asked him. He nodded his head. I asked him if he was a friend of hers. He didn't look like he would be a friend. He was much younger, you see." Greta smiled impishly. "I was curious. But he said, no, he wasn't a friend. She was his mom. Then the attendant rushed in, and I stopped her and asked her to take the boy with her into the back."

"Miss Tennerud, what kind of employee was Liz Goldenstern? Was she easy to work with?"

She hesitated, long enough for that to be my answer. "A store like this, it must have been difficult for her to see. It would have been unkind to flaunt my muscles. She needed to concentrate on her work. So I left her alone. That's why I don't know more about the boy."

I moved to the door. "Can you think of anyone who would want to kill Liz Goldenstern? Did she say she was afraid? Did anyone come in here and make her uneasy?"

"My customers are not back here. They don't know when she is. No one visited her but those two, unless they came in by the back when I was out front. But I am in and out of the back. They would have had to come in like that." She snapped her fingers.

"Think, Miss Tennerud. This is important."

She shook her head again. "Perhaps with her son she was not on the best of terms. But that is common with children that age, is it not?"

Children that age must have been about five years younger than Greta. "What gave you that idea? Did she say something to you? Or did you overhear something?"

"No, no. It was not her. It was him. He left quickly each time. He had the long face."

CHAPTER 12

It was already twenty to eight as I raced back to the station. Detectives' Morning Meeting started in five minutes.

In many ways we are more liberal than other police departments, more "Berkeley" than "Police." But maybe because of the laid-back atmosphere of the town, in which arriving on time takes second place to finishing an incisive conversation or appreciating the first daffodil of spring, running in late to Morning Meeting is viewed much the same as leaving the keys in the ignition of your patrol car. In my few months as a detective, I had been late for two meetings and missed one entirely. Inspector Doyle, the head of Homicide Detail, had called me in each time.

As the traffic light turned from amber to red, I stepped harder on the gas and hurried on past the high school, blowing my horn at a covey of ambling adolescents who had stopped to argue in the crosswalk.

With a burst of bravado I circled in front of the station. Parking was at a premium. It was not unknown to find the only available spot five or six blocks away. As I passed the station, and the full curb opposite, Howard slowed his Land Rover and pointed to the garage he rented from a woman across the street. "Take it," he called.

I could have asked why he could do without it—he could no more miss Morning Meeting than I. Howard and I had started on patrol together, walked the same beat. We had worked on many of the same cases and stuck our necks out way too far for each other on more than one occasion. And when I had gotten the prestigious promotion to Homicide, and he only to Vice and Substance Abuse, he had swallowed his disappointment. There was little I wouldn't do for Howard, or he for me. But giving up a parking spot was beyond the limits of even our friendship.

I waved a thanks and pulled into the driveway.

It was just quarter to eight when I slid into an empty chair at the conference room table. I glanced at Clayton Jackson, one of the two old-time homicide detectives. Jackson had been in Homicide when I joined the force nearly four years ago. For all I knew that might have been his first day in homicide. But for me, he and Al "Eggs" Eggenberger were institutions.

Jackson grinned and shoved a thermos cup toward me. We had a deal, the Jackson family and I. Once a week I coached Jackson's fifteen-year-old son, Pernell, who had been cut from the junior varsity swim team. In return, Pernell made me a thermos of Peet's strongest coffee every morning. There had been a few disasters the first week (after Pernell realized that his mother was not going to make the coffee for him). But compared to the machine coffee, which I never got to work in time to get anyway, Pernell's brew was superb. This was one of those days I counted on that coffee to get me through.

Howard slid into the seat next to me at the same time the captain took his. Grinning at me, he leaned his elbows on the table. His arm length, fingertip to fingertip, was a foot more than mine. (We had had a bet. We measured, and he won a beer.) I shifted my coffee to the left.

The captain circulated the hot car list. Edison, from Crimes Against Property, gave an update on a VCR theft ring that had been hitting Berkeley stores on and off for three months. Pereira, doing a "guest shot," reported on the running shoe thief.

"The shoes," said Ortiz, from Internal Affairs, "are they any particular brand?"

"No," Pereira snapped. "Just new, expensive running shoes that the owners refuse to take inside with them. They put them outside because they want to think Berkeley is the kind of place where you can leave your door unlocked."

A groan came from the guys in Burglary.

Howard leaned back in his chair, balancing precariously on the rear legs. "Hey Connie, we could set up a Berkeley Marathon and check the shoes of all the runners." Howard loved stings. But at six foot six, with blue eyes and curly red hair, his picture had graced more newspaper articles than any other officer in the history of the department. His days of leading stings were pretty well over. Like an aged athlete, he satisfied himself by coaching others. And others, like Connie, tried to steer clear.

"Smith, you have a murder," the captain said.

I summarized the Liz Goldenstern case. Just as the meeting was finishing, Murakawa rushed in to report that his crew had canvassed the entire marina area and hadn't found one vehicle that didn't belong there.

As I headed to the door, Magill, the press officer, caught my arm. "Don't you have anything more than that, Smith? My phone's been going nonstop, and there were four reporters and a photographer at the door when I got here this morning. This Goldenstern murder is a natural for the papers. The schmaltz will be running like molasses. And unless you come up with the killer pronto, you're not going to look too sweet."

"Magill, you've been doing news conferences too long. In another month you'll sound like something out of *Variety*."

"My question, Smith?" he demanded. I wasn't the first to comment on Magill's seduction by the press.

"The case isn't twelve hours old. I've been up all night. What do you want? If I had anything else don't you think I would have told the captain?"

"Well, check in with me before noon." He turned and strode down the hall.

"If it's convenient," I called after as I headed toward my office.

Murakawa came up beside me. Without commenting on my grumblings he said, "I called AC Transit. The driver of the bus with the lift on the Marina route last night knows Liz. She wasn't on the bus between six and ten. I checked the victim and Stuart and Summerlight through files. Nothing in California Identification Index. None of them had been arrested for a retainable offense in this state. According to Corpus Files they've never been arrested at all. There's nothing in PIN—no warrants out for them. As for Motor Vehicles, they've got no record of an Aura Summerlight or"—he flipped open his note pad—"a Penelope Lynn Garrett. No license, no I.D."

"She could have an out-of-state license. Where's her truck registered?"

"New Mexico. I sent a request to Motor Vehicles there."

"Don't hold your breath. This won't be top priority for them. What about Stuart?"

"He got a California license last year. Turned in one from British Columbia."

"And Liz?"

"She's on file. Took her last test five years ago and re-registered by mail last year."

I laughed. The motor vehicle department had instituted a new system wherein randomly selected good drivers were allowed to reregister without coming down and taking the test. It was a popular innovation with those who benefited, and maddening for the rest of us who were not among the chosen. But clearly it had its drawbacks. According to Liz Goldenstern's driver's license, she had no limitations.

"I'm on my way to C.I.L." Murakawa said.

"Wait. What about the hedge by Rainbow Village? Did you find the place that twig in Liz's sweater came from?"

"Possibly. It's by the top. The lab's checking the twig against the broken samples."

"Good." But I knew better than to expect the report today, or tomorrow.

Giving him the names of Laurence Mayer and Greta Tennerud to run through files, I walked into my office and slumped in my chair. Settling in his, Howard pushed it against the outer wall and stretched his legs. "You ought to hire Murakawa permanently, Jill," he said. "He's been up all night and he looks like he's ready for a few sets of tennis. While you . . ." He grinned.

"I know. I look like something grabbed out of the 'free box.' I'm counting on Jackson's coffee to help me pass for a human being," I said, pouring another cup of coffee. "It would have been gracious of you not to mention my appearance. But I suppose you're entitled to one free dig after the favor you did me. This isn't my day for your garage." I had done Howard a favor a few months back, in return for Monday and Friday use of the garage he rented.

"If that's the trade-off, I should be able to publicize every defect in your body, and your soul," Howard said, grinning. That grin had charmed no small number of Berkeley ladies, several of whom, from time to time, had rented him a coveted garage near the station.

"What are you planning to give me for that kind of presumption?" I demanded.

"My parking spot."

"For how long?"

"Until further notice. Maybe forever."

"For that you could repeat every malicious word I've ever spoken. And a few so damning I've only thought them." I finished the coffee. "How come, Howard? I mean, it's twice as hard to find a parking spot for your Rover than for my bug. With the size of that thing you could be among the elite in Rainbow Village."

His smile faded. "Well, I've got another parking spot."

"Another local lady wants you to park in her driveway?"

He shifted in his chair. "Well, actually, it's Nancy, the woman I've been seeing for the last couple months. She lives two blocks away."

"Oh." I could feel my face flush. I lifted the coffee cup to my lips, putting it down slowly when I realized it was empty. "Forever, huh?" Howard and I had discussed our various relationships, but it was only when they were on the way out and we needed each other to gripe to. When I had been going through my divorce he had sympathized with a string of complaints that could only have interested another ex-wife. But afterward, when I found an intriguing man, I tended to keep it to myself. And I only suspected Howard had a new lady friend when he seemed preoccupied. Neither of us had talked in terms of forever before. I swallowed. "Pretty serious, huh?"

"I don't know. We're going to see what it's like, my staying at her place. You know what a zoo my house is. There are five other guys living there now and three have their girlfriends staying most nights. And Dwight's got that Irish Setter, and his girlfriend's got a parrot that squawks half the night."

"It's probably got good reason. Setters are bird dogs."

"Well, this one's not too bright. Or at least he hasn't learned to open a cage." He drew his legs in toward him so his knees pointed sharply to the transom. Shifting his gaze to the door, he said, "You know I've been thinking about moving out of that house for ages, or getting all of *them* out. And then Nancy offered, and well . . ."

"Oh." I said. It was more serious than I had thought. "Well, best wishes. I hope it goes really well. My house-warming gift to you is going to be no advice based on my own years of matrimony."

Now, as Howard laughed, I could see him relaxing. "How about some breakfast?" he asked.

"I had breakfast," I said, too quickly. "I had a couple of Night Watch's donuts a few hours ago."

"I mean real food, or as close to real as Wally's serves. You can tell me about your murder."

"Okay, maybe I could use some food." Maybe hashing out a case, like we'd always done together, was what we both needed now. We stood up and headed out. I said, "I can't help thinking about Liz yesterday, when I was pushing her chair. She wasn't like the other times I'd come across her. She was more open, or at least she was sporadically. I didn't think about it much then, but now, looking back, it seems like she was apprehensive, that she wanted to talk about something, or to be reassured, or even just to connect with someone who . . ."

"Someone she could trust?" Howard asked as we crossed the street.

"Well, yes. Liz knew enough of me from our encounters on the Avenue to have some sense of me. I'd always been straight with her."

"And you *were* pushing her home yesterday. That has to count for something."

We headed into Wally's and settled on stools at the counter. Without asking, Wally filled two cups with coffee and set them in front of us. It wasn't Peet's, it wasn't even good, but as Howard had said early on, "We're cops; we're tough. It'll take more than Wally to make us give up caffeine."

I considered ordering pancakes, the nearest thing to respectable junk food, but decided on a fried egg sandwich.

Wally nodded. "Your body will thank you, Smith."

"My sweater will thank me. At least a sandwich I can hold in my hand while I eat." I had been known to get too caught up in pondering a case. It wasn't a thing to do with maple syrup dripping from your fork.

Howard ordered the Wallaroo—three eggs, a waffle, sausage, home fries, toast, and a couple pieces of fruit. Wally had been to Australia over Christmas. To commemorate the trip he had renamed his specials. The standard two eggs, home fries, and toast was now the Wallyrag (runt of the litter). The large breakfast was the Wallaby (small to medium sized kangaroo). And Howard's Wallaroo was the former Gigantic Breakfast. But Wally hadn't been sated with his menu changes. Over the counter in bright red letters he had painted, "WALLY—1. Fine, first-rate. 2. Ample, large, strong, or robust. 3. Pleasing or agreeable." When pressed, he had admitted that Wally and Wallyrag were not Australian but Scottish. But he was so proud of his sign that neither Howard nor I could bring ourselves to mention the other definition of Wally, the noun: a toy, gimcrack, or bauble.

"If Liz Goldenstern drove her chair to the waterfront, it must have been quite a trip," I said. "There's no sidewalk on the freeway overpass. And according to Murakawa she didn't take the bus."

"And no suspicious vehicles down at the marina, right?"

"Right. No one I interrogated turned up on any of the files. And the only question mark now is Liz's son, and he hasn't surfaced."

"So where does that leave you, Jill?"

I took a swallow of coffee. "I don't know. I'm not the best person to be handling this case."

Howard nodded. I had told him as much about my fears as I was willing to admit to anyone. "I wasn't surprised you hadn't been home. Didn't think you could sleep, huh?"

"The chance didn't arise, but if it had I would have been staring at the ceiling."

"Jill, the idea of paralysis is awful. Most of us just don't think about it. Why this big thing with you?"

I took a long swallow of coffee, picked up my sandwich, looked at it, and put it back down. "I told you about my father's cousin, John."

He nodded. "A little. Were you very close to him?"

"No, on the contrary, I only saw him twice a year—at his birthday in June and sometime around Christmas. I resented him every moment of each visit and for days before and after. He died the summer I was fourteen. I was at camp when they held the funeral. I didn't realize he was dead till after New Year's, when it occurred to me that I hadn't had to see him. Then I didn't bring it up for two weeks, in case my parents had forgotten and we might still have to go."

Howard fingered his cup. "So this guilt is what's been eating you all these years?"

"No, no. I did feel bad, but it passed. No, Howard. I guess I never mentioned what happened to cousin John. I know I didn't. My father told me one Sunday in August when we were watching the white caps break on the beach at Asbury Park. We'd just eaten lunch, so of course we couldn't go in the water for an hour. That was a strict rule in those days. The water was calm that day. Beyond the breakers, people were lying on air mattresses, barely moving any more than if they'd been stretched out on a blanket on the sand. Even under the umbrella it was scorching. A hundred and three. I remember that. It was the hottest day of the year. My father opened a beer, leaned back on one elbow, and stared out at the ocean. The beer foamed over the edge of the can and ran across his hand. When he spoke it was like he was talking to himself. He said, 'I came here with John on a day like this. Hot. He was sweating. We both were. He had his clothes half off before we put the blanket down. He flung them at me. His shirt landed on my head. He looked at me and laughed. He had a big, booming laugh then. He was still laughing as he ran down to the water. He dived in through the breakers. His head hit the bottom. He snapped his neck.' Howard, Cousin John was eighteen years old then. He never moved an arm or leg again."

I swallowed, lifted the coffee cup to take a sip, but my throat closed. "The family didn't hold my father responsible, but he never forgave himself. He went to see John every Sunday afternoon. He never said where he was going and we knew not to ask. And when he got home it was as if he had taken on the pall of the sick room. As John got weaker over the years, it got worse. But as kids, we didn't make those connections." I looked out the window. Gray cars moved through the fog. "For years when I went in the water, it was all I could do to make myself stay in long enough so no one asked me why I was getting out so soon. I never let my feet leave the bottom. And then, finally, I decided I had to deal with it. I had to learn to swim. But even now, I never go in the water without thinking about Cousin John. And I never see anyone in a wheelchair without feeling that pall, and that awful fear."

Howard put his hand over mine. "Jackson or Eggs could take this case. You could swap with them."

I shook my head. "No. It's just something I have to deal with. Look, I can dive off the high board at King Pool. I'm tough."

Howard grinned, releasing my hand.

"Besides, I've spent all night on this case. I'm not about to plop it in Jackson's lap."

Wally set my dish in front of me. I reached for the mustard and ketchup. Eyeing my hand, Wally shook his head and set down the serving platter that held Howard's breakfast.

"So now what, tough detective?" Howard asked, forking a mound of scrambled egg.

"I don't know. Before I left her, Liz let me turn her phone machine on for her. That was very unlike her. She was anxious for me to leave. I had the impression there was something she was waiting to hear on that tape."

"You could hardly have stayed and eavesdropped. It wasn't like she was a suspect."

"Howard," I said, holding my sandwich in mid-air. "I did stop outside. I could hear the tape through the window. Guess who the call was from?"

"Got me."

"Herman Ott."

"Well, now there's a pleasant prospect for you. And you, Ott's favorite cop."

Plunking the sandwich on the plate, I stood.

"Hey," Wally called from the end of the counter. "You eat that."

"Got to run." To Howard, I said, "I have to catch Pereira before she gets to Ott herself."

CHAPTER 13

"Gone? Where is she?" I demanded of Pereira's fellow beat officer.

"Doing her rounds. A bottle of milk here, two creams there." It was an old beat officer joke.

"Did she say anything about where specifically she was going?"

"She had to make a check on some vandalism outside a dental office at the top of Solano. After that, who knows."

"Thanks."

My next stop was at accounting. "I requested two hundred dollars from the discretionary fund. That was three weeks ago, Mrs. Vorkey," I said. Plump, gray-haired Mrs. Vorkey had ruled accounting when Jackson and Eggs were eyeing their first play pistols.

"I'll check." She pulled a ledger from her second drawer. "March twenty-fifth. Right here," she said in a tone of crisp satisfaction, as if my question had thus been answered.

"I haven't gotten the money," I said. "But I can take it now," I added, businesswoman to businesswoman.

She started to nod, then stopped. "Now wait, eh, Smith." I suspected Mrs. Vorkey knew every employee of the department by sight, if only to avoid handing Jackson's money to Howard, or Pereira's to Eggs. But she never addressed one of us by name without that regal pause. To her we were only names to be filled in after "authorized by" or "disbursed to." Without looking up, she said, "This requisition has never gotten proper authorization."

"I put it through Inspector Doyle."

"He has not authorized it." She held out the form. The line over "authorizing officer" was blank.

"Why didn't you send it back, then?" I demanded.

"Officer, it's not the purview of the Accounting Department to question an inspector's decision."

"Well, then why didn't you send it back to me? How long has it been sitting here unsigned?" I said, furious.

But Mrs. Vorkey wasn't ruffled. "We in Accounting assume that officers will follow up their requests. It is not our function to track down requestees."

I grabbed the authorization form and stomped out, up the stairs, and down the hall to the inspector's office. "He in?" I asked the division secretary.

"Working on a report," she said, which meant he would be anything but agreeable.

"I need to see him. I'm in a hurry."

"Okay," she said, shaking her head. Picking up the phone, she announced me. "Go on in."

Inspector Doyle was slumped behind a desk covered with a mound of white papers, some mimeographed, some Xeroxes, some printouts, and a few just typed. Atop the pile, like the hard yolk of my fried egg sandwich, was a clump of wadded up sheets of yellow paper. The pad from which they'd been ripped was on his lap. He looked irritated and haggard. His face was almost the same color as his short, gray-laced carrot-colored hair. Behind him, the sun was beginning to singe the fog, breaking through in short-lived bursts. It showed the dirt on his window.

"So, Smith?" he demanded.

This certainly wasn't the time to see him. "Quick item, sir," I said. "Accounting needs a signature on this authorization. It got sent on without one."

He nodded, taking the form.

I waited. When I'd joined the Detail, there was a rumor that Inspector Doyle had cancer. He'd lost a lot of weight. He looked tired and worried. Now four months later, he looked exactly the same, no worse, but certainly no better. The rumor mill had stalled.

His ruddy forehead wrinkled. "Sit down, Smith."

I sat.

"I thought I had sent this back to you."

"No."

He shrugged. "It should never have got to Accounting." He laid the form atop the yellow pad. With both hands he shoved the piles of white papers toward the sides of the desk, as if he were treading paper-strewn water. "The thing is, Smith," he said, propping an elbow in the space he'd cleared, "I don't like this type of pay-off. Informants! These guys, they spend half their time thumbing their noses at the law and the other half picking our pockets."

It's a bit late in the day for this kind of idealism, I thought, particularly for the head of Homicide. There had to be something behind Inspector Doyle's reaction. "Sir, this is Herman Ott. He'd never flaunt the law in public. He's too careful. Sometimes I wish he would; we'd have a little more to bargain with."

His color deepened. I had taken the wrong tack.

Quickly, I said, "He did give me information I couldn't have gotten anywhere else. I collared the South Side Basher because of him."

"Still, Smith . . ."

"Sir, I did discuss this with you then."

"I don't recall any mention of two hundred dollars."

"I didn't know the amount then. I hadn't done the actual bargaining." I added, "I assumed you would expect me to check with you first."

Grudgingly, he nodded. "I'll look this over, Smith. It won't do Ott any harm to wait."

"Maybe not, but he left a message for Liz Goldenstern. It could be important. If I don't come through with that money—money I promised him—you can imagine how much he'll tell me."

Inspector Doyle leaned back in his chair. His shirt hung

oose. It was obviously a garment from his heavier days. "Ott talks enough when he chooses," he grumbled.

Rats. I'd forgotten Herman Ott had testified before the police review commission last month. It was his testimony that had convinced the board to hold another week of hearings, and to call in Inspector Doyle. Ott hadn't won his point, but his accusations had triggered the board's request for another, more detailed report, a report Inspector Doyle had to write up, a report that had caused him to miss a three-day conference in sunny Santa Barbara.

I took a breath, trying to decide on the right tack. I said, "Sir, it's not a question of Ott. It's a matter of my reputation. I made a deal, and I'm not holding up my end. If I don't pay Herman Ott, I'll never get another thing out of him, or, when the word spreads, any other informant."

He pressed his lips together.

"And everyone else in the department will be tainted. There will be borderline deals that won't get made, collars we won't get."

With a sigh, he said, "All right, all right, Smith, you've made your point. You'll have your money. But it'll go through channels like anything else. I'm not shaking up the department for Herman Ott."

There was no point in arguing. Muttering the minimum necessary pleasantries, I walked out. The division secretary eyed me for wounds. I shrugged. I'd won the battle, after a fashion, but lost the war. The operation had been a success, but the patient had died. I'd get my money, but by then it would be too late for it to be any use in bargaining with Herman Ott. By then it would just be payment for services rendered. Without it, I could kiss Herman Ott's reason for calling Liz good-bye.

The only possible leverage was Pereira's tax knowledge. To get any use of that, I'd have to catch her before she spent it all on leads to the shoe thief. After an all-nighter learning the intricacies of Form 45-whatever, Connie wasn't going to be in a mood to share the reward. But she'd be easier to bargain with than Ott. She owed me. I glanced into the bullpen. Her desk was still empty.

But there was one more place to check for Ott's message. Leaving word with the dispatcher to have Pereira meet me at Ott's office at eleven A.M., I signed out a car and headed for Liz Goldenstern's phone machine.

It was just after ten A.M. when I passed Liz's flat. There was a blue van in the driveway by Laurence Mayer's cottage, a patrol car in front of the triplex, and not another parking spot on the street. I could have left the black and white in the driveway, but I didn't want to block in Mayer's patient. I needed to question Mayer about Liz Goldenstern's son but I could do that after I had listened to her tape. I drove around the corner. A yellow Volvo was pulling out, which saved me from testing just how considerate I was willing to be. Even with the walk, there was ample time to deal with everything here and still meet Pereira before she got to Herman Ott's office.

In front of Liz's triplex, Heling, a rookie, slumped against her patrol car seat, her eyes on Liz's flat.

"Anything new in there?" I asked.

She raised her eyebrows and sighed deeply. "Nothing has changed since I got here"—she looked down at her watch—"two hours and twenty-six minutes ago. It's been like staring at a photograph. If I had known police work would be this boring I'd have stayed in word processing."

"Which *wasn't* boring?" When she didn't answer, I said, "I expect to be in here for forty-five minutes. Why don't you take a break?"

"You don't have to ask twice, Smith. See you then."

I walked up the ramp. The breeze that had blown the palm fronds early this morning had disappeared with the fog. In the stillness, the sweet smell of freesias drifted up from the box beneath the windows. I opened the door and stood as I had yesterday afternoon when I'd pushed Liz's chair inside. Then Liz had dominated everything. But now, with her gone, I was struck by the emptiness of the room—not a spiritual vacancy, but a lack of furnishings. The room looked like it had been cleared, repainted, and was waiting for the furniture to be brought back in. All that stood on the green wall-to-wall carpet were four floor lamps, one by each wall, and the small table under the front windows that held the phone and answering machine. Across from the door was a beige-tiled fireplace with an empty mantel. The only chairs were pushed against the waist-high partition that divided this room from the next. It took me a moment to recall that Laurence Mayer had remodeled this flat to suit Liz. There was no furniture to maneuver around, no area rugs to get caught in her wheels, no chairs to come between her and the lamps she needed to turn on.

As I walked in, I realized that the barrenness of decoration on the floor was balanced by the profusion of color on the one full wall, by the door. A two-by-three-foot weaving in thick red and gold wools hung next to water colors: one of a fishing troller with the sun tinting the ocean swells, the other of the fog lifting off the towers of the Golden Gate Bridge. Beside them were posters of a Greek village at sunrise, Guadalajara on a cloudless day, and the Berkeley pier at dusk. None of the works looked valuable in itself, but their placement drew my eye from one to the next, following the warm golden lines and the clear blue of freedom. I swallowed, surveyed the room again, and moved on to the next room.

Clearly, it had been intended to be a dining room. Most houses in the Berkeley flatlands had built-in china cabinets. They varied in size, and in tastefulness. Some were of the original stained wood, with leaded glass doors to stand guard over the good Dresden. Some had been painted over to blend with the walls. Others had been "updated," the original wood yanked out and replaced with varnished pine.

But it was a rare house that had none at all. When Liz had turned the dining room into an office she had left the china cabinet—one of the leaded glass ones—but she'd had the bottom doors removed and filled the shelves behind them with phone books, municipal directories, and annual reports of public agencies. Despite the leaded glass, there was nothing homey about this room. The walls were covered with bulletin boards, and those boards were laden with schedules of committee meetings, proposals from those committees, a calendar that listed nothing for last night but the meeting she had missed, and nothing for today at all.

The only decoration, if it could be called such, was an artist's sketch of Marina Vista. In it, the building could have passed for the Greek village. It stood a crisp white against the pale blue of the sky, the darker blue of the bay, and the fresh green of the imagined landscaping. The building looked to be six stories high, with the ramp both Brad Butz and Laurence Mayer had bragged about coiling around it. They had been right about that ramp; even in the sketch it gave the building a sense of community. I could picture the tenants joining friends on the flat portions, chatting as the sun set over the inlet. Looking at the sketch, I could see why Liz had pushed for it. I could see why she was willing to give up this desirable flat to move in there.

The kitchen, bedroom, and bathroom were sparsely furnished. They were rooms in which Liz would rarely have to back up to turn. The bathroom had more empty floor space than Inspector Doyle's office. It had been more than revamped. Berkeley houses didn't have bathrooms that size; to create this, walls had to have been moved.

I stood in the doorway of the office, trying to see it as Liz would have. It was a command post, with the spheres of her activities segregated into modules. Once she had stationed herself at one of these, there would have been nothing out of reach. There were even two phones—besides the ones in the living room and the bedroom—one on each work table. And the bulletin boards, hung low on the walls, made me feel Brobdingnagian.

I walked back into the living room. Covering my finger with a tissue, I pressed the rewind button on the machine and then "play."

This is Liz Goldenstern. Leave a message. I'll get back to you as soon as I can. Some recordings sound metallic and fake, but this one sounded just like Liz. I had the feeling that if I looked around she would be rolling in from the dining room, demanding to know what I was doing here.

"This is John, at C.I.L. Call me."

This is Liz Goldenstern . . .

"Liz, I can't make it tonight. Can you get someone else to help you to bed? Sorry." It was a woman's voice, familiar but I couldn't quite place it. I'd have to play that one again.

This is Liz . . .

"Call Dr. Green's office to make an appointment for a prophylaxis."

This is Liz . . . I could see why she had chosen such a succinct message. How many times a day had she listened to her voice?

"Liz, you were right; only they were up-to-date. My fee is dinner. Let me know when."

Herman Ott! I reached out to stop the tape, then decided to hear it through.

This is Liz . . .

"Liz, I'm at the meeting. Where are you?" A male voice, one I didn't recognize, asked in a tone of exasperated concern.

I ran the tape back and played Herman Ott's message again. His voice sounded different. I wouldn't have recognized it. I played it once more. It was not the voice I heard when Ott was telling me he didn't deal with cops. It was the voice of a friend, inviting himself for dinner. It was a side of Herman Ott I wouldn't have thought existed.

But his message—who were they, and what were they up-to-date about?

There was no point wasting my time trying to figure that out. I got out my pad to note the other messages.

The front door opened.

CHAPTER 14

"What are you doing here?" the woman demanded. She was a little taller than I, maybe five nine. Her well-worn jeans stretched across her stomach and hung loose over her thin legs. But her gray sweatshirt looked freshly washed. A violet bandanna covered her hair. As she stared at me, her deep-set eyes widened in horror.

For an instant I wondered if she thought I was a burglar. Or perhaps she was. But as I looked at her sharp features, set so incongruously above her thick shoulders and full breasts, I recognized her as Aura Summerlight, the woman who had discovered Liz's body. Without the bright Punjabi cape and the light hair blowing in the night wind, she looked less like a creature of the sixties. In jeans and a sweatshirt, she was just another middle-aged woman lined from years of hard work at low pay.

But she had no trouble recognizing me. I, of course, looked exactly as I had the previous night when I questioned her. I was still wearing the same clothes. "What are *you* doing here, Ms. Summerlight?"

"I have a right. I work here. I'm Liz's attendant. If you don't believe me, you can ask Dr. Mayer."

"You knew Liz! Why didn't you tell me that last night?" I demanded.

"I have a right," she insisted.

"Sit down," I said, indicating the two chairs in the living room. "I'm not questioning your taking care of Liz. After all, you do have a key." I waited for her to relax at my reassurance. Any questions I had about that arrangement would be easy enough to check later. Right now, I needed her to be calm enough to deal with the important issue. "About last night. You found Liz's body. Then you acted like you didn't know her."

"That was Liz?" she said. But she wasn't a good actress.

"You just told me you were her attendant, right?"

She nodded.

"For how long?"

"Almost three months."

"Then you recognized her."

"No. I didn't. I told you her head was in the water." The words tumbled out. Her voice had the same frantic quality it did last night. "I never saw her face. It was dark there."

"Don't lie to me!"

She stared down at her old purse, gripped the zipper, and yanked it half open, then let it drop. "You're just badgering me because I live in Rainbow Village. You cops, you're always on us."

I took a breath, planning my approach, trying to work out the proper balance between comfort and authority. "Discovering the body of someone you know is a great shock. But lying to the police isn't going to make that go away. There is no way you could *not* have recognized Liz Goldenstern. We both know that." I paused, letting my assurances sink in. I had dealt with people like her before, poor people whose only contact with the police had been at the wrong end of a gun or a nightstick, people who were so used to being scoffed at that they wove the anticipated disbelief into their explanations.

She looked up from the purse. In the daylight, her dark eyes looked even more wary than they had at night. And her sharp features seemed pointier. She'd probably been awake all night, frantically watching the collage of fears, grief, regrets, and the hopeful glimmers of escape that then faded in the light of consideration.

"Now tell me what really happened."

Her eyes darted toward the door, evaluating the distance.

Softly, I said, "You said you got home late because you were waiting for a client who owed you fifty dollars."

"Yes, that's right. Like I said, I stopped to get a pizza—the girl at the counter, the one who gave me a hard time, she'll remember me. Then I missed my bus, and I got home late." Dealing with the peripheral established facts seemed to calm her, as I hoped it would. Whether this part of her story was true or not I could decide later. For now I nodded.

"Like I said, I wanted to be alone. It had been a shitty day. I walked down by the water, and"—she swallowed—"I saw the chair. It was like I knew it was her as soon as I saw the chair. I couldn't bring myself to look at her. It was like if I didn't see her she wouldn't be dead. You know what I mean?"

"Yes, I do."

"I don't know how long I stood there. Maybe if I'd pulled her out instead of just standing there she wouldn't be dead. But I froze. Like I told you, I've seen death before. I knew she was dead. I couldn't make myself touch her." She clutched her mouth, and for a moment I thought she was going to be sick.

Steeling my face to cover my horror and fury, I said, "What did you do then?"

Her face was clammy. She stared down at her shaking hands. "It was awful. It's the worst thing that's ever happened to me. If I had just stayed in town longer, I wouldn't . . ." Her eyes widened. She looked around frantically. "I can't stand this. I'm not supposed to strain my nerves. The doctors all warn me. I need a pill." She yanked at the purse zipper again. It stuck. "I shouldn't get upset like this. The doctors always tell me that." The zipper gave. She rooted down in the deep bag and extricated a small plastic bottle. "I need a glass of water."

"What is that?"

"It's phenobarb. It's prescription. See?" She extended the bottle. "I'm epileptic. If I get too upset I'll have a seizure. I need water to wash down my pill."

I kept the bottle and motioned her to the kitchen. I ran water in a glass and handed her one pill. She tossed it in her mouth and swallowed slowly, sipping at the water until the glass was empty. "I'll be all right now," she said. "I just may be a little out of it. I don't like to take these things. They're so strong. Sometimes I'm really out of it afterwards."

Handing her back the bottle, I walked back to the two chairs. "How serious is your epilepsy?" I asked as we sat back down.

She shook her head. "Not bad. I haven't had a seizure in six months. And then it wasn't a big one. It really doesn't keep me from doing anything. I know when they're coming. I have time to stop whatever I'm doing, to put things down, to sit down if there's a chair nearby. It's been years since I fell out on the street."

I thought of her truck. It was a safe guess she'd lied to get a driver's license, if she had one. "Did you come in contact with Liz because of your illness?"

"I said it's not that bad," she snapped.

I nodded.

She sighed. "I never went to C.I.L. for services, but in a way you're right. It's because I'm an epileptic I can't get a lot of jobs. Most jobs. There's plenty of work I could do, but companies are afraid hiring me would raise their insurance rates. They're afraid I would fall and injure myself, or break something. They're not about to take the chance. I can't even get a waitress job."

"Unless you lie?"

She hesitated, then said, "Sure." Her breath seemed calmer now. I wondered if the drug could have kicked in so soon. "Liz knew. She didn't care. She said the chances of me having an attack when I was transferring her to her chair were as great as her having a spontaneous cure. She understood. But most people don't."

"But if you lied, then you could get other jobs, right?" When she hesitated, I said, "I'm investigating a murder, not your employment history. I just want to clear up this discrepancy. If you could get a better job by concealing your illness, why were you working for Liz?"

She sighed impatiently. "Because, for one thing, a lot of jobs require physicals. The pills work, but the doctors have to find the right balance—it changes from person to person. With me it took years. I thought they'd never get it right. I figured I'd never be able to do a lot of things and I didn't get the training. I got married and figured I'd have a bunch of kids. And when I didn't have kids, I figured I'd spend my time working the phones at the gym. My husband, my ex-husband, ran a gym in Santa Fe. By the time the business went belly-up—that'll tell you something about him: it's really hard these days to have a gym fail. Every third person, even in Santa Fe, wants to firm up. Anyway, when the business went, so did he. And by the time I realized I was going to have to make it on my own, I was forty-five and hadn't done more than answer the phones and mop up the gym floor. But I did know something about the body after all those years. And I'm strong. You can't do attendant work without a strong back, I'll tell you. So I answered Liz's ad."

"What did Liz pay you?"

"Dr. Mayer paid me. Ten bucks an hour."

Ten dollars an hour was a fortune compared to the usual pay for attendants. "How come so much?"

"She had strange hours. Like some mornings she wanted me here at seven because she had to get to an early meeting.

But then if she had a late meeting, she might need me to come and put her to bed at eleven."

"Then why weren't you here last night?"

She nodded more slowly. The drug was beginning to take hold. There wouldn't be much time for answers I could be sure of. "Sometimes there was someone at the meetings who came home with her and got her in bed. Yesterday morning she told me she would be late and she wouldn't need me, and she wouldn't be getting up till after ten."

"So normally she let you know just the day before?"

"Right. That's part of the reason she paid so much. I had two other jobs to shift around. Not everyone could do that. But I clean house for students. They don't remember when you're coming anyway. They don't put away their clothes like normal people so that I can get to the beds or the rugs. With them I have to spend half my time just picking up before I can start cleaning." She shrugged. "It's their money."

"But yesterday Liz didn't tell you she could do without you. You called her. You left a message that you weren't coming."

"No, she—"

"Ms. Summerlight," I said in exasperation, "your message is on the tape." It was no wonder this woman didn't expect anyone to believe her. "Now tell me, when were you supposed to be here last night?"

"Ten," she said in a small voice. "I told you I got hung up. I called her while I was waiting for the bus, the one I missed."

"No, you didn't. You called her in the afternoon. Did you kill Liz Goldenstern?"

"No. No." But her protest lacked fire. Her voice was mushy.

"Then stop acting like you're guilty. Tell me the truth. Why did you call Liz in the afternoon?"

She took the moment and several more. "If Liz had found

out," she said even more slowly, "she would have canned me. But I guess that doesn't matter any more, huh?"

"Right."

"Well, see, I had a date." She smiled, her eyes half closed. Then letting her gaze fall to the mound of her belly, she said, "I know, it's hard to believe, huh? After my husband ran off, I was depressed. Let myself go. Used to be in good shape, when I worked at the gym. Sometimes, then, I worked out . . . a couple hours a day. Nick, my husband, said it looked good . . . to have someone on the machines, looked like the place was busy. I was . . . in good shape."

"About your date?" I prodded.

"Well, I don't have . . . many dates. This guy asked me . . . to dinner, and I . . . wasn't about to say no."

"I'll need his name and address."

Slowly she shook her head. "Don't know."

"You're going to have to do better than that."

Her thin mouth tightened in fear. I could almost see the spurt of adrenaline. "It's the truth. I lied about the fifty bucks and the pizza and all, but this is the truth. You've got to believe me."

"Then give me proof."

"He took me to a place on the Bay. They'll remember me. I had on my shawl, the one with the red roses on it. They'll remember."

"Just like the girl at the pizza place would remember you?"

"No, but this is true. I was there. We had dinner. I had prawns stuffed with crab. And white wine. I haven't had a dinner like that since I left Santa Fe."

"A dinner like that and you don't know this man's name?"

"Barney. That's all I know." Her eyelids drooped again. The phenobarb was stronger than fear. In another minute or two she'd be completely out of it.

"Where does he live?" I demanded. "Didn't he invite you back to his place?"

"He did, yeah. And I'm not going . . . to try . . . to tell you I wasn't going to go. You're too smart . . . to believe that." Her cheeks pulled up into a lopsided attempt at a smile. "I didn't go. He thought I would. We were walking . . . out of the restaurant. He started talking about ropes, and tying me up . . . in the bathtub. Real kinky stuff. I could have drowned. I'm no fool. I split."

"Which restaurant did you go to?"

Her eyes shut completely.

"Which restaurant?"

Her eyelids flickered but didn't open. When she spoke her voice was so low I had to lean in to hear. She said, "The Shanty."

The Shanty had been closed for five years.

"Aura!"

She slumped in her chair, completely out. She had said that the phenobarbital was strong, but not so potent as to knock her out in twenty minutes. She must normally have halved the pills. She had been exhausted from last night. This dose had been her escape, at least for a few hours. And for those hours I wouldn't know what it was she had been doing the night when Liz was killed. I'd only know she'd gone to lengths to avoid telling me.

She didn't look in danger of doing more than drifting off into a comfortable and probably much-needed sleep, but I couldn't take any chances. Irritably, I called the fire department for medics. And, as I suspected, when the medics finished their assessment, they pronounced Aura in no danger. She just needed to sleep off the effects. But they couldn't take a chance either.

As they carried her out, on her way to the county hospital, the white coat in the rear said, "Hey, man, move it. We got forty-five minutes to lunch."

I looked at my watch. Eleven-fifteen! I was supposed to

meet Pereira outside Herman Ott's office fifteen minutes ago. By now, she'd have left and taken my only leverage with her. Or she'd have seen him and bartered it away for information on the shoe thief.

I motioned to Heling. She could continue her surveillance from inside. "Keep an eye on the driveway. If Mayer tries to leave, find out where he's going. I have to talk to him. And while you're here, catalog the contents of the office—every file, every note, every name on the calendar, particularly anything that has to do with her son. Got that? And check in with me before you leave," I said. And ran.

CHAPTER 15

I left the black and white double-parked in front of Herman Ott's building and took the stairs two at a time. As I reached Ott's floor, the ponderous sounds of soap opera music oozed from the corner apartment. Three preschoolers on big wheels careened past the landing. I hurried by two small girls huddled conspiratorially in the safety of the corner, past an open door through which came the aroma of curry and ginger cooking. I rapped on Ott's door just as the tiny cyclists began their next lap.

"Who's there?" At the best of times Herman Ott, with his strange passion for yellow, resembled a large canary. But this morning he didn't sound like a creature anyone would pay money for.

"It's Smith, Ott," I said, catching my breath.

The door opened. But Herman Ott was not standing in the doorway.

I glanced around it to see a blond woman in a tailored

gray suit and black high heels. Under her arm was a leather briefcase. I did a double take realizing it was Connie Pereira. I'd never seen her in her financial district garb. She looked more formidable than Mrs. Vorkey in Accounting. She looked like a woman who would stare disdainfully down the full length of her nose at your financial shambles, then sigh, settle down, and set things right. She looked as out of place in Herman Ott's shabby office, in front of Herman Ott's disheveled self, as anyone I'd ever seen.

"Sorry, I'm late," I muttered.

"No problem," she said. "We've arranged everything, and I'm just about to start on these forms." She indicated a small stack topped by the infamous 4562. "It's not complicated if you understand the mentality behind it. But the instructions," she threw up her hands. "Anyone unfamiliar with the tax system wouldn't have a chance."

I nodded. I hoped she wasn't laying it on too thick. I glanced at Herman Ott. He nodded. His eyes were bloodshot, the skin beneath them was blue-gray. Everything about him sagged. If he resembled a canary at all now, it was one about to be flushed. It didn't take a detective to see he had spent the sixteen hours since I'd left him staring at the tax forms and getting no place. When Connie Pereira arrived, she must have looked to him like the angel of salvation. I said, "So you've taken our offer, Ott."

Eyeing Pereira as she settled in his chair and began straightening up the co-mingling piles on the desk, he said, "We worked out a deal."

"For?"

Ott's red eyes narrowed. "The deal's made, Smith. Done. Doesn't matter what's involved."

"So then, tell me."

"Okay, Smith, but don't take this as an opening for renegotiation. There's more than one boy grabbing those shoes. They're college kids. And the shoes aren't being fenced at the flea markets."

"That's it?"

"That's plenty."

I glanced at Pereira. She grinned. "I'll save you two a couple of rounds. He said he'll keep his eyes open."

I nodded. She'd gotten all she could hope for. She'd also gotten all that could be squeezed from her tax work. I knew Ott's unshakable ethics where his work was concerned. Once he made a deal, he'd stick by it no matter how dangerous it made things for him. And he expected the same good faith from those on the other end. Delayed payments were poor faith. But going back on a deal, trying to squeeze more out of it, was no faith at all. I said, "I need to talk to you, Ott."

"Smith, I said—"

"Not about this."

"You brought me my money?" he asked mockingly.

"You'll get it."

"When?"

"As soon as the paperwork clears. You know you haven't made yourself Mr. Congeniality around the department."

The hint of a smile flickered at the corners of his pale lips. It was a sign how tired he was. In prime form Ott would never exhibit a friendly emotion to an adversary. He'd spent too long on the streets where a dominating glower was de rigueur. "The police review commission, huh?"

"You've got it."

"But Smith, we had a deal."

"We *have* a deal. But you made it almost impossible for me to come through."

"A deal's a deal. You should have taken that into account."

"Ott, you testified the day I submitted the form. Instead of requesting a routine payment to a local P.I., I found myself asking for money for a man who'd created an entire week of work for the department. You changed the balance, Ott."

He rubbed his palm against the leg of his tan chinos. "You still owe me two hundred dollars."

I almost smiled. With that pause, he'd conceded the point. "It's going through. I had to stick my neck out, but you'll get it. But that's not what I came to talk about."

"Could you two barter somewhere else?" Pereira grumbled. "I'm trying to concentrate on the Accelerated Cost Recovery System here."

I pulled open the door. The big wheels clattered past.

"Come back tomorrow, Smith," Ott said.

"It's about Liz Goldenstern. Tomorrow's too late."

His eyes almost closed—another sign of his exhaustion.

I wasn't surprised he didn't ask what. Even though Ott had been holed up here with his schedule C's, I never questioned that he would know about Liz's murder. His sources were not the types to be home doing taxes.

Giving his head a shake, he said, "Okay. In the other room."

The times I'd peered in through the doorway into that room, his folding bed had been bare, and his clothes, blankets, and books had covered the floor. During those long pauses, while he considered whether to deal or not, I'd wondered absently how he managed to get across this mess without breaking his neck. Did he place each foot with care? Or were there tiny, camouflaged clearings where he could touch bare floor? I watched as he passed through the door. His normal gait changed; his feet dragged, as if he were trudging through mud.

I followed, nearly tripping over two large wicker baskets. Each was half filled with yellow clothes—one batch rumpled but clean, the other shaded with dirt, smeared with grease, or spotted with liquids that had turned to brittle brown. When all the garments had made it to the second basket, I could picture him hauling them to the Laundromat, ready to transform basket two into basket one.

He poised his butt over the visible springs of his once over-stuffed chair and lowered himself down.

I sat on the bare mattress. "You called Liz yesterday."

He started to answer.

I held up a hand. "I heard the tape. That's not what I'm asking. What you said was, 'You were right; only they are up-to-date.' What did that mean?"

He looked down, at a coffee stain on his chinos. He wouldn't give me the line about his call having nothing to do with the murder. He was too professional for that. He knew I could haul him in as a material witness. I knew he could tell me enough to pass for cooperating, and too little to be worth anything.

"Okay, Smith. She was thinking of taking a class at U.C. Extension. Liz wanted to know how U.C. compared to other schools."

"Jesus, Ott. You are tired. The kids on the big wheels could do better than that."

He shrugged.

"Ott, whatever you said, it was virtually the last message she had before someone drowned her. I won't insult you by asking if the connection occurred to you."

"It was a computer class."

"Sure." Behind him on the radiator sat a pot caked with salt and chemicals. A thin mist rose from it—the poor man's humidifier. Beside it was an under-the-counter-type refrigerator, with dark scuff marks from being kicked shut. There was no counter. A hot plate sat on the floor, dangerously close to the edge of a blanket.

I looked back at him slumped in his chair. I recalled Ott's sociable voice on the tape when he said, "My fee is dinner. Let me know when." It was a tone I had never heard from him. I doubted many had. "Ott," I said, "we're on the same side here. This is more than just another case for me."

His eyes opened a fraction.

"Someone flipped Liz in the water and watched her

drown. They didn't even have the decency to throw her in all the way. Ott, just her head and shoulders were underwater. Don't you understand the viciousness in that? This wasn't a killing of convenience. Someone really hated her. The killer was taunting her as she died."

His eyes opened wider. He hadn't known that.

Slowly I said, "Liz Goldenstern wasn't just another client, was she? You cared about her?"

"Back off, Smith," he snapped.

I sighed. "Okay, okay. You're going to have to come across with the real story sooner or later. You know that. The only one who'll thank you for holding out is Liz's killer."

"Liz was a woman you could trust," he said, almost to himself. "With her a deal was a deal."

I hadn't considered Liz as a female Ott. But now that he mentioned this similarity, I could see it. Ott irate about my late two hundred dollars, Liz furious at the man with the four-pronged cane who deserted her picket line—they were indeed birds of a feather.

Ott pushed himself halfway up. His shirttail caught on a spring from the seat cushion. Without turning around, he ripped it free and stood, the torn flannel still in his hand. "This is what I'm going to give you, Smith. Before the accident, she crewed in the bay for herring. You know what that's like? Fish and Game sets a limit. In thirty-six hours, sometimes less, it's been filled. A crew can make thousands of dollars in one night. It's pitch black. The fog's thick. No one runs with lights for fear someone else will check out their spot. The bay's so jammed up the boats are smashing into each other. Nets get cut 'accidentally.' It's as cutthroat as it comes. Liz was with one of the Capellis, Tony, the youngest. He was high when he went out. About three in the morning the nets got tangled. He dove in. And when he didn't come up, Liz had to go in after him. There were only the two of them on the boat. Leaving it to bounce around on top of you while you hunt in the dark is asking for it. But Liz pulled Tony in. And the Capellis never forgot that. They've got money. There was nothing they wouldn't have done for Liz. They paid for her trip to Mexico last winter, two weeks, her and her attendant."

I hadn't heard the story, but it didn't surprise me. Still, I didn't see the relevance. The Capellis wouldn't have killed Liz. I nodded. Herman Ott didn't reminisce for no reason.

"Ott? What are you telling me?"

He shook his head. "I've told you. If you can't use it . . ." He shrugged. With a sigh of decision, he said, "Okay, Smith, I'll give you something easier. Liz was married."

"Married? To whom?"

He looked me full in the face. "Ian Stuart."

"Stuart, the guy in Rainbow Village with the hot tub on his truck?"

"One and the same."

CHAPTER 16

True to his word, Herman Ott offered not another word about Liz Goldenstern. But for the moment that hardly mattered. He had told me Ian Stuart was Liz's husband.

As I raced down the stairs of Herman Ott's building to my patrol car, I thought of Ian Stuart, who had inaugurated the day yesterday by threatening to drown Brad Butz and who had ended the day by reporting Liz's death and then disappearing. Although I hadn't seen Stuart myself, I had a vivid picture of him standing at the Marina Vista site yesterday morning, his long blond hair escaping from a blue wool cap, blowing in the bay breeze, his face screwed up in anger as he threatened Brad Butz. By the time Murakawa and I arrived all that had been left of him was the hot tub. He was out of sight until ten P.M. when he called us about Liz's—his wife's—body. He had a lot of explaining to do.

I pulled into the maddeningly slow one-way traffic on Telegraph. It was lunch time. Students swarmed along the sidewalks—pizza, pita sandwiches, frozen yogurt, or fresh fruit slushes in hand. In front of me horns honked as drivers spotted friends they hadn't seen in half an hour or so. Across the street a dark-haired boy in red running shorts hurried into Racer's Edge, just as Laurence Mayer strolled out. Mayer was wearing the same running shorts he'd had on that morning. He strode down the sidewalk with the easy gait of a natural athlete, smiling at a girl in sweatpants, slowing his pace to join a boy with a tennis racket briefly, and then moving on. I could see him as the competitors' psychological guru. He must have been a natural at that, too.

I was tempted to put on the pulsers, but the Avenue was nearly in gridlock; the only action the pulsers would get would be hostility. I gritted my teeth, reminded myself that patience was widely esteemed as a virtue, and rode the tail of the car in front.

On University, I did hit the pulsers, and it was less than five minutes before I pulled up at the gate to Rainbow Village.

Ian Stuart still was not at Rainbow Village. His parking space was empty. And the person who might know where he was—Aura Summerlight—was asleep in the county hospital. I knocked on the door of the purple school bus, the one occupied by the woman who was having the party the previous night. It didn't surprise me that there was no response. Liz's death might have changed the tone of the party, but I doubted it had ended it. I knocked again.

"Who is it now?" A woman demanded. I wondered who else had been banging on this metal door today.

"Police."

"Again? Well, just a minute."

In the daylight, splotches of rust shone through the fading purple paint. Black burlap curtains hung behind the windows where once small, crew-cut heads had looked out at Dwight David Eisenhower Elementary School or P.S. 139. From the looks of it, this bus, like so many others, had been gutted and revamped for the sixties' hippies—carpeted with foam mats and huge pillows, with a stereo secured to the wall, rows of orange crates holding albums, and the aromas of marijuana and incense permeating the fibers as they battled for supremacy.

The sixties were over. They'd been over for close to twenty years. Most of the hippie fleet had been abandoned to junkyards. Most of the hippies had changed with the decades. Life was no longer infinite, and one day floating into the next was no longer a sign of freedom but simply meant one less day to finish what had to be done. Poverty had lost its charm. The hippies were middle-aged now. Many had gone back to school. Some were lawyers, some social workers, some even cops.

But the woman who pulled the lever to open the bus door couldn't have been pegged as either a lawyer or a transient. In jeans and a sweatshirt, with long dark hair parted in the middle and a pale face still mashed from sleep, she could have represented any stratum of Berkeley. She rubbed her knuckles in her eyes, then took a drag of a cigarette. "I was up late."

If she was looking for sympathy she'd picked the wrong person. "I'm trying to find Ian Stuart."

Now she grinned. But the muscles on the right side of her face still hadn't shaken off sleep. Her cheek hung. The whole effect was of a soft doll that had been crammed in a suitcase. "You sure you're a cop?"

I pulled out my shield and held it out.

She shook her head in quick snaps. "Nah, that's okay. I'll take your word. I can't be bothered to put my contacts in this early," she said, leaning back against the arm of the black Naugahyde swivel chair that served as the driver's seat and motioning me in.

The sixties had indeed ended. There was no smell of marijuana and incense here, or at least none strong enough to hide the stench of tobacco. There were no pillows and mats on the floor, no padded floors and walls so the most athletic of orgyists wouldn't bruise a part he might need later. This school bus looked like a trailer park mobile home. An old plaid love seat backed against the far wall. Across from it was a dinette set with a portable typewriter on the table. Beyond that was a tiny stove and apartment-sized refrigerator under a counter so small that even Herman Ott would have winced. And on every surface was a full ashtray. In Berkeley, where city law mandates non-smoking sections in every theater and restaurant, coming across a smoker was unusual enough. I hadn't seen this much tobacco in years.

"You're not dressed like a cop." It wasn't an accusation, just a statement of fact.

"I'm a detective. Detective Smith."

She stuck out a hand as she said, "Marie Denton."

I shook the proffered hand. "About Ian Stuart?"

"Oh, Ian. Well, if he's not here, he's probably at work. At the heliport on University."

"And if he's not there?"

"Off with one of his ladies."

"Where?"

"Wherever one will have him."

"Can you give me a name, or an address, or even a description of these women?"

She took a long drag of her cigarette, then shook her head.

"Did his ladies include his wife?"

"Wife?" She perked up. "That's a new one to me. Are you sure?"

"Yes."

She laughed. "Well, there will be a lot of surprised half-soaked ladies when that word gets out."

"Do you have any other ideas where he might be if he's not at the heliport?"

"Like I said, no. But he's probably there. The only thing he's really interested in is helicopters. I barely know the man and he's carried on so much about lift off and hovering that I'm sure I could fly a copter myself. He came on like he'd chosen me to share his secret—the fact that he's trying to discover some sort of important improvement in the rotor blades. He made a big thing about not letting anyone in the village know what he was doing or where he was. As if they'd care! I mean he acted like everyone here was sitting around all day plotting to rip him off. I told him we're not all deadbeats here, or on the needle, or transient. Some people have just had a string of bad breaks, some just don't want to be tied down; a lot, like me, are walking our tails off trying to get jobs, any jobs." She shrugged. "I might as well have been talking to his rotor blade."

"Then why was he leading the protest against Marina Vista?"

Again she shook her head. "Got me. Got everyone. There was a lot of speculation about everything here. People with endless time have endless opinions. Some of the guys figured he was on something. A couple thought maybe he knew that guy Butz from Canada. Ian's Canadian, you know. And he sure acted like he had something personal against Butz."

"How so?"

She blew out a column of smoke. It hung suspended between us. My throat was getting scratchy. "Well, hardly anyone here paid attention to him carrying on about Marina Vista. We all know this place is temporary. But a couple of times someone did pop up ready to mount a protest at City

Hall. You should have seen Ian back off. He only wanted to harass Butz. Like I said, it seemed personal." She stubbed out the cigarette in an ashtray already precariously full. "Of course, one guy insisted that Ian just wanted to get some free publicity for his hot tub. You've seen his ads, haven't you?"

"No."

" 'Portable hot tub looking for driveway to park in.' Ian's been hoping some lady would take him and it in. Women find him attractive. Or they do until they realize what a bore he is. So, anyway, if he's not at his beloved heliport, then your best bet is to cruise the streets till you spot the hot tub."

CHAPTER 17

If Marie Denton's assessment of Ian Stuart was accurate— his heart was in the helicopter shop and he was looking merely for a spot to stash his body at night—then no place could have been more convenient than Rainbow Village. A quarter mile east of the turn-off to the village, I found Ian Stuart's hot tub-laden pickup parked behind a square metal building. A small plastic sign on the wall whispered "Calicopter." Even though the shop was alone on this narrow rim of bay frontage here on the extension of University Avenue, it was such an innocuous, ill-marked building that probably ninety-five percent of Berkeleyans had no idea what went on inside.

The southern wall of the building had been rolled back. Inside I could see a blue and white helicopter with its roof panels removed and its rotor gears exposed, like a corpse halfway through autopsy. A slight man was lowering himself to the floor, holding a three-and-a-half-foot metal tube. His hair was caught back in a ponytail, but the afternoon wind flicked the ends of the soft blond strands against his sweatshirt. Without realizing it, I had been expecting the hangar to resemble the inside of a garage, with circles of oil here and there, piles of tools that should have been put away last month, and the smell of gasoline rising all around. But the hangar had no stains, no discarded tools, and the only smell was the musty odor of low tide.

He carried the pole across to a small enclosed room. He was shorter than I expected, a good six inches shorter than Brad Butz and probably fifty pounds lighter. His threat to Butz must have looked like something out of Laurel and Hardy.

Still, he had disappeared. I poised my hand over my gun and waited until he put the helicopter pole down.

"Ian Stuart?"

"Yes?"

"I'm Detective Smith, Berkeley Police Department. I need to talk to you about your wife's murder."

His eyes scrunched together. For a moment I thought I'd caught him off guard. Then he nodded and motioned me inside the enclosed room. His expression didn't change. His nose and cheekbones were narrow and pointy. His eyes were naturally scrunched.

"Your wife was murdered last night. You called us and then you disappeared. You've got a lot of explaining to do, Mr. Stuart. Tell me about finding Liz's body."

"I didn't find it."

"It! Your wife is dead less than one day and already you're referring to her body as 'it'!"

He looked away, toward a wall covered with numbered circular pieces of metal—parts of tools, I guessed. "I didn't know it was her."

"You called us."

"Aura found her. Aura was hysterical. Someone had to call in."

"What exactly did Aura tell you?" I was coming on stronger than I had intended. His dispassion had gotten to me. I decided to go with my anger.

"She said there was a woman in the water. She was dead."

"And?"

"That's what she said."

"She was hysterical, and that's all she said? I don't buy that. I've talked to her twice. She's not the type of person who clams up when she's hysterical. She's the type who talks. She told you more than that. What?"

"Well, she repeated a lot. She must have said the same thing four or five times. Do you want me to tell you that often?"

"I want you to tell me exactly what she said."

"I can't remember her words. She was babbling."

"You're not being straight with me, Ian. Yesterday you were threatening to drown a man outside of Rainbow Village. He didn't press charges. He could have. He still could. That's one offense. Then, your wife is drowned on your doorstep. You disappear. And now you're concealing information from the police. Do I have to tell you how suspicious this makes you look? Now tell me everything Aura Summerlight said to you."

His pale face paled further. "Okay, okay. It probably can't make me look much worse. But you've got to understand my situation."

"First, tell me what she said."

"She told me there was a woman dead at the water, and there was a wheelchair overturned next to her."

"Didn't you go to see if that woman was your wife?"

He hesitated. Behind his pale skin, I could almost see the choices he was considering.

He sighed. "It was very odd. Look, the whole thing was

very odd. Aura told me she was dead." He swallowed, and the first blush of color swept up his face. "Aura said Liz's head was in the water. She had drowned." He swallowed again. "Aura said she panicked. She knew Liz was dead." He squeezed his eyes shut. "She left her head in the water."

"What did you do?"

"Nothing." His voice broke.

"Your wife was drowning and you couldn't go a hundred yards to pull her out?"

"She was dead. Even if she'd been alive when Aura saw her, she would have been dead by the time Aura got to me. There was nothing I could do. And I just couldn't bring myself to go and see her like that. I couldn't bring myself to talk about it. It was all I could do to make the call to you guys. I'm surprised I held myself together for that. I must have sounded shaky. If Aura hadn't been so spun out herself, she would have noticed."

I sighed. Only the density of my own exhaustion kept me from reacting to this new horror of Liz's death. "And then?" I prodded.

"Then I got out of there."

"Where'd you go?"

Again he hesitated.

"We'll check."

"Okay. I came here."

Had I pressed too hard? Maybe he had spent the night with one of the women friends Marie Denton had mentioned. Maybe he made the decision that for a husband in his position admitting extramarital relations was more incriminating than having no alibi at all. But there was no way to dispute his claim. For someone else spending the night here would have been cold and uncomfortable at best. But for Ian Stuart, who was used to curling up on the seat of his truck, this would be like a room at the Marriott.

I decided on the roundabout route. "What kind of work do you do here?"

"I'm a mechanic."

"Licensed?"

"Well, no. I could pass the written test for the A and P license—"

"A and P?"

"Air frame and power plant license. The test would be no problem. I could have passed it years ago. But I need someone to vouch for my experience before I can sign up. That's why I'm here." He pulled the door of the small room shut. "Dust. I don't want it blowing on the transmission." He nodded at the machinery on the work bench.

"How long have you been as assistant mechanic here?"

His pale face reddened. "You think I'm some kind of flunky here. You think I mop the floors and carry the parts around, and maybe at the end of the day they let me hold the wrench or turn a couple of screws, don't you? Look, Quade isn't doing me a favor letting me work here. He's getting license-quality work for unlicensed pay. I'm here just for the hours and because Quade lets me use the space for my own work."

"And that work is?"

Without thinking he glanced behind him at the area outside the dust-free room, as if spies might be lurking behind the tail of the helicopter. "It's a modification," he said, nearly whispering.

I was still considering whether to press him on the exact nature of his work, when he said, "It has to do with the drag-lift ratio. That's basically what helicopters are all about. You've got to get enough lift to overcome the drag, and then you've got to keep it. You get into moister air, you get more drag. You go higher, you get more drag. Then you've got to give her more throttle to keep your lift, see? Look, come over here," he said without pause. He hurried out toward the helicopter, still careful, despite his enthusiasm, to shut the workroom door. "See, a helicopter is really a very easy ship to run. It's simpler than a car. You don't have a gear stick, or a clutch, or stuff like turn signals to worry about."

I looked into the cockpit. Between the two seats was a dashboard that must have held fifteen gauges. "It doesn't look that easy to me."

"Oh, those. Well that looks more complicated than it is. But once you get used to them you just need to check to see that everything's all right. But look here, you don't have a steering wheel, you just have this one stick that moves the ship forward and back—the cyclic." He pointed to the stick that rose in front of the driver's seat. "And this one, the collective"—he pointed to a gearstick to the left of the driver's seat—"controls altitude. It goes up, you go up. It goes down, you drop. And this is the throttle, just like you have on a motorcycle. It works with the collective; that's why it's on the end of it. When you go up, you need more power, so increased collective means an increase in the throttle."

So far Marie Denton's assessment was correct. The man was obsessed, and already he was boring me. "Ian—"

"And these pedals work the tail rotor so you don't spin out. See, whenever a copter loses power, it has a tendency to torque, so when you're coming down, you need to adjust—"

"Ian," I insisted. I couldn't tell whether he was actually pausing to listen or just catching his breath. "Tell me, briefly, what modification you are working on."

He frowned. "Well, I don't know how brief I can be."

"Try."

"Well, okay, but I can't promise you'll understand."

I waited.

"I'm experimenting with a new blade design to cut down the drag."

"So the ship will lift more easily and run more economically," I said in a tone so condescending that anyone who was not so totally caught up in his project would have been taken aback. "Do you spend a lot of time working on it?"

"Whenever I'm not doing overhauls for Quade. I don't

have time to waste. Someone else could come up with a similar modification, and then, even if mine's better, companies aren't going to change twice in a year."

I nodded. The signs of distress he'd shown talking of Liz had vanished. He seemed to have handled her death more easily than anyone I had talked to. Disguising my skepticism, I said, "It must have been difficult being here so much, when your wife was in a wheelchair and needed some care."

But if he noticed any undertone in the question, he gave no indication. "She had an attendant," he said matter-of-factly. "Actually, she had a lot of attendants. Liz wasn't the easiest person to work for. But in fairness to her, attendants aren't always the most responsible people around. Sometimes they partied at night and overslept the next morning and didn't bother to get her up. Sometimes they just split without warning."

"Didn't she need you then?"

"Sure. And I came. There's a phone here. Look, we haven't been together for a long time. Actually, we've been apart more than we were together."

I kept silent, counting on its nervous-making quality to keep him talking.

"We just weren't very alike. Or at least we had different priorities. Liz knew how important my work was. She knew that when this modification works, helicopter companies will be fighting to get it. I can sell it for more money than I've ever seen, enough to start my own company. She understood that." He nodded toward the standing copter. "Besides, even if I had been doing nothing but sitting on my butt, I wouldn't have seen her much more. She was hardly ever home, and when she was she was busy at her desk, or on the phone to one of her committee members, or to Brad Butz. Christ, if it hadn't been for Liz that Marina Vista project would never have gotten anywhere. He couldn't have done that himself. He was just a ne'er-do-well carpenter when he latched onto Liz. He didn't have influence with the city. They would never have considered him without Liz pushing them. And after he got the job, he didn't understand politics like Liz did. He could never have battled all those boards and committees—he thinks too small. He's the perfect nuts and bolts man. Of course, he doesn't know that. He struts around like the idea for Marina Vista grew in his own prissy-faced head. Marina Vista's going to make him hot stuff in the construction world. The whole shorefront project is a bitch. It's going to force a hundred people with no other place to go out of Rainbow Village. Even Calicopter is going to lose its lease here. But do you think he cared? I told Liz, I said, 'Look, this guy is using you. What are you going to get out of his million dollar project? An apartment? The honor of being manager and listening to people complain?' " He shook his head. "That building is going up on fill. You know what that means."

Fill, or filled land, was the land created at the edge of the bay from projects like the Berkeley dump. A hundred years ago San Francisco Bay had been twice its present size before man-made "land" gobbled its edges. Fill, of course, was not attached to the bedrock deep beneath, and when a sizeable earthquake came, the fill would melt back into the water it had displaced.

"It's one thing for commercial buildings to go up here. People don't sleep in them. That's why the regulations aren't so stiff for them. But apartments . . . I can't believe the city is allowing an apartment building to go up there, particularly one for people with disabilities," Ian said. "It's crazy. In a quake, those people won't have a chance. But then, the city wouldn't have okayed it if it hadn't been for Liz's lobbying. She was always off at some committee or speaking in front of some board or other." He sounded like any spouse would have. I could remember my own ex-husband complaining when I worked Night Watch.

I took a breath, trying to decide how to phrase my question. Stuart was clearly fascinated with motion. He hadn't given any indication of being adaptable to a life without it. I wondered if the pressures of Liz's accident, and the changes that her paralysis had brought—the physical inconveniences, the sexual limitations, all the things that were no longer possible—had been more than he was able or willing to adjust to. "You said you didn't live with Liz long. When were you married, and exactly how long did you live together?"

"I don't know. It was a long time ago. And you don't just move out, not when it's out to sleep in your truck. You do it gradually."

"When did you get married?"

"I can't remember the exact date."

"Ian, I can check. It'll just take my time, and my patience."

"Okay, okay. Three years ago."

"Three years!"

"Right. It was *after* her accident. She was already in the chair when I married her. That's what you were wondering about, isn't it?"

I nodded. "Yes. Now what I'm wondering is why you moved out."

His eyes were half closed. I knew he was weighing his possible responses, but this time I didn't press him.

"Okay, I'll tell you the truth, but I can't have it go any further."

"This is a murder investigation. You'd better be straight with me."

He shrugged. "The truth is that we never really lived together. It was a marriage of convenience. Liz did me a favor."

My buzzer beeped. "What kind of favor?"

His scrunched features pushed closer together. "Well, I needed a wife."

The buzzer went off again.

"I have to go. If you don't tell me what you're leading up

to now, I'm going to have to take you with me to the station."

He shrank back, his thin chest hollowing. "Can I get some immunity?"

"Don't talk immunity. I've just explained your choices."

"Officer, I don't—"

"Okay, get your coat." I stepped toward him.

"No, wait. Okay. I'm a Canadian. I needed a green card to work here. I needed to be someplace like this, where there's variation in the weather. Canada's too cold. You can't test a rudder design in weather like that. I had to be here."

"Liz married you so you could stay in the country and work on your invention?"

He nodded.

"What did she get out of it?" Obviously, not the pleasure of his company.

"I told you, she did me a favor. She said she didn't get much chance to do things for other people."

I sighed. "Get in the car."

"But you said—"

The Liz I knew would never have made a deal like that. "You're lying. I don't have time to coddle you. You've just halved your choice." I herded him to the car and opened the rear door. He protested again, and when I closed the door after him, it took all my self control not to slam it.

For this, I thought, I've been up thirty-two hours!

"Officer, this isn't fair."

"Hey, keep it down. You had your chance." I started the engine and, while it warmed, called in to the dispatcher.

"Smith?" he said, "Contact Heling. She says she's got something you'll be real pleased with."

CHAPTER 18

With a burst of adrenaline I drove back to the station, Ian Stuart complaining the entire way. The Liz Goldenstern I knew, the fisherwoman who had plucked the young Capelli out of the bay, might be pleased to help someone out, but I was willing to bet that that someone would have a more compelling need than Ian Stuart. Or if not a dire need, at least an appealing personality. I could see why they had never lived together. From what Marie Denton had said, which Stuart had unintentionally confirmed, he would have been willing to park his truck wherever he could find a bed to park himself. The fewer obligations the better. Living with Liz, as long as there was an attendant to do the work, would have been perfect. Living with him would have driven Liz crazy.

I stopped the car by the station and turned to him. "I'm going to give you one more chance, Ian."

For the first time he was silent.

"Tell me about Liz's son."

His narrow-set eyes scrunched. "I told you it wasn't that type of relationship. How many times do I—"

"Not your son. Liz's son."

His eyes grew even narrower; they seemed ready to squeeze the bridge of his nose off his face. Shaking his head, he said, "Liz didn't have children."

"How do you know? It doesn't sound like you were around any more than you had to be."

"Still, I was her husband. I'd know that."

"There are witnesses who saw her son coming to see her."

Continuing to shake his head, he said, "If Liz had had a

kid, don't you think that kid would have been around? Liz would have seen to that."

Silently, I admitted he had a point. To him, I said, "Not good enough," and headed him into the station. I'd have another go at him after he'd spent a few hours in one of the few rooms in Berkeley he found unacceptable. But booking takes time—the forms, the fingerprinting, the computer checks of the Corpus file, even the receipt for belongings. No one step takes long, but altogether you never book a suspect in less than half an hour.

It was nearly four o'clock when I got to Liz Goldenstern's flat. Leaving the black and white double-parked, I ran in.

I expected Heling, whose shift had ended an hour ago, to be fuming, but she greeted me with a grin.

"Smith," Heling said, "you remember you told me to go over this place? Well, I figured I had hours," she added with a meaningful glance at me. "So I went through every drawer, every closet, every shelf, every—"

"Heling!"

Her grin widened. "You know those bags people hang over the back of their wheelchairs? The ones they put books or groceries or whatever in?"

"Yes."

"Liz Goldenstern's wasn't on her chair when you discovered it, right?"

I recalled the chair on its side in the dirt. There was no bag in my picture. "No."

"Well I found it."

"Where?"

"Under the desk in her office, back by the wall."

"And?" I hadn't realized Heling had this theatrical ability to turn a simple statement into Masterpiece Theater.

"Guess what was in it."

"Heling, I've found Liz dead. I've been up all night. Now what is it?"

"Running shoes," she said triumphantly. "Size 9-B, New Balances. New."

"Whew!"

"And that's not all, Smith. That was just the beginning, in a way. After I found those—actually that was pretty soon— I really went over this place inch by inch. And guess what else I found?"

"A buyer's list?"

Her face fell. "Well, no. Not that. But something pretty interesting," she added, regrouping. "In the back of the bedside table drawer, in an envelope, all by itself," she said, slowing her delivery with each phrase, "I found four hundred fifty dollars."

"Nine pairs of the stolen shoes were from Racer's Edge. Fifty per pair. And these shoes were waiting to be traded for another fifty, eh?"

"Jill, it's so little. I can't believe what people will risk jail for."

"Yeah. Of course, the proceeds from this would have been split two ways—half for the mastermind and half for whoever did the actual stealing. A hundred per pair sounds about all the market would bear."

Heling nodded.

"It's nice that four fifty's still here. Have you notified Coleman, or Pereira?"

"Coleman's sick. And for all I knew Pereira is in Timbuktu. I left a message for her hours ago."

I smiled. After all day with Herman Ott's taxes, Timbuktu would be an appealing prospect for Pereira.

"But that's not all, Smith," she insisted. "Guess what else was in that envelope."

"Other than a signed confession, I can't imagine."

"Check it out." Heling thrust the envelope toward me.

I plucked out the bills, all crisp fifties. A slip of paper fell on the floor. Picking it up, I read, *"New Balance—9-B.*

Dusty Wilson. 4–13. It's even got his phone number. How considerate. I'd say, Heling, that Pereira owes you one."

"Great. I haven't started my taxes yet."

"Maybe not that big a one. In the meantime, have someone from Day Watch relieve you. We'll get someone to the hospital to pick up Aura Summerlight when they release her. She was the attendant here. Let's see what her connection was in this operation."

"She didn't have any." The words tumbled out of Heling's mouth. "I mean, I've given this a lot of thought. And it had to be Liz's scheme. I mean, look where the shoes were —in Liz's bag. Common sense says Liz put them there. If Aura had stashed them here in the flat she would have put them on a top shelf, someplace where Liz wouldn't come across them. That bag is the last place she'd put them. And the bag was hidden in one of the few places she wouldn't look. And the money . . . well, my first guess is that she'd have spent it. She must have needed it. But even if she didn't spend it, she wouldn't hide it in the bedside table where Liz would find it. The bedside table is one spot where Liz would keep things she needed, and where her attendants would have no reason to go. It's the logical place for Liz to stash the money."

I nodded slowly.

"I figure, Smith, that Liz just got sick of pushy runners thinking everyone should get out of their way, and she came up with this plan. It doesn't look like she really needed the money, but who knows. Maybe she just wanted to get even."

If Laurence Mayer had been buying her this building and paying her attendant and the Capellis were underwriting her vacations, Liz shouldn't have needed money. "Okay, when you dictate it, include every inch of your investigation of the flat. But keep to the facts. Don't interpret. And make copies, six of them."

* * *

I had seen Pereira at five A.M. stake-outs, and after half-hour chases, but I had never seen her look this gray and worn out. She was hunched over Herman Ott's desk. What had been a shambles of papers this morning was now four tidy piles. What had been a fashionable hairdo then looked like a haystack now. From the other room came rhythmic snores that were audible from the staircase. In all the time I had been coming here, pounding on Ott's door in the middle of the night, I had never heard a snore. I had assumed Ott was a light and very wary sleeper. Today's performance could only be a show of trust in Pereira to protect him.

"How's it going?" I asked.

Pereira did a double take. "Jill, I didn't even hear you come in. I think my hearing's gone. Ott must be doing eighty decibels in there. I know my vision is permanently impaired. Jill, I just can't see how this man runs a detective agency. I can't see how he runs anything. His records. Jeez. Look at these revolting scraps of paper. I know I'm going to get hepatitis from touching them, and probably black lung from breathing the air above them. Half of them don't have dates, or addresses. The mileage! I can't believe it. It took me all morning just to get them into the right piles. I didn't get to the forty-five sixty-two till half an hour ago. I can't believe it."

In the next room Herman Ott snored on.

"Listen to him," Pereira continued. "It's like going down into the Sea Lion Caves."

"How much longer will the taxes take you?"

She leaned back in the chair. "I don't know, an hour, the rest of my life, who can say?"

"Well, how would you like to take a break—"

"Oh, I can't, not with—"

"And solve the shoe thief case!"

Resurrection must be a startling event, but hardly more so than the rejuvenation of Connie Pereira. In an instant she turned from a tax-hag back to the infuriated sidewalk-kicker who had just lost her thief. I explained Heling's find. "It's hard to believe that Liz was behind this," I said slowly.

"Jill, you've let yourself get too close to her, or her memory. Look at the set-up. She did the books in a running shoe store. She could find out who'd bought what shoe. She could be on the Avenue when she chose. The thieves could steal the shoes and slip them in her bag. No one would suspect her because she was a cripple."

I had to admit that that irony would have appealed to Liz.

"It's perfect."

I nodded, slowly. "She even had a college-age son who could introduce her to his larcenous friends. No wonder we haven't heard from him. Still," I said, "I just can't see her . . ."

"A little Robin Hooding? Or at least taking from the rich. No one with two-hundred-dollar running shoes can't afford to replace them."

"Maybe the adventure appealed to her. She used to fish. She must have missed the excitement." I leaned back against the wall. What Pereira said made sense. What Heling had said made sense. Why couldn't I accept the conclusions they reached so easily? It wasn't a question of breaking the law. Liz had done that in demonstrations. But then there had been a good cause; these thefts were different. They weren't socially motivated—they were done for greed, or spite. "Connie, can you see Liz Goldenstern setting up these thefts for spite?"

"Sure. Why not?"

I shrugged. "I don't know. Maybe I'm thinking of her as a Noble Savage. Maybe I'm so caught up in my outrage about the way she was killed that I've lost sight of her as more than a body to fill her chair."

Pereira nodded. "It's safe to say that being disabled isn't likely to make you a nicer person."

"Maybe you become more patient, of necessity, though Liz didn't show any signs of that." But I knew there was more to my discomfort than that. Paralysis was still a subject I didn't want to think about. If I were forced to consider it, I wanted there to be a silver lining, even if that lining were only patience. But I was too tired to deal with that. "Maybe Liz just enjoyed the thefts," I said. "Anyway, shall we give Dusty Wilson a call about his New Balance 9-B's?"

Pereira shoved the phone toward me. "What if he's already talked to Liz? He'll recognize a different voice."

"I thought of that. I'm prepared to handle it if he did, or if he didn't. This is known as the Howard Method Three, Dilettante Crook Division, perfected when we cracked that Hindu art ring that had statues of Shiva flying around town like Archangels." I dialed. "Dusty Wilson?"

"Yes?"

"I've got your New Bal—Hey, you're not Dusty Wilson."

"Yeah, I am."

"You sure?"

" 'Course I'm sure."

"You sound . . . well . . ."

"Listen, you sound a little odd, too. It must be the connection."

I held up a thumb. Pereira pursed her lips and nodded approval. "Okay. Well, your shoes are ready," I said to Wilson. Had Liz worked out the pick-up arrangement with him or would she have waited until now? If there was nothing set, there was no problem, but if Liz had arranged a spot, then we needed to know where.

"What time should I come?" he asked.

"Half an hour."

"Right."

"Repeat the address."

I could hear his swift intake of breath. "How do I know—"

"I've had problems with this. One guy forgot the pick-up

place. Someone else swiped the shoes. I don't go to all this trouble to donate shoes to passersby. I want to know you'll be there."

"I'm not a moron."

"Forget the whole thing."

"Okay, okay. Twenty-seven eighty-six Channing. Good enough?"

CHAPTER 19

Dwarfed by apartment buildings, 2786 Channing Way sat three blocks above Telegraph Avenue. On another street it would have been recognized as a sizable brown shingle house. On another street, its weed-tossed lawn would have caused comment. But here, amidst the dormitories and fraternity houses, it was understood that lawns occupied space more properly covered with decks, deck chairs, and kegs of beer. All three were in evidence.

After a stop at her patrol car to change shoes, fix her hair, and notify the beat officer of our plan, Pereira had settled herself at the bus stop on College Avenue, half a block east of the house. Seeing her in her suit and running shoes, ten out of ten people would have said she was a businesswoman on her way home. Once Dusty Wilson started toward the Channing Way door, she would move in. Pereira might have had a few hours sleep last night, but neither of us was in sprint condition.

At nearly five o'clock, the wind off the bay blew fitfully, bringing with it a covering of fog. Cars raced down Channing, ready to join the rush hour clog on all Berkeley's main streets. A motor scooter sashayed from lane to lane, its engine ripping through the equilibrium of urban noise. A trail of exhaust fumes hung in its wake. I glanced up the driveway, noting that there was no step up to the side door. Easy access for a wheelchair there. Carrying the New Balance 9-B's in a brown grocery bag, I climbed to the deck and rang the bell. In five minutes Wilson would be here to get them.

The door opened. The boy who looked out had shaggy dark hair, jeans, sweatshirt. He was the boy who had called to Liz Goldenstern when I was at her door. I remembered her telling him pointedly, "The *officer* is helping me." But if he was Liz's son, he resembled his father.

I pulled out my shield. "Detective Smith. I'm investigating a murder. Let's talk inside?"

His hesitation was long enough for me to describe it as acquiescence, should the question arise. I walked past him into a dark foyer. Through an archway, I could see the living room. Its oak paneling seemed to shrink back against the studs, as if humiliated by the cast-off Danish modern sofa and chairs scattered before it. It was one of those Berkeley houses coveted for its dark wood and charm, a house in which you were never warm enough to take off your sweater. It smelled of dust and stale chili. "You live here, Mr. . . ."

"Yeah. That a crime?"

"Impeding an officer is a crime. Your name?"

"Blaine Horton Morris. One four five, eight six, three . . ."

"Fine." I put the bag on a table and pulled out my pad for effect. "Now I'm going to tell you about the aspect of the crime I'm working on now. Have you heard about running shoes being stolen?" I glanced down at his feet. They were wide and long, like the feet of a six-foot duck. They were encased in the largest pair of grey and maroon-striped running shoes I had ever seen.

He followed my gaze. "Hey, you aren't accusing me . . ."

"Not now, Blaine. But someone has been making the drops here, and—"

"Here? Passing the hot shoes here?" He laughed. His teeth were too big for his mouth. They overwhelmed his otherwise nondescript face. "The thief is coming here? I'd like to see that."

"Fine. The buyer is coming. You can see him in a few minutes. Stand back there." I motioned toward the hallway that led back to the kitchen."

"That'd be a kick to see the guy come up hot for his racers and get busted. But you need my permission, right?"

"You're in a very dicey position here, in a house where someone's passing stolen goods. If you're not involved, you can show it now."

He drew those big incisors up over his lower lip. "Well, I don't think so. Maybe they need the money. The guys they steal from can afford it."

"You don't know that."

"Oh, sure. No one's panhandling in new Nikes."

Dusty Wilson would be ringing the bell any moment. I took a breath. "I'm not here to argue sociological theory. Theft is theft. It's your duty to cooperate with the police."

He laughed. "Lady, my only duty is to me."

"Well, then, look at it this way. Do you have classes you have to go to, papers you have to write, quizzes you have to take?"

"So?"

"Questioning about a case like this isn't over in one day. You can spend a lot of time coming down to the station and going over your story. And when you come, Blaine, it isn't at your convenience, it's at ours. If you happen to miss a quiz, well . . ." I shrugged.

"Hey, are you threatening me? My father—"

"Your father would expect you to cooperate. Your father wouldn't be amused to find his son involved in a ring of thieves. You're an adult now. We're not talking about your being suspended from school for a couple days. We're talking felony. Jail."

The blood drained from his face. He was thinking. I reached in my pocket for the note, ready to answer Dusty Wilson's ring.

I motioned him back into the hallway.

He started to move, then stopped.

On the deck I could hear steps.

I glared at Blaine.

"No," he snapped.

The bell rang.

I pulled open the door. "Dusty?"

A tall sandy-haired man in shorts and a T-shirt nodded.

I stepped out, pulling a shoe from the bag.

He reached into his pants pocket.

"Hey man," Blaine yelled. "She's a cop."

Wilson spun, covered the deck in three steps, flung himself over the rail, scrambled to his feet, and headed full-out for Telegraph. Pereira was twenty yards behind.

To Blaine I said, "Stay put or you're in bigger trouble." I ran down the steps, up the driveway, and through the tangle of discarded deck furniture to the hedge in the rear. Catching the top, I leapt, thrust my foot up to hook it on the far edge. It fell to the ground with a thud. It hadn't even come close. I'd done plenty more than that in training. I tried again. No go. I had no reserve left. Shoving my arms forward in diving position, I threaded through the hedge, the branches scratching my arms, the bitter-smelling sap sticking to my skin. The yard on the other side looked like an upscale parking lot. I ran around the clutch of Triumph sports cars and BMW's to the driveway. At the front edge of the building I stopped and glanced right, onto the sidewalk. Pereira had planned to herd Wilson up here. But there was no one on the sidewalk but four women students lugging books. I sighed. Chasing is not shepherding. If Wilson was not here, he could be mingling in the crowds on Telegraph or hiding in the bushes on campus.

Walking toward Telegraph, I restrained myself from kicking the sidewalk as Pereira had done yesterday.

I turned the corner.

Dusty Wilson was lying spread-eagled on the sidewalk. Connie Pereira was smiling.

CHAPTER 20

The station is old, the paint none too recent. Dusk mutes what colors there are. The institution-beige walls of the bullpen seem to press inward. The walls of my own office look scummy gray. But the holding cells are the worst, with their army drab walls, with the stench of urine that no amount of ammonia ever removes, and with the very public openness that makes a prisoner feel naked even under four layers of shirts and sweaters. The interrogation rooms are a little better, but after a couple hours in a cell, few prisoners appreciate the improvement.

Dusty Wilson was Pereira's collar. She got first go at him. Coleman, the Avenue beat officer whose case this was, had rousted himself from his sick bed when he got the word. He was on his way to take charge. The Day Watch beat officers were waiting for the other tenants of the Channing house to come home. But Blaine Morris was mine.

Morris bore scant resemblance to the cocky kid who had stood in the doorway, deciding he wouldn't deign to help me. Now he fidgeted in the plastic chair, nervously running his long fingers through his hair, oblivious to the fact that the combing was thrusting clumps up from his skull.

I sat on the other side of the scarred green table. Between us were the symbols of officialdom—the pen and pad and the tape recorder. "You're entitled to a lawyer, Blaine," I said, making a great effort to keep any hint of triumph from my voice.

He nodded.

"You don't have to have one, but it's your right."

"I know that," he snapped defiantly, then slumped back down. "I don't want a lawyer."

"If you had one, he'd tell you that you are in a lot of trouble. This isn't a school prank. You're not a minor any more. This is grand theft."

His mouth stiffened.

"It's not something your parents can get you out of now. You're on your own. What your lawyer would tell you is that your best chance, your only chance, is to cooperate with us."

His breath caught.

"Your house was the center of a theft ring," I said, stretching the truth. "We're going to bring in everyone who lives there. We're going to start off assuming that all the tenants were equally involved in this ring. Of course, you've already refused to cooperate once . . ."

"Hey, you can't convict me because of that!"

I let a moment pass before saying, "I'm not judging you. I'm just telling you the lay of the land. Now, anyone can choose to be the one who tells us about the theft ring. We'll remember that help. But we only need one to tell us. We'll talk to whoever decides first. Only one of you can help himself."

"And rat on his friends!"

"This isn't junior high, Blaine. We're not talking about who threw a spitball across the room. We're talking jail. If you'd rather read about your friends' graduation from a cell, then you keep quiet. It doesn't matter to me who gets the benefit of cooperating. I'm only dealing with you because you're here. When your friends get home, I'll see them."

He ran his big teeth over his chin, catching them at the edge of his lip and pulling the soft flesh in.

I doodled—a goose on a platter, though an uninformed observer might have taken it for a pigeon or an anteater. "There are what, four, five of you living there? I can tell you from experience that one of you will decide to help. It may not be you." I leaned back. "Actually, I'm hoping it won't be. You caused me a lot of trouble this afternoon. We could have blown the whole operation because of you. You're not my favorite person. I'd really hate to see a smart-aleck rich kid like you get the advantage of cooperating."

Again he pulled his teeth over his lip.

I flipped the pad shut, stuck the pen in my pocket, and pulled the pad to my edge of the table. Then I unplugged the tape recorder.

"Okay," he said. "I don't like doing this, but I don't have any choice."

Now I allowed myself a smile. Plugging the recorder back in I said, "We'll record this. For my use, and your protection."

He leaned forward toward the recorder, his face suddenly relaxed. It made me a bit uncomfortable to see how easily he had assimilated my offer of rationalization.

"Give me the full names of your parents."

I expected him to fuss, but he simply said, "Edward Horton Morris and Pamela Blaine Morris Dixon. They're divorced."

So he wasn't Liz's son. I'd have to check his roommates. "Tell me how the ring operated."

"She set it up. We just kind of went along for the fun of it. When she first suggested it, it was like a game. I mean, we didn't really think she could run a scheme like this. I mean she is, well, like they say, limited."

"How exactly did she run it?"

"She got the word that someone wanted a pair of say, Nikes, size 10-C. Some common size. I mean, she would never have taken an order from me." He glanced down at the table, as if peering through to his huge feet. "Sometimes the guy would take any of a number of shoes. That made it easier; it gave us a bigger pool to choose from."

"Where did she get the shoes?"

"*We* got the shoes. She just took the names of guys, or women, depending, from the sales slips in the running shoe store. You know the one, Racer's Edge."

"But they weren't all from Racer's Edge."

"No, it would have been too suspicious that way. We all know that. So every so often we just grabbed another pair and tossed them in the Good Will or something."

"Go on with the Racer's Edge operation.

"She got the names and addresses of all the people who had bought the shoe we wanted in the last week. There were a lot. I mean, everyone on campus and half of Berkeley must be going through running shoes like the streets are burning. She gave us the names and we followed them. If we could, we struck up a conversation, casual-like, like on line for a frozen yogurt. Then we could ask them about yoga, or dance, or meditation. Listen, half of Berkeley is into one of those things. You know this isn't a scam you could pull off in Lakewood, New Jersey. People are really big on leaving their shoes outside, here. I'll tell you it really made me think. Now I never leave the house without locking the door. Can I have a glass of water?"

I turned off the tape and filled a paper cup from the fountain outside. Flicking the tape back on I said, "Repeat the last thing you said so we have continuity on the tape."

He gulped down the water. "You mean when I asked for this, the water?"

"Yes."

"Can I have a glass of water?"

"How did you actually get the shoes?"

"Oh, well, we just followed the guys till they went to a class and lifted them. I mean we couldn't follow a guy if we'd already talked to him. Then we had to switch off."

"And then what did you do with the shoes?"

"Brought them home."

"And?"

"She picked them up."

"What did you get paid?"

For the first time he smiled and his eyes softened. "You could say we got half. Fifty dollars a pair. But most of the time it just worked out that we didn't pay her."

"You didn't pay *her*?" What was the four hundred and fifty dollars Heling found? "You didn't pay her because she was one guy's mother?"

"Mother?" He laughed. "She wasn't anyone's mother. She was our house cleaner."

CHAPTER 21

Aura Summerlight had been running the shoe theft ring. I greeted that knowledge with a variety of emotions: relief that Liz Goldenstern had not been involved, and at the same time discomfort with that relief; delight that the mastermind was so easily accessible, under guard at the county hospital, yet disappointment that this discovery lead nowhere. At least if Liz had been involved, this case might have given me a clue to her murder. Now I had nothing but the solution to a small-time theft ring.

As for the murder case, I was left with less than I thought I had before. I had hoped that Liz's son would turn up and bring with him the key to her killer. But as Ian Stuart had assured me, Liz had no son. Not only was none of the shoe thieves related to Liz, none but Blaine had even heard of her. Blaine Morris was the boy Greta Tennerud took to be Liz's son. Blaine had admitted seeing Liz once or twice when he left a note for Aura at Liz's flat or passed her on the way to the back room at Racer's Edge. But he hadn't gone back there to see Liz; he'd gone to meet Aura. (Why hadn't he waited until she came to clean his house, I'd asked in amazement. Rush orders, he'd replied, sounding like head of General Motors.)

What I didn't know was why Aura had hidden the shoes in Liz's bag and the money in her bedside drawer. But that could wait until morning. She'd still be here, and I'd be awake.

It took me an hour to finish the minimum paper work and sign out. In my IN box was a note from the patrol officer who had contacted Liz Goldenstern's lawyer. It verified what Laurence Mayer had told me about their financial arrangement. He gave her the building and paid her attendant.

I considered stopping for a hamburger, but it seemed too great an effort. Even eating ice cream was a more daunting task than I could handle.

I have a better-than-average ability to manage without sleep. I'd learned all the tricks in school, and afterwards, when normal people let all-nighters become memories of a wild or procrastinatory youth, I had stayed up with my graduate student husband. Then, I had started in the department on Night Watch. And now, working what the guys on shifts call banker's hours, I frequently found myself staying up too late and jolting awake in shock when the alarm rang. But thirty-six hours of chasing suspects, of psyching myself up for confrontations, or of being taken aback by ones I hadn't expected—of seeing death—had shown me my limits. When I got in my own car, it took me two tries to find the ignition.

I headed home, relieved that night had fallen and it was

too dark for Mr. Kepple to be dervishing around the yard. He wouldn't be traipsing after a power mower louder than the snoring Ott. He wouldn't be futilely trying to start his rip-cord edger. He wouldn't be scattering the fifteen or so leaves that dared to settle outside my jalousies with his hurricane-force power blower.

I pulled up in front of the house and walked up the path —or what used to be the path, and was now the bare earth I had tripped in last night—around to my flat. The yard was empty, except at the back, where there was a tarp with a long cylindrical object under it. Mr. Kepple was nowhere in sight. I smiled. There was, after all, some fairness in life. The forces that be were repaying me for last night's mishap. Tonight Mr. Kepple would be making the circuit of garden shops, assessing every redwood burl in the East Bay.

I opened the door and walked across the green indoor-outdoor carpet, ignoring the piles of magazines, newspapers, and catalogs that could provide for my every need throughout eternity. I should root out the ones I was never going to read and clear off the table. But they would still be there when I got around to it. For now, a quick shower, and into my sleeping bag before dusk darkened to night. (I should think about getting a futon. But that project would be there, too, when I got around to it). I turned the water on high, hung my clothes on the hook, and stepped into the shower. It was almost as good as sleep. The staccato spray from the shower head massaged my tense neck and shoulders, then worked its way down my back. I almost forgot to soap up, and stepped out reluctantly when the hot water ran out. Pulling on a nightshirt, I dashed through the kitchen and drew the sleeping bag up around my neck.

I had just set the alarm when a spotlight lit the yard. I scrunched down and pulled the sleeping bag over my head. The air inside was thick and hot. I thought of Liz Goldenstern gasping for breath in the inlet. I told myself to blot out that picture before it gave me nightmares. But the scene grew dimmer before I could will myself to action. My body gave that moment-before-sleep jerk, as if I had stepped off the sidewalk by mistake.

The whirr of the chain saw shrieked from the yard.

I jolted up.

The noise stopped.

Warily, I lay down. I could hear Mr. Kepple's footsteps in the yard. The tarp flapped. I pulled the bag back over my head.

The saw shrieked again.

I put the pillow over my ears.

The pitch lowered. Mr. Kepple was sawing wood. Eight-thirty at night, in the dark, and he was sawing wood! Now he lifted the saw away, its frustrated blades caterwauling.

Furious, I sat up in the bag and edged toward the jalousies. Opening the bottom half, I yelled, "Mr. Kepple!"

He lowered the saw back to the ten-foot log.

A light came on in the kitchen of the house behind us. Bert Prendergast peered irritably through the window, shut off the light, and stepped out onto the porch.

"Mr. Kepple!" I yelled.

Of course he didn't hear me. He lifted the saw with reverence and attacked the spotlit log.

I slammed the jalousie shut, grabbed my robe, and slipped on shower shoes.

"Hey, Kepple," Bert Prendergast yelled. "Cut out the noise!"

I stalked into the yard. The manure-heavy soil had just been watered. It sucked my feet ankle-deep.

The porch light went on in the yard to the right. To the left, the back door slammed open. I curled my toes to keep the shower shoes on and trudged forward.

Mr. Kepple continued to saw.

"Cut it out or I call the cops!" Prendergast yelled.

More porch lights came on.

"Mr. Kepple," I yelled from a foot behind him.

The saw bit deeper.

I tapped him on the shoulder.

He turned, his sparse gray eyebrows pulled up in wariness. Recognizing me, he smiled, turned off the saw.

"And keep it off!" Prendergast slammed his door. Two porch lights went out.

Mr. Kepple pulled the plugs out of his ears, oblivious to the scene he had caused. "Redwood," he said, looking back proudly at the log. "You wouldn't believe how much burls cost, Jill. I looked all over. I told you about my plan, didn't I, for the walkway. I—"

"Mr. Kepple. I can't sleep."

He shook his head. "Such a problem. My ex-wife, God rest her soul, used to be like that. Myself, I've never had any trouble. I just lay my head on the pillow and I'm gone. I—"

"Mr. Kepple. The saw. It's annoying the neighbors. You're keeping me awake."

His eyes widened in astonishment. Then he looked sadly down at the saw. I felt like I had kicked his dog. Then he glanced at his watch. "It's only eight-thirty. What's a pretty girl like you doing in bed at this hour? You should be out with your friends. I didn't want to tell you, Jill, but you work too hard. You should have more fun. You're only young once. You get old before you know it." Under the spotlight I could see his eyes misting. "You put off the things you want to do till you have time, and then just when you're ready . . . she dies." Swallowing, he looked behind me toward my flat, which, he'd once told me, had been planned as a sun room for his wife. "Then, Jill, you're old and all you have left is"—he glanced around at the sodden dirt—"this."

I put a hand on his shoulder. "Well," I said resignedly, "at least it will be the best garden in Berkeley."

"It will indeed," he said, turning back to his saw.

"Mr. Kepple, you can't go on sawing now. The neighbors . . ."

He smiled. "They're all gardeners, too. Bert Prendergast's the one who told me I should use redwood burls for the path." He pushed the plugs in his ears and started the motor. But his enthusiasm was muted now.

I trudged through the mud to my door and carried my shoes to the bathroom to rinse off. Then I put on a turtleneck (from the Eddie Bauer catalog) and a pair of corduroy slacks (L.L. Bean), stalked back to the bathroom for enough makeup to cover the dark circles under my eyes, rolled up the sleeping bag, and walked out.

All the porch lights were on again. In another few minutes the beat officer would be pulling up out front. The neighbors would be traipsing over to make their complaints. Mr. Kepple would be recounting Bert Prendergast's advice. And when the beat officer discovered a detective he could defer to . . .

If I planned to get any sleep I needed to get out of here fast.

A slice of redwood fell. Mr. Kepple turned off the saw. Spotting me he smiled. "Taking my advice, huh? Well, you have a good time." He poised the saw over the log and turned it on.

At the station, I hurried to my office, grateful to avoid anyone who might ask what I was doing with a sleeping bag under my arm. I spread the bag out between the desks, hung my slacks and turtleneck over the back of my chair, and crawled in, smiling. A sleeping bag may not be a bed, but when you're used to sleeping in one, it gives you a lot of freedom. One floor is like another.

My last thoughts were, again, of Liz Goldenstern. Again, I failed to push them from my mind and feared I'd spend the night dreaming of the murky bay water filling her nostrils. But I didn't dream of anything. I didn't even move until the light went on.

In bleary outrage, I parted my eyelids.

From the doorway, Howard stared down at me. "What are you doing here?"

I dragged my arm out of the bag and held it in front of my eyes, taking a moment to focus on my watch. "It's five in the morning. Why are you here? I didn't invite you over."

"Jill, you're in the office."

I rolled to the right and found myself face to face with my bottom desk drawer. "Oh." Rolling back, I propped myself on my elbows. "Mr. Kepple was sawing off burls of redwood for his path last night. The neighbors were ready to riot. I'd been up all the night before. I thought," I said, bitterly, "that I could get some sleep here."

"Oh, sorry. Go back to sleep." He stepped back to the door.

My eyes focused enough to take in Howard's appearance. His thick carrot-colored hair stood out in unruly curls. His skin looked drawn, and the dark gray under his eyes was not unlike my own. "Hey, wait. How come you're here?"

He shrugged. "Nothing to rival your reason."

I started to sit up, then realized I was only wearing a bra. "Come on, Howard. You've got to have some fairly good reason to be in the police station at five in the morning."

"Well, I thought I could get an hour or so of sleep." The parties Howard's roommates gave could be even louder than Mr. Kepple's mower.

"But I thought you were staying with Nancy."

"I am." Leaning back against the door jamb, he said, "Did I mention that she has a dog?"

"No." I was tempted to say he hadn't mentioned much of anything about Nancy, but grogginess prevented what tact might not have.

"Well, she does. Gander. I like dogs. I had a Weimaraner as a kid. He went everywhere with me. I was broken up for months after he got hit."

I nodded, letting Howard take what time necessary to get to the point.

"And God knows, my roommates have had enough dogs, cats, parrots. One even kept a tarantula." He squatted down and flicked my feet with his hand. When I bent my knees, he settled cross-legged on the end of the bag. "The thing is that Nancy's dog hates me. He's jealous. If we close the door and leave him out, he barks. If we let him in he clambers onto the middle of the bed. And Jill, this dog, he's a Newfoundland."

I laughed. I had had a Newfoundland as a child. I knew about their patience, their responsibility, their loyalty. But they weighed over two hundred pounds. Picturing the mass of black fur maneuvering Howard toward the edge of the bed, I laughed harder.

"Some friend you are," he muttered, but even he couldn't resist a smile. "I haven't even told you the worst. He crawls up, wedges himself in between us, rolls over so his back is against Nancy, then he shifts himself around, with a scratch here and there, and ends up with his mouth by my ear. And Jill, do you know how much a Newfoundland drools?"

I pounded the floor in laughter, with each let-up bringing new pictures of drool-related disasters in my childhood house, which only made me laugh harder. I rolled onto my stomach and buried my face until the chortling and gurgling stopped. Only then did I realize that Howard was staring blankly at me. His freckled face was flushed, but it wasn't with amusement.

"It sounds ridiculous," he said slowly. "It's like something sitcoms are made of. But it's really gotten to me. I mean, dammit, Jill, it's insulting to take second place to a dog."

Clutching the bag in front of me, I reached out the other hand and put it on Howard's arm. I knew him well enough to realize that he wasn't so much insulted as hurt. He might be more than a little shocked. Howard had always had women willing to give up apartments, lovers, or careers for him. His only problem had been choosing among these women. In his more serious relationships, the ones he hadn't told me about until they were over, he had had the women stay the weekend at his place. He had gone with them for weeks to Tahoe or Mazatlan. But he had never come close to giving up his own place and moving in with a woman before.

My teeth jammed together and I could feel my face coloring. I wanted to get up and stalk across the street to wherever this callous woman lived and smack her silly.

Howard weaved his fingers in among mine. "I feel like a fool," he said.

His hand was cold. "That's okay. I felt like one every time I complained about my divorce."

"It's not the sex I'm complaining about, though it's hard to get in the mood with the growls coming under the door. It's not even the dog himself." His fingers squeezed into the flesh of my palm. "It's just that there's this thing between us, and there's nothing I can do about it. Nancy won't even talk about it."

The cold flowed down my unprotected back. I shivered. Howard leaned over and tossed me my turtleneck, but he didn't let go of my hand. Awkwardly, I draped it over my shoulders. He settled back against his desk, his long legs bent over my knees. And we sat, not moving, with time, in that stillness, ceasing to exist. By tacit agreement we had never taken the chance of endangering a friendship that had been vital to both of us. But I could feel it all balanced on the tip of an atom now. It wouldn't require more than a word, or even a look. Just one movement.

It would be so easy, so comfortable to stroke his hand with the tip of my finger, to draw him in.

But not this way, when he was deflated by someone else. I sighed. "You know, Howard, a dog is almost like a child. So trusting, so emotionally helpless. You can't explain to a dog that it just looks like he's being replaced. How long has Nancy had this dog?"

"Six years," he said hoarsely.

"Look at it from Nancy's view. It must be an awful situation for her. Would you want a woman who didn't care about her dog? It doesn't mean she doesn't love you. You're just able to handle the situation better than the dog. Give her a little time."

He nodded.

His fingers felt waxy, like a mannequin's. He drew them out and, without looking at me, made the offer that had always eased uncomfortable situations here. "Let's go to Wally's and you can tell me about your case."

CHAPTER 22

At six A.M. Wally's was nearly empty. Howard and I sat at a small table by the window, and when Wally came over Howard ordered the huge Walleroo. I hesitated. I felt like I hadn't eaten in days. Indeed, the last meal I had had was in here yesterday morning. I ordered the Wallyrag and hoped I wouldn't be too tired and depressed to get through it. My voice was lifeless. I hoped Howard would credit that to my lack of sleep, or to mid-case blues. I hoped Wally wouldn't carry on in his normal way about my lack of appetite.

"So, how's the murder case going?" It was the same question Howard had asked me many times, even the same words, but it sounded hollow now. I wished I had begged off breakfast. By now, he probably wished I had, too.

But we were here. And no matter how out of sync, we had to make it through breakfast. I said, "Liz was killed between ten and midnight, night before last. That morning her husband-of-convenience threatened to drown the Marina Vista contractor at the same spot."

"Why there?" he asked, looking into his coffee cup.

"Ian Stuart, the husband, lives in Rainbow Village," I answered observing the view out the window.

"He's the guy who was railing about Marina Vista?"

"Yes, but helicopters are his passion. He says—and other residents agree—that he didn't really care about Rainbow Village, or Marina Vista."

"Then why the fuss?"

"Best guess is animosity toward Butz." I sipped at the hot coffee. "Then there's Liz's landlord, Laurence Mayer, who says he spent the night with his girlfriend."

"Good alibi for both of them."

"Exactly. He's a psychologist who says he's committed to helping people with disabilities. He was driving the car that put Liz in the chair."

"Whew! A little guilt?"

"A lot. He bought Liz the building to provide her a decent place to live. And Liz asked him to be on the board of Marina Vista. It's pretty clear that he and Brad Butz, the builder, aren't crazy about each other."

"Butz isn't a real likeable guy," Howard said, with a small shake of the head.

"I'm surprised he hasn't had someone from City Hall on my tail by now. Maybe he doesn't have as much influence as he says."

"More likely, City Hall's as sick of him as we are."

I nodded. "He's certainly taken his position at Marina Vista seriously. You'd think he was Berkeley's Contractor Laureate."

"Loathing Butz could be viewed as a plus for Mayer, and Stuart. But what's Mayer's gripe?"

"They both claimed credit for the special features of the building, like the outdoor circular ramp."

"Both wanted to see themselves as top dog." Howard

jerked back infinitesimally as he realized the allusion to his own predicament.

"And neither of them was," I said quickly. "Liz had the power. She's the one who got the permit to build apartments on the waterfront. It's illegal to put housing on fill. The consensus is that no one else could have managed that."

"Still, there's no question that both the shrink and the builder wanted to see themselves as the power behind the throne. There has to be a lot of prestige in this project. They'll want everyone else to know who Number One is."

Wally put Howard's platter in front of him with a nod of approval. And, showing hitherto unseen self-control, he said nothing as he set down my eggs, home fries, and toast. He even brought the mustard and ketchup without grimacing.

"I'll tell you the thing that's been bugging me, Howard. Why did Liz go down there that night? And how did she get there? It takes a truck or a van to transport a power chair, and a ramp to get it into the vehicle."

"Well, who of the suspects has a van?"

"Let's see," I said, forking a wad of egg. "Butz, the builder, has a panel truck with a ramp. Greta Tennerud, the shrink's girlfriend, has access to the one that belongs to Racer's Edge. Aura Summerlight and Ian Stuart have pick-ups—no ramps—but hers doesn't run, and his has a hot tub on the back."

"His has what?"

I shrugged. "We *are* in California. And Laurence Mayer doesn't drive at all."

"That doesn't sound very upwardly mobile," he commented before stuffing a piece of waffle in his mouth.

"After the accident, Mayer swore he'd never drive again. It was one of the promises he made to Liz."

Howard shook his head. "That doesn't fit with a middle-aged guy who's peacocking around his beautiful, young, athlete lover. Let me tell you about the male ego, Jill."

I smiled. This was a classic Howard line. And it sounded the way it always had.

"If a guy plans to spread his tail feathers, he doesn't take the bus to do it."

"When I saw Mayer yesterday morning he'd just run home after a night with Greta."

"Running home in the morning is the hard-muscle thing to do. Walking to the bus stop at night is not. Mayer may not own a car—I'm betting he does, but I'll give on that— but when he takes out his peahen, I'm willing to bet my . . ." He rolled his eyes up in thought. "What? You've already got my parking space."

"Skip the prize. When Greta and Mayer go out, you bet . . . ?"

"He's behind the wheel."

I nodded. "I'll check."

Howard shook his head. "I could have made a bundle on this one." He turned his attention back to the dish before him. Howard had ordered a breakfast fit for the Forty-Niners training table. He hadn't appeared to be gulping his food. But in record time his platter was empty.

"Hey," I said, "you're eyeing my toast."

"I thought you'd forgotten it."

I stuffed a piece in my mouth. Then, relenting, I handed him the other half. Without a second thought he ate it.

My throat tightened. With time, the time I had pressured Howard to give her, Nancy would deal with her dog. Or the dog would adjust to Howard. Then everything would be fine for them. There'd be no more breakfast sessions like this. Howard would be eating at home, with her. The beers after work, the lap swims at the pool—there wouldn't be any more of those. He'd be too busy buying charcoal for the barbecue. And the piquant tension that underlay it all, that certainly would be gone. Rats. I had done the decent thing. And I was sorry. Maybe there was reincarnation and I would get a reward in the next life—a big one.

"But, still," I said, "that doesn't tell me how Liz got to the waterfront."

"You should have made Herman Ott tell you that instead of making a big deal about Liz being married. That you could have discovered yourself."

"She had a driver's license, from before the accident," I said, ignoring the jibe about Ott. Ott was a sore point with Howard. In four years, Howard had gotten zilch from Ott. "The D.M.V. sent her one of those renewals through the mail, so it's still good—no restrictions."

"But with that kind of paralysis . . ."

"You'd be surprised, Howard. They make vans to be driven almost as easily as power chairs. Some have a board of push buttons, some have a knob on the steering wheel, some are driven by the same hand controls that work the chair. Liz could have driven . . ." I stopped, cup poised mid-air.

"What is it, Jill?"

"It's just that I've never seen Liz drive."

"So?"

"So, Howard, knowing what you do of Liz, can you imagine her choosing *not* to drive?"

He shook his head. "But she'd still need something to drive. You checked with the D.M.V. Nothing's registered. So, like I told you, Jill, you should have made this your freebee from Herman Ott."

"It was." I stood up. "Herman Ott laid it in my lap." I headed out the door. Grabbing the last piece of toast, Howard followed. As I reached the corner, Wally yelled from the doorway, "Whose tab?"

"Mine," we called together.

"No, Howard," I said. "My discovery, my tab." I held up my hand to Wally as I raced across the street.

"The damned thing is," I said as I crossed the freeway to the marina, "the van's been sitting under our noses the whole time. I had Murakawa go over every vehicle down here. It took him and his buddies four hours, and it's been right here."

One of the things that kept Howard and me friends was the ability to let the grumbler berate himself—without attempting to mitigate or join in. So now Howard sat silently, his knees pressed against the handle above the glove compartment of my Volkswagen, his hair grazing the roof with each bump in the road.

I passed the helicopter shop and turned right toward the docks. "The night of the accident when Mayer hit her, Liz had just gotten out of the company truck. The company," I said, pulling in by the boats, "was the Capellis. The truck was their van. Murakawa checked for any vehicle that didn't belong here."

"And that one," Howard said, unfolding himself from the car, "is here every day. Right down there." He pointed to a spot at the end of the lot.

I ran. When I reached the window of the van, Howard was already peering in. "Just as you said, Jill, she drove it like a wheelchair."

It took only a few minutes to discover the Capellis weren't around. Six forty-five was the crack of dawn for me, but for a commercial fisherman it was midday. Another task for Murakawa.

Walking back to my car, Howard said, "So Liz drove herself here Thursday night. Why?"

"And more to the point, if she was coming to meet someone at Marina Vista, why didn't she drive there? Why did she park here, a quarter of a mile away?"

CHAPTER 23

Howard could have ridden with me to the county hospital, but there's a limit to friendship. And while driving to Oakland at seven in the morning to spend twenty minutes waiting in the lobby of the county hospital when I interrogated a patient may not have strained it, doing that on a Saturday morning, when he only came into work to get some sleep, would be worthy of a hernia. But Howard was too caught up in the question of why Liz Goldenstern drove to the marina Thursday night to let go easily. He was still offering theories when I dropped him at the station, where he could make use of my sleeping bag.

I had, at odd moments, wondered what it would be like sharing my bed with Howard. I'd never thought it would be like this.

I headed for the county hospital and Aura Summerlight.

No one looks her best in one-size-fits-all. And when the garment is a faded blue gown that has been washed, bleached, and sanitized every day for half a year, it can't help but make the wearer look as if the bleach has seeped inward from the gown. When I had first seen Aura Summerlight she had looked like a bright but rather shabby Ghost of Christmas Past. At Liz's flat yesterday, her face had revealed just what her life was. Now, under the limp sheets in a crowded four-bed room in the county hospital, she looked haunting, like the Ghost of Christmas Yet to Come.

The chatter from a morning news-talk show flowed irregularly from a television suspended over a bed across the room. Beside Aura, a gray head was crumpled into the pillow. Each breath came with painful wheezes.

"How are you?" I asked Aura, already knowing the answer.

"Okay. They're going to release me this morning."

"Officer Coleman will come for you."

She paled, nearly fading into the sheets.

"We caught the boys last night. We know about the shoe theft ring."

She started to protest, but I held up a hand. "Now what I want you to tell me is what part Liz played."

Her eyes closed. Under the lids I could see the eyeballs shift to the right and back to center as she considered her choice of answer. When her eyes opened, I caught her gaze. "You're not only up for theft, but conspiracy. And if any of those boys is a minor . . ." I let that threat hang. "You don't have much to bargain with, but you can buy yourself some good will by giving me the truth, now."

Slowly, she said, "Liz wasn't involved."

"What about the boy who came to see you at Racer's Edge?"

"It was the easiest place to pass him the information. Liz was too busy to notice."

I recalled Liz at her door, warning Blaine Morris I was a cop. "But she *did* know, didn't she?"

"No."

I braced my hands on the bed table. "Don't lie to me."

"Okay," she sighed. "She figured it out."

"When?"

"I don't know. She didn't mention it till that day."

"The day she died?"

The volume rose on the television. The jingle for Florida orange juice spread through the room. Aura nodded weakly. "She said she couldn't have my petty crimes—that's what she called it—going on in her house. She said if word got out it would smear her and Marina Vista. She said she had worked her butt off for Marina Vista—that was true, she had—and she wasn't going to let anyone screw it up. So she fired me. She said she was sorry. I was the best attendant she'd had. We were friends, in a way. But she said she had no choice."

"But you called her to say you weren't coming that evening. Why would she have assumed you were?"

"We agreed I'd stay on till the end of the week."

"That's very civilized," I said with more sarcasm than I'd intended.

The gray-haired woman turned over, grimaced, and pulled the sheet over her ears. The public address system called for Dr. Something, then repeated the call, further garbling the name.

"She needed time to find someone else. I needed the money."

"You had four hundred and fifty dollars in an envelope. The few dollars you'd earn for the rest of the week wouldn't have made you stay."

Aura seemed to sink further into the pillow. "I wasn't surprised she caught on. I wasn't surprised she fired me. But she could have turned me in to you guys. And she didn't do that."

I sighed. Prosecuting her seemed like the final slap. She was like an old dog that's been kicked around so long it cowers at any approach. I could see her accepting Liz Goldenstern's dismissal as her due. What I couldn't see was her setting up the scam. "Liz is dead. There's nothing to be gained in protecting her."

Aura's eyes widened. "I told you the truth. She didn't know. Ask the boys, they'll tell you. You'll believe them."

"We found the shoes in Liz's bag, the one she has on her chair. You could have hidden those anywhere, on a top shelf where she'd never find them. Why did you keep them in her bag?"

"I didn't, usually. I never would have put them there if I hadn't been so rushed. I always kept them in the kitchen cupboard. But that night I didn't have time."

"What about the money? If it was yours, why didn't you take it with you?"

"I couldn't keep that kind of money in the village. How could I know who would come in at night? Lots of stuff gets stolen. Besides, I was saving to get myself a place. That's why I kept the money in fifty-dollar bills, so I wouldn't be spending it on beer and pizza."

"But why did you put it in the bedside table? It's one of the few places Liz would have looked."

"I didn't usually. I always kept it in the cupboard, where I had the shoes."

"Then why didn't you put it there Thursday night?" I asked, attempting to mask my exasperation.

"I didn't have time. I—"

"Okay, Aura," a surprisingly cheerful nurse said, as she reached for the curtain ready to pull it around the bed. "We just need to do one or two things."

"Can you do someone else first?" I said, trying to sound somewhere near that pleasant. "This is police business. It'll only take a minute."

She hesitated, then said, "I guess. But I only have so much leeway."

"Thanks."

To Aura, I said, "Why didn't you have time to put the money and the shoes in the cupboard?"

"I heard the key in the door. I was standing in the bedroom, looking at the money. I did that a lot when Liz wasn't there. The bell rang. I froze. Then I heard him call out 'Liz?' "

"Who?"

"The Marina Vista guy. Brad. I didn't have time to stop in the kitchen and fiddle with the cabinets. I stuck the shoes the first place I saw—her bag—stuffed the money in the drawer, tossed the bag under the desk, and ran out the back."

"Didn't you expect Liz to look in that drawer when she got home?"

Aura shook her head. "I panicked. When I got outside, and I had time to think, I figured if I came early in the morning before she got up, I could get to it first."

"But wouldn't she have opened the drawer at night?" Bedside tables weren't called night stands for no reason.

"No. She knew I wouldn't be there, so she would have had someone from the meeting help her to bed. She hated to do that, impose. When she did, she was as quick as possible. She wouldn't have asked for anything extra. She didn't take sleeping pills or anything."

I braced my arms on her table. "So you heard Brad Butz at the door. You panicked, and ran. Why didn't you just wait till he went away?"

Her pale eyebrows narrowed in unbelief. "I'm no fool. I know what a temper he has. I heard them arguing."

"When? That day?" I asked, straining to contain my excitement.

"No. They'd argued all along. Liz wasn't the easiest person to work for. And him!" She laughed weakly. "It wasn't a match made in heaven. But the fights—him yelling and her icy cold—they were about a week ago. But then they stopped. Everything wasn't lovey-dovey like before, but they weren't fighting. It was . . . you married?"

"Not any more."

She nodded knowingly, "Then you'll understand. It was like nothing had been settled but they didn't want to go into it. You know what I mean?"

"Yes." I'd lived in that state for nearly a year before I moved out. "But, Aura, if you only heard him call out one word—'Liz?'—how can you be sure it was Brad Butz? Do you recognize his voice that easily?"

"It wasn't his voice. It wasn't that clear. I heard his key go into the lock. I heard him jiggle it, like he always did. You have to pull back on the key to make it work. He never could remember that. He always jiggled it. The more he jiggled it the madder he got. I knew what he'd be like. That's why I didn't just wait for him to leave. I knew he had a key."

When a suspect emerges as the victim's lover, it makes him worth another look. When he's been overheard fighting with the victim, and has kept that a secret, he moves to the front of the pack. For me to drive to confront Brad Butz, a patrol car was in order. I stopped at the station to sign one out and headed to Butz's house.

His truck wasn't there, and five minutes at the door told me he wasn't either. I drove on to Marina Vista.

The sun sliced through the fog only long enough to stun my eyes; then the gray-beige sky sucked it back in. The musty smell of low tide seemed to penetrate with the morning dampness as I drove past the gray metal Calicopter building for the second time that morning and made the turn to Rainbow Village, passing the grassy field, the future sites of sports boutiques and soccer clinics. Rainbow Village seemed to sag and pale under the weight of the fog. Even the Rainbow sign looked like it had been out in the sun—sun we hadn't seen much of since November—too long.

Some of the residents might have been awake, but none was outside to see Brad Butz fitting a new Marina Vista sign into the pole holes.

"Mr. Butz," I called.

With one hand on the heavy redwood sign, he spun toward me, planting himself with the same belligerent stance he had assumed Thursday morning before Liz was murdered, when he was fuming about his stolen sign. Ever since Aura Summerlight's revelation about Liz and Butz, I had wondered what she saw in him. Whatever it was, it certainly was not visible to the untutored eye.

I stood a moment staring at his doll-like face. I remembered Liz telling me that she'd thought it would be nice to have someone around she could count on, someone malleable. Was Brad Butz malleable? No one in our department had found him so. But for Liz? She'd picked him as the contractor for Marina Vista. Knowing Liz, she wouldn't have chosen someone from whom she expected an argument. Since I had questioned him after the murder I had wondered why Liz went to the trouble of backing him for the job. It wasn't for his experience. Was it because they were already lovers?

"Now what?" Butz demanded.

"You didn't tell me you and Liz Goldenstern were lovers."

He glared at me. "You find that hard to believe? Does it surprise you to know that people in chairs have lovers? Liz had some undamaged portion of her spine. She had some feeling, some control. It's different person to person. Being in a chair doesn't make someone helpless. All relationships aren't based on dexterity, you know."

"Spare me the lecture," I snapped. "If you cared about finding Liz's killer you would have been straight with me yesterday. Were you still lovers when she died?"

"Yes, we were still lovers. We had the project and we had each other. Just because I don't go hanging my feelings out for the world to finger doesn't mean I'm not broken up by Liz's death."

"What were you fighting about?"

"Huh?" I could tell from his expression that he hadn't been quick enough to assimilate my knowing about the fights. He was playing for time to create his story.

"You had big fights. What about?"

He sighed. "What do you think?"

"You tell me."

"That jerk of a husband of hers. You knew Liz was married, didn't you? To that jerk in there." He glared at Rainbow Village.

I nodded, but Butz barely noticed.

"Here she did him this big favor, marrying him so he could stay in the country, and all he gave her was grief. She couldn't even count on the bum to come and get her out of bed if she needed help."

"Why did she marry him? Charity?"

Butz laughed. "Hardly. She didn't want to talk about it. I just figured it was a mistake."

"But she didn't divorce him."

"No." His porcelain skin flushed.

"First you told me you argued about him, now you say she didn't want to talk about her marriage. Which is it?"

"I talked. She didn't. She just said she had her reasons for staying married and I could take it or leave it." Coming up behind him, the wind off the bay thrust his halo of wiry curls on end, adding to his look of outrage. But the pain and frustration in that anger was so clear that I felt a rush of compassion. I could almost see the basis of whatever feelings Liz had for him. "I don't know why I bothered arguing. With that woman I never came out on top," he mumbled.

Filing that conclusion away for future consideration, I said, "Tell me about Thursday morning. What really happened?"

"Not much different from what I said. Stuart did scream about Marina Vista dispossessing the derelicts over there. That jerk didn't care any more about those people than he did about Liz. He happened to live there, so he wanted people to think he was running the place. But when he got closer, he lowered his voice so no one could hear him, not that there was anyone listening. He told me to keep away from Liz. It was real cheap melodrama. Ridiculous. I couldn't have avoided Liz if I'd wanted to. We spent half our time working on the project. But what I told you about him threatening to drown me, that's true."

"He told me you were using Liz. Were you?"

"Hardly." Butz shrugged. "It's the type of thing he'd

come up with. Liz only had to hear that once. Boy, she took his head off." A triumphant smile crept onto Butz's face.

"He said Marina Vista would endanger the people who lived in it."

His smile vanished. "I told you, I've lined up the best—"

"The zoning laws prohibit apartments down here. Filled land is too dangerous. Ian Stuart could be right. When the big earthquake comes . . ."

Butz threw up his hands. "Don't you think the city considered that? Before they issued the permits, I had to show them a soil engineer's report. Those engineers had our plans; they knew what the building will be. They insisted we sink concrete piers, ten inches in diameter; we've got to have them every six feet under the building. These piers, they go down till we hit bedrock; that can be fifty, seventy, a hundred feet. And I'll tell you, they're a pain in the ass. You drill down and the auger gets caught in a rusted-out car door, or in old tires—there are hundreds of them down there. That's what fill is—more junk than soil. And even when you can drill straight down without stopping fifteen times, you've still got to pour your concrete, and half the time the sides of the hole cave in first and you have to repair those. But when the piers are in, they'll keep Marina Vista as secure as any place in Berkeley. The guys in the building department aren't dummies; they insisted on that before they'd issue the permit. Besides that, we had the BCDC assessment, and the Environmental Impact Report, and the building department, and zoning going over our plans. Look, that jerk Stuart doesn't have the first idea of what goes into getting a permit. He's just shooting his mouth off. The plans for Marina Vista have been checked, and rechecked, and checked again. But let me tell you, Liz and I didn't stop there. Liz and I weren't speculators. Liz was planning to live in this building. So I lined up QuakeChek to go over the building. I worked there. I know how thorough they are. As soon as the building is up, they'll have their computers going over it. They'll have to okay it before the first tenant moves in." He sighed, looking beyond me, not to the city on the far side of the inlet, but into the waters lapping against the shoreline. "Even with all the hassles involved in her condition, Liz was still better to be with than any woman I've had. I've lost my lover, and I could lose the chance of a lifetime with this project. Without Liz, anything could happen. Like I told you, I'm the last person who would kill her."

"You were her lover, and her business partner. Ian Stuart said—"

"Ian Stuart! Jesus, how can you believe anything that guy comes out with? Let me tell you about him and his great concern for the tenants in Marina Vista. He didn't want this building here. Do you know what he wanted in its place?"

"What?"

"A heliport!"

If Howard thought Butz and Mayer were looking out for Number One, he should hear about Ian Stuart. And knowing Stuart, the heliport he had in mind would be one with his own planned helicopter company as its major tenant.

Butz looked back over the inlet, his color normal again, a smug half-smile on his face.

"One more thing," I said. "What were you doing at Liz's flat Thursday evening?"

His smile vanished. "I wasn't there."

"You have a key, right?"

"Sure. Liz gave it to me."

"A witness heard you opening the door."

"I'm not the only one with a key."

CHAPTER 24

I called the dispatcher from Marina Vista and had him relay my message to Murakawa.

Murakawa was waiting in the Spenger's Fish Grotto parking lot when I pulled in. Rolling down the window, I told him about Brad Butz and his protestations about QuakeChek. "He assured me they'd go over the building before the first tenant moved in. See what you can find out. Brad Butz told me he couldn't set a date with them yet. But find out what he did do. And see exactly how they're going to come up with this assurance. No one but mystics promise to protect people, much less buildings, in the big one."

"Do you think Butz killed her, Smith?" Murakawa asked eagerly.

"I don't know. He doesn't seem to have gained anything by her death."

"Yeah, but the crime, the passion of it. Suggests a lover. I've given this a lot of thought. I could see him going into a rage and hurling her in the water." He leaned further out the window toward me.

"But Paul, the killer cut her seat belt. That's not something that could be done in one angry swat. He'd have to have been virtually nose to nose with her as he loosened it enough to get the knife under it. Then, after it was cut, he'd have stood up and pushed the chair over. It's too slow a sequence of actions for passion. Passion is slap-slap-you're-dead."

Murakawa nodded. "I should have thought of that."

"You will the next time. What did you come up with on your checks of Laurence Mayer and Greta Tennerud?"

"Nothing on her, except a red Triumph, two years old,

registered in her name. As for him, there are two D.U.I.'s four years ago, and then the reckless driving when he hit Goldenstern."

"Just reckless driving? Not under the influence?"

"Not according to the D.M.V. files. And he doesn't show on any of the other files for that."

"But he told me he was drunk when he hit her."

Murakawa shook his head. "I guess he didn't tell the arresting officer."

"I'm surprised he admitted it at all, then."

Laurence Mayer pulled open the door to his earthbound cottage. In gray sweat pants and a striped rugby shirt, he looked prepared for a long relaxed weekend. His curly gray hair was dry now. If he had run and showered this morning, it had been well before now.

"What can I do for you, Detective?" he asked, as he might have of a new patient.

"A few more questions."

"Come in, then. I've just made a pot of coffee. You'll have a cup?"

The thick, inviting aroma floated through the doorway. "Thanks."

He led the way through the barren white waiting room to the tiny kitchen. "It's New Orleans blend," he said, as he poured the coffee.

From Community Kitchens, I noted. One of the many catalogs I had on my dining table pile.

"Cream?"

"Lots."

When it was ready, I followed him up the circular metal stairs to his airy studio and settled on the sofa facing the French doors. A plate, with abandoned flakes of croissants, sat on the coffee table. I smiled. "I would have pictured a runner breakfasting on steak and herb tea."

Mayer laughed. "Heresy! Tomorrow I'm planning a ten-k

run. So today I'm doing what's called carb loading—croissants for breakfast, pasta for dinner. And before I start the race I'll have some coffee. The caffeine will burn fat more effectively."

I nodded. "Was this part of your suggestions when you were counseling athletes?"

"No, it wasn't in fashion then. I don't keep up on the trends now, but Greta does. She's superb at guiding her customers, from footwear to diet to training schedules. In Norway, sports management programs like the one she was in cover all aspects of sports: body, mind, varieties of training, clothing, facilities, everything. Very thorough."

I sipped the coffee, savoring the first decent cup since Jackson's thermos. "Dr. Mayer," I said, "the motor vehicle department records of your accident, when you hit Liz, doesn't mention drunk driving . . ."

"And you wonder why. I've been expecting this." He took a swallow of coffee. "A little deception, I'm afraid, and a lot of luck. It's ironic how luck finds the least deserving, isn't it?" He held the cup between both hands on his lap. Looking out the French doors at the foggy sky beyond, he said, "My luck was that I hit Liz right across the street from Herrick Hospital. I had barely gotten out of my car before the hospital crew was rushing her into emergency. I went along with them. I was so horrified at what I had done that I didn't think of anything but her, certainly not waiting for an officer to take an accident report. In emergency there was a lot of flurry, coming and going. If anyone realized I was the one who hit Liz, they forgot it. By the time anyone spoke to me, they assumed I was a friend, a very upset friend. I waited while they took the x-rays and did the preliminary tests. I was terribly upset; I drank a lot of coffee, peed a lot. Maybe it was that, or the adrenaline in my system, or maybe just the amount of time that had elapsed before the officer found me. But by the time he gave me the breath test, I passed. He could have gotten me for leaving the scene of the accident, of course."

"I guess he realized you weren't making a run for it."

Mayer shook his head. "I was too stunned."

"Is that why you promised Liz you'd never drive again?"

"Right. I was stunned. I would have promised her anything if it made her feel better."

I took another drink of coffee. "But you do drive now, don't you?" I asked, reasonable woman to reasonable man.

With a quick nod, he said, "I don't own a car. It's very inconvenient for me. But I did promise Liz. I promised her a lot of things a good lawyer would have advised me against. As I said, the emotion of that time overcame any sense of personal protection, much less the ability to conceive what things would be like three years from then. The not driving was important to Liz. With time, she would have relaxed about it. But a few months ago, I finally decided that commitment was ridiculous. Liz had made a decent life for herself. There was no crisis anymore. There was nothing to be gained by my making Greta do all the driving whenever we took a trip. I haven't had a drink since the accident. I doubt I'll ever feel comfortable drinking again. I'm a better risk than half of the drivers on the road."

"Still, you didn't buy a car?"

"That would have been rubbing it in Liz's face. I didn't want to make a big thing of this. This way, just using Greta's car at those times, I could accommodate my own feelings without irritating Liz."

That was the best rationalization for sneaking I'd heard in a long time, but if he realized that, he gave no indication. I finished the coffee. Standing to go, I said, "Where do you keep your keys for the tenants' flats?"

He finished his own coffee. "On a hook in the kitchen, why?"

"Someone used a key to get into Liz's flat Thursday night."

"Well, it wasn't my key. It's still there. You can see when you go down, if you want. I kept Liz's key for her own safety. If she'd had to call me, she wouldn't have been able to get to the door." He stood up and started down the stairs. "As for keys to the other flats, my son's and his friends', those I keep for my own safety."

He insisted I see Liz's key, though its presence this morning proved or disproved nothing. It only showed that Greta Tennerud could have picked it up and put it back, with or without Mayer noticing.

In the car, I headed toward Racer's Edge.

Traffic moved more easily on Telegraph today. On Saturdays, without classes at Cal to draw students out of bed, life starts later. Now, at ten forty-five in the morning, the two lanes for traffic seemed quite adequate. The few people on the sidewalk hurried purposefully through the unbroken fog, anxious to get to their destinations and out of the unexpected cold. Only the most dedicated of street artists were setting up their tables or spreading their blankets. It was one of those days when the fog wouldn't lift at all. The gray layer that normally covered the sky was thin, like a blanket of fiberglass "snow" we spread out under the Christmas tree as children, snow that had been packed away and dragged back out each December for a decade. But today's fog was loaded with dingy lumpy clouds, like the pillows on a bachelor uncle's bed.

They told me at Racer's Edge that Greta Tennerud was out training, running up one of the longest, steepest streets in Berkeley to Tilden Park, through the eucalyptus-covered roads in the park, to the town of Orinda ten miles beyond. If I didn't spot her on the road, I could try the Bay Area Rapid Transit station in Orinda. She'd be taking BART home.

But I was lucky. I spotted her easing past a pair of chatty weekend joggers whose conversation was more animated than their gait. As she moved out in front of them, Greta

Tennerud looked like a representative of a different species, running with long, smooth strides on her long, lean-muscled legs. Her pale blond hair wafted out away from her tanned face and red sweat band. In red striped nylon shorts and a tank top that said "Racer's Edge," she was so superb an advertisement for running, and for the running shoe store, I found it hard to imagine her boss letting her go if she didn't win the Bay to Breakers race. But from the intense look on her face, it was easy to see she believed he would.

I waved her over.

"Can't stop," she called, coming alongside the window.

"I have to talk to you now. It'll only take a few minutes," I said, braking the car.

Without appearing to shift her tempo, she ran in place beside the window. "No, no. If I stop, I have to start all over again. I need the distance. Besides, I am monitoring my stride. Like most runners I advise in the store, I have a little"—she held her thumb and forefinger a quarter of an inch apart—"pronation to work out." She gave an amused, conspiratorial smile.

"I'm sorry," I said as I got out of the car. I was sorry. She was hard not to like, to root for. "This is business."

Her clear blue eyes narrowed in a scowl. "Excuse me, but my training, this is business, too."

"A murder investigation comes first. I have to talk to you now."

She let her feet settle on the road for a moment. "I am not a citizen here. I have no choice."

"You wouldn't have a choice even if you were," I said, for what it was worth. "Do you have a key to Liz Goldenstern's flat?"

"No," she said, beginning to run in place again. "There would be no reason."

"But you do know where Laurence Mayer keeps his keys to the flats, don't you?"

She hesitated.

"They're in plain sight. It would be odd if you didn't," I offered.

There was a long pause before she said, "You mean the ring in the kitchen? That I saw, but I didn't know what they were for."

I took her explanation with a grain of salt. I was about to thank her for her time when the odd omission of this conversation struck me. Even though the apprehension of the shoe thief had been reported tongue-in-cheek, it had made the front page of every local newspaper and, as far as I knew, was featured on the ten and eleven o'clock news last night. One reporter had interviewed Pereira live when she left the station. Greta Tennerud, who had been central to the case, should have been eager to hear every detail about it. I said, "Have you seen the news this morning, or last night?"

"Yes? Ah, our thief. That is fine work. My boss will be pleased." Her voice sounded strained. It was not the delivery of a relieved party.

"We've spent all night questioning the boys involved."

"The lady who cleaned house for them, she was the mastermind?" Greta raised her eyebrows in an attempt at amusement.

I nodded. "Tell me about the sales slips at Racer's Edge. What is written on them?"

"Their purchases: shoes, shorts, socks, whatever."

"The make of shoe?"

"Officer Coleman and Officer Pereira asked me these same questions."

"I know. It's a nuisance to answer them again. Did the sales slip list the make of shoe?"

"Yes."

"And the size?"

"Yes."

"And the customer's name?"

She shook her head. "No, there was no need for that. We

used the sales slips to keep records for reordering, not for payment records."

"Aura Summerlight was just a pawn, wasn't she? You let her keep half the money. But it was you who set up the shoe thefts."

Under her tan, the color drained from her face, leaving the appearance of a gray mask. "No," she said in a small, unconvincing voice.

I took out the card and read her her rights. She reached for the car to steady herself. I said, "Liz Goldenstern worked with the sales slips. As for the checks or credit card receipts, the checks went to the bank the same day you got them, right?"

She nodded warily.

"And the credit card slips you stuck in a manila envelope each day. It wasn't till the end of the month that they got filed, right?"

"Yes. Liz's friend, the mastermind, she did that."

"She alphabetized the credit card slips."

"Yes. Only she saw them all together. At first I couldn't believe she had staged the robberies." Greta was shaking her head in dismay, or what she expected me to take for dismay. "She *said* she stopped in to find out when Liz wanted her at her house. But she was always there when Liz was working on the sales slips and she had the credit card copies, with the names and addresses on them. I saw how she could have done it."

"But she didn't get the credit card receipts till the end of the month. By that time ninety percent of the shoes would be too worn to steal. In order to orchestrate the thefts she would have needed them the same day. She didn't have that chance. Liz Goldenstern certainly didn't. She didn't see the credit card receipts at all. Only you had that opportunity."

She tried to feign shock, but the muscles around her eyes and mouth were too taut with wariness to move quickly. The look of fear merely intensified. "No, no. Why would I do that? I am an alien here. If I break the law, you will deport me. I will be sent back in disgrace, to those long, long winters. I would be a fool to do that for nine pairs of shoes."

"You would indeed, if that were your reason. But when a runner has expensive shoes stolen, he doesn't go barefoot, he buys another pair. He buys them from the store he got them from before. Nine of the pairs of shoes stolen came from your store. So, the thefts mean that you sold nine more pairs. If they'd gone on, you would have sold more. Nine pairs at two hundred dollars a pair makes a difference in the store receipts. It's enough to show the boss that you're being there is worth the money."

She shook her head. "If I win Boston, I'll make seventy-five thousand. Why would I jeopardize everything?"

"Because without a job, a job that only you can fill, you lose your green card. You'd have to go back to Norway."

I loaded Greta into the car and called the dispatcher to alert Coleman I was bringing her in.

Coleman met me at the station and claimed Greta Tennerud. I walked on to my office and opened the door to find Murakawa standing in front of the small dark window, tapping his foot.

"Jeez, Smith," he said, "I thought you'd driven by way of San Francisco."

"It's only been fifteen minutes since I called in."

"Really?" He glanced at the clock. "Well, maybe so. But when you hear what I have to tell you you'll know why it seemed like eternity."

I swung my chair around and sat. But Murakawa continued to stand, shifting his weight from one foot to the other.

"After I left you I came back here and called QuakeChek. I was all set to ask them how they evaluated the buildings for earthquake resistance."

I nodded.

"But when I called, the woman who answered said they don't give out information on the phone."

"That's interesting."

Murakawa tapped a finger. "Just what I thought. So I told her I was a police officer. It didn't make any difference."

I groaned. Surely we wouldn't have to hassle getting a court order for this.

"I could have argued, but I thought the simplest way to handle things was just to go down there. So, I did. And guess what they said, Smith?"

"No idea."

"They said they do computer checks for earthquake safety."

I knew that.

"Not just on the buildings, like you said, but on the plans and their own soil engineer's report, and the latest earthquake data. They know every tributary and trace in Berkeley, whether it's growing and how fast. Seismic engineers are finding new traces all the time. QuakeChek has records of new traces that won't show up on the fault maps till the next revisions, a couple of years from now. When I asked them if their data is more current than the city's, they laughed. They said the most competent building department in the world couldn't keep up with every shift in every fault, much less the new traces—most of them aren't visible from above. The city has to go by the fault map, and by the time that's printed it's probably already out of date."

"Whew!"

Murakawa was grinning. He had a shallow nose, but a wide strong mouth. His grin took over his face. "And that's not all, Smith."

"What?" I was thinking Murakawa should team up with Heling. Between the two of them the suspense could be dragged out forever.

"They said a guy was in Thursday asking the very same question."

I held my breath. "Did they get his name."

"No."

"Oh."

"But, Smith, they gave me something just as good—his description. They said he was a short Caucasian, had limp blond hair, and was dressed entirely in shades of yellow."

"Herman Ott!"

CHAPTER 25

Herman Ott had been investigating QuakeChek! That explained his message—"Liz, you were right; only they are up-to-date"—on Liz Goldenstern's answering machine. And while I was up all night, racing around, searching for a key to this case, he had it. And at the time he was bartering with me, carrying on like he was selling his favorite daughter into slavery, he knew about QuakeChek. He could have told me then. When I was convincing Pereira to spend her night finding out about esoteric tax forms for him, he knew. And while she created order amidst the morass of his files, and I listened to Ian Stuart go on about the collective moving a helicopter up and down, and the throttle starting the craft just like a motorcycle's, Herman Ott was curled up around the QuakeChek information, covered with his clutter of blankets, snoring away.

I stormed out of the station, slammed down into the driver's seat, started the car, and put it into gear without waiting for the engine to warm. It jerked. I stepped harder on the gas, racing the engine. Then I headed through the fog to Telegraph.

Despite the chill, the sidewalks were crowded with students and graduates meandering from displays of stained-glass panels, to blankets of hand-tooled belts, to tables of turquoise jewelry. Parents fingered tie-dyed baby shirts for the future members of the class of '08, while the strollers that held the incipient scholars blocked the sidewalk. By Herman Ott's corner, melted-glass wind chimes clattered atonally in the sharp wind.

Cutting in front of a station wagon loaded with ficus and potted palm trees, I pulled into a loading zone, got out, and slammed the door. No space was wasted in this sidewalk commercial district. There was barely eight inches between displays. I squeezed between a table of ceramic toothbrush holders and one displaying hand-dyed shirts, shorts, and sweat pants, letting my butt bang against the latter. I had bought a forest-green shirt there once. Every time I washed it, it ran. Now it was running for the Salvation Army or whatever charitable soul took it off their hands.

Despite the cold and fog, the kitchen fans at the pizza place were on high, blowing the smells of garlic and tomato sauce across the sidewalk. Dammit, I'd even bought Ott pizza Thursday night!

I took the stairs in Ott's building two at a time, arriving at his floor winded. The couple by the landing was still going at it, their retorts keeping pace with the television chase music. I raced down the hallway, skirting two six-year-olds playing catch, and banged on the office door.

There was no answer. It hadn't occurred to me that Ott might be out. How could he not be here when I was so furious!

Before I could pound again, he pulled open the door. There was a sleepy look to his small hazel eyes. Crossing his arms over his saffron sweatshirt and gold-and-mustard-striped shirt, he said, "You've brought my money?"

"Forget your money, Ott." I shoved past him.

"What's with you? I'm the one who's owed."

"You've had a day and a half to toss yourself into that

heap you call a bed. You wouldn't have had that if I hadn't gotten Connie Pereira to do your taxes."

"It wasn't a gift, Smith. We had a deal. I kept up my end."

"Some deal! Pereira spent hours on your return. If it hadn't been for her, you'd still be sitting here dredging through scraps of paper and trying to figure out those forms. And what did you give us? A few asides, information so extraneous that we solved the case without it."

Ott shrugged. "A deal's a deal. Sometimes you get an edge, sometimes you don't. You shouldn't get so worked up, Smith. You don't see me down at your office, huffing and puffing because my money's late."

Pulling the door from his hand, I slammed it. "Don't give me this philosophical garbage. You and your flaunted ethics! Some friend you are."

Ott's eyes widened in true disbelief. "Smith, have I ever given you the impression that you and I are friends?"

"Not me, Ott. Liz Goldenstern. You were her friend. I heard her tape when you called and suggested dinner. That was the voice of a friend. And now your friend is dead, and you are so hidebound, so busy justifying your life by your own self-imposed rules that you don't care whether her killer is caught or not."

He said nothing. No muscle in his face moved. Someone else might have taken that for impassivity. But I knew it was the skill of a detective who'd spent twenty years working on the streets. And I knew, too, that I'd gotten to him.

"You don't need to worry now, Ott," I said, "I'm not going to ask you about that message. I'm going to *give* you something. But then I expect you to cooperate, completely."

His pale eyes narrowed. "What do you take me for, Smith, that's a sucker's deal."

"Wait till you hear it."

He shrugged.

"QuakeChek had stairs, but no ramp, right? They don't

give information over the phone. So Liz asked you, her friend, to go there for her. And you found out that they have the most current knowledge of earthquake faults and their tributaries and traces, that *only they are up to date*, right?"

"I'm waiting for your gift, Smith," he said, showing no surprise, much less interest.

"They told you that by the time a fault map is printed it's out of date. They said, in essence, that there are earthquake traces so new that only they know about them. And that's what you told Liz. And Ott, that's what killed her."

His thin lips squeezed together until the darker color was entirely covered. Still, he couldn't control the quiver at the sides. This was far and away the most emotional I had ever seen him. I could have saved him begging, but I didn't. I waited until he said, "How?"

I walked to the window and stared at its soot-covered surface. The building had been erected in the twenties. Sixty years of soot. There was only an air shaft out there, but I couldn't see the wall on the other side. That show of contrition, so out of character for Herman Ott, still wasn't enough. I could hear the bitterness in my voice as I said, "You didn't even bother to find out why she needed that information, did you?"

"It's not my job to question clients," he said. But his usual caustic tone was missing.

I walked back to his desk. Yesterday afternoon it had resembled the bedroom. Now it was back to normal, completely orderly, a desk where any needed item could be found in less time than it took to pronounce its name. It epitomized the Ott Detective Agency. Shoving aside a yellow legal pad, I sat on the cleared spot. "This is what I'm giving you, Ott. Brad Butz followed all the steps to get his building permit, including getting a soils engineer's report. Those engineers take soil samples every twenty feet or so. If two samples are the same they assume what's between them is the same. Their reports stipulate that. If the soils engineer's report had shown evidence of an earthquake trace, Butz would never have gotten a building permit. So we can assume it didn't. If the soils engineer didn't find a fissure, why would Butz think there was one, and why would he wait till after the building was up to contact QuakeChek?"

It only took him a moment to reach the same conclusion I had. "He knew there was a trace because he'd worked for QuakeChek, a trace new enough so it wasn't on the map. The trace wouldn't be right under the building, but it'd be near enough to make the city decide not to risk housing people with disabilities there."

"Exactly." I waited till he nodded. Herman Ott's personal code of ethics could be a pain in the ass, but one of its positive points was that he stood by his commitments. And that nod, we both knew, was his agreement to come in on this. He owed Liz Goldenstern that much.

"Fucking bastard!" he muttered. "Butz was a small time, barely licensed contractor. He didn't have connections in the city. Liz made him the Marina Vista contractor. Without Liz there would have been no Marina Vista. Without Liz there would have been no variance. He could never have gotten it himself. He used her to get a variance for a building he planned to have declared uninhabitable."

"And she realized that, or at least she suspected it strongly enough to call you about QuakeChek."

"Jesus. When she found out about this, she must have been furious. I wouldn't want to have been Butz when she got to him."

"Or vice versa, as it turns out." I propped my feet on the edge of his waste basket.

He shrugged. His gold and mustard collar scrunched against his plump shoulders. "She could have turned him in, of course, but it wasn't her style. Racing down to the site and giving him hell; that was Liz."

"Maybe. Liz certainly had a temper. If she had heard this

like you have, she probably would have taken off after him. But she had had enough time to formulate her suspicions. If she hadn't been fairly sure beforehand, she wouldn't have called you. So when you told her about QuakeChek you were just confirming what she already suspected. She'd had time to cool down and think clearly. She'd had enough time to call Butz at the site and make sure he'd be there. And she'd had time to consider what it all meant, which is what we have to do." I hoisted myself atop the desk.

"Mmm." Ott pulled his chair from behind the desk, set it to face me, and plopped down in it. A lemon-colored sweater fell off the back. "He needed the variance just to get the building up. It's not only the sole dwelling down there but it's the only building over two stories. Then when the building was up . . ."

"He planned to spring the QuakeChek report."

Ott leaned forward in his chair. "And the city would renege on the deal. I've seen these boards, Smith. The same five or six citizens who patted themselves on the back for okaying the variance to begin with would be hollering that they were the ones who were protecting the disabled now. There'd be enough righteous indignation to fill in the rest of the bay."

"And if Brad Butz realized that, Liz had to, too." I sighed. "But once the city canceled the variance, what Butz would be left with would be an empty building."

"An empty, six-story building on the waterfront."

"The question is, why go through that elaborate deception? What does he want that building for?" I waited for the answer to arise, but it didn't, not to either of us. "Let's shelve that for the moment. Let's posit that he planned to turn it into a warehouse."

"Why a warehouse?"

"Well, anything but apartments. The restrictions for commercial use aren't so strict as for dwellings. Ian Stuart wanted it to be a heliport."

"That's a little more like it. The thing is, Smith, that building is one of a kind. He could do a lot better than a warehouse."

I was beginning to be sorry I'd mentioned warehouses and annoyed that Ott stubbornly insisted on following this sidetrack.

Pushing off with his feet, he rolled the chair back against the wall, running over the sweater on the way. "This is a complicated, dangerous scheme you're suggesting Butz hatched. He'd have to have had a goal that made it worth his while. He'd have to have planned to put something in that building that paid a helluva lot more than the prospective tenants and whatever government grants would come with them. But with a building on the waterfront, the only one of its kind that shouldn't be hard."

"It won't overlook the bay, remember. It'll look out on the inlet and the city. For the next year or so the main sight from there will be the construction sites for those sports stores and playing fields. . . . Jesus, Ott, do you know what the plans of Marina Vista include?"

He made a "come" motion with his hand.

"The first two floors will have a weight room and a basketball court—supposedly for chair sports—a dining hall, a big swimming pool, and an outdoor ramp that winds around the whole building. What does that sound like to you?"

"A waterfront spa."

"Exactly. He wouldn't have needed a variance for that. A spa would fit right into the city's waterfront plan. Even if he had to reinforce the structure and the foundation, it would be a small price to pay for Berkeley's only waterfront spa." I jumped up. "I suppose there's no point in telling you not to follow me. But stay far enough out of my way so you don't create a loophole for Butz when we take him to trial."

CHAPTER 26

In the car I called the dispatcher for back-up, who would preferably be Murakawa. I waited until I got off Telegraph to turn on the pulser lights. While I'd been hashing things out with Herman Ott, the fog had thickened to a rainy mist, heavy enough to coat the windshield but not thick enough to smooth the path of the wiper blades. Even on low they squeaked with each arc.

The mist thinned the traffic—foot and vehicle—on Telegraph. I turned left and headed around the campus to University Avenue, slowing behind a Mazda driver looking for a parking space he was unlikely to find, then switching lanes, only to jam on the brakes as a trucker decided to turn left. I wondered about Brad Butz and the plans for Marina Vista. Had he intended from the beginning to build a spa? Had the idea come to him when he saw the soils engineer's report and realized it didn't mention the earthquake trace he knew was nearby? Or having known where the trace was, had he realized beforehand that there would be no evidence of it in the engineer's report?

The light at Martin Luther King Jr. Way turned from amber to red. I turned on the siren, cut around the Volkswagen in front of me and stepped on the gas, barely missing a beige Chevrolet making an illegal left turn against the light. Who were the backers for Marina Vista? (I'd have to have Murakawa check in City Hall.) They, of course, would be in for a hefty profit, having gotten the benefits of government incentives for building housing for people with disabilities—if we couldn't prove they'd conspired with Butz from the beginning. How did Butz find them?

I crossed San Pablo Avenue and kept on going west past

tiny Indian cafes, sari shops, delis, and corner bars. Recalling Brad Butz as I had first seen him—standing irate at the Marina Vista site, denouncing Ian Stuart, screaming at me —I couldn't picture him calmly putting together such an ambitious, such a risky plan as this one. I couldn't picture him feeling out the backers and risking his career, if not his freedom with each carefully phrased question. That suggested a subtlety that Butz wasn't likely to attain, not in this life, anyway.

I pushed that consideration aside. I certainly could see Liz Goldenstern discovering Butz's betrayal. I could see her dropping everything and driving the Capelli van—much as I was maneuvering the patrol car now, weaving in and out, hitting the horn, teed off with every dawdling vehicle. I could see her arriving at Marina Vista, pulling into the parking space where she knew she had room to get out, lowering herself on the rear platform, and pressing the chair forward toward Marina Vista at full speed. It must have been dusk when she came up to the shack.

But why, I wondered as I headed onto the freeway overpass, had she gotten out of the truck at all? She had no more mobility in the chair. As events proved, she was only making herself more vulnerable. When she planned to confront Brad Butz, wouldn't she have been better off physically, and psychologically, to stay in the truck and yell down at him from the window? So why had she chosen to park the truck by the docks and get out? To catch him off guard? Chairs aren't as noisy as vans, but they're also not vehicles for stealth. The small advantage the lesser sound might have given her would have been overcome by the time she spent coming up the unpaved road, completely visible to anyone in the shack. The only way to avoid that would have been to go along the path on the ridge, on the landscaped area that used to be the dump, and from there look down on Butz. That would explain how that twig caught in her sleeve. But why did she go up there?

As I headed up the back of the neck of the marina, past the squat aluminum Calicopter building, any euphemism of mist ceased. The rain struck hard against the windshield. Gusts of wind and the undulating pavement made the patrol car seem like a tiny fishing boat in a Pacific storm.

It would have been more sensible for Liz to stay in her van. Liz was no fool. She might once have been an impulsive fisherwoman, but she'd spent long enough in her chair to learn patience and planning. The Liz Goldenstern I had seen orchestrate demonstrations, the woman who had shepherded Marina Vista through the mazes of city bureaucracy, didn't fling herself thoughtlessly into the fray.

But she chose to get out of the van. Why? I turned left along the chin of the marina, past the field where the tennis boutiques and playing fields would be. To my left, the bare masts of the sailboats thrashed fitfully. In front of them was the empty space where the Capelli van had been. I passed the Marriott Inn and came to the end of the pavement where the macadam path veered behind the hedge of bushes up along the crest of the hillock. Walking, a man or woman would be spotted there with no trouble. But in a chair, only Liz's head would have topped the bushes. Not expecting her, there would have been no reason for Butz to notice her dark hair moving in front of the dusky sky. And she would have been too far away for him to hear the chair.

Of course, she also would have been too far away to chew him out, or hear any excuses he might have made. She would have been too far away to hear, period. Up there was not a place to listen; it was a place to watch. It was not a spot she would have chosen if she wanted to know what Butz was saying; it was the place to see who Butz was saying it to. It was the place Liz chose because she wanted to know who was in this scheme with Butz.

It was after dusk when she got here. Brad Butz could

have been home by then, he could have stopped off somewhere for a drink, he could have been anywhere. As I had told Herman Ott, Liz would not have driven down here without calling first. But if she called, she could hardly have planned on surprising him. Unless she told him she was coming later.

What was it she had said when I was pushing her chair? "It would be nice to have someone around again, someone I could count on to do things I need." Then she'd laughed ironically. "Of course, the problem with malleable people," she'd said, "is that what attracts you, attracts a lot of other people. You're not the only one who can manipulate them." That afternoon she had been waiting for Herman Ott's call. She'd been thinking about Brad Butz. She'd been wondering how much he'd been manipulated, and by whom. And when she called him and told him she'd be down to talk to him about QuakeChek, she knew he would panic and call whomever he'd worked the scheme with. And that's who she wanted to see.

The Marina Vista site was empty now except for the construction shack and Butz's white panel truck parked behind it. The rain dribbled down over the sign he had put in this morning. Beyond, Rainbow Village looked less rainbowlike than ever. I pulled the car up next to the shack, took my gun out of my purse, and strode the three steps to the shack door. Butz wasn't visible inside.

"Butz," I called. "Open up."

Nothing.

"Butz, this is the police. There's no point putting me off. Open this door."

The rain hit my hair and dripped down my neck. Butz didn't answer. I reached for the door and yanked it open.

Brad Butz lay on the floor, his china blue eyes opened wide in horror, his cheeks rosier than ever against his death-pale skin. On his white shirt was a ring of blood, which spread from a bright red hole to a brick-brown rim four inches away.

He was dead. But he hadn't been dead more than a couple minutes.

CHAPTER 27

Shutting the shack door, I hurried back to the car and called the dispatcher. "Five twenty-seven," I said, giving him my badge number. "I'm at the construction shack for Marina Vista, by Rainbow Village. I've got a D.O.A. in there. Get me an ambulance, code three"—(red lights and siren going) —"the beat officer, the Watch Commander, and the I.D. Tech. And have Murakawa or whoever's nearest here block off University Avenue west of the freeway. I don't want anyone entering or leaving the marina."

Judging from Brad Butz's wound, he hadn't been dead long enough for his killer to get to the freeway or the front-age road before I arrived. Once I crossed the freeway, I hadn't seen another car moving. There was a scabbily-paved road at the front of the neck of the marina. It had been used mainly for access to the dump. But now it was blocked off. University was the only way out. Which meant that the killer was still down here. Somewhere. Hiding in Rainbow Village or behind the hedge on the ridge, under the land-scaping of the waterfront park, in one of the junk boats in the inlet. Or in the men's or lady's room at the Marriott, cleaning off any signs of conflict. Maybe the killer had es-caped untainted, in which case he or she could be in the Marriott bar having a brandy or headed to one of the other bars along the waterfront. It was a search that would take a lot of manpower.

I walked back into the shack and, in hopes that I hadn't rubbed off any fingerprints when I opened it before, used a handkerchief to open the door. Brad Butz looked even more like my grandmother's doll as the waxiness of death seeped across his face. His bowels had emptied with the shock. The stench was nearly overwhelming. Perhaps that was part of the reason, but I felt none of the shocked sorrow I had when seeing Liz Goldenstern. There was horror—there always is —but my strongest reaction was anger and frustration.

Forcing myself to stay inside, I glanced around the tiny room. Cartons lined one wall. A desk jutted out from the other. Between them there was just enough room for Brad Butz to die in. I understood why Liz expected to see Butz and his partner talking outside. In here they would have been cheek to jowl.

I stuck my head out the door and took a deep breath. When I pulled my head back in, the stench seemed worse. I surveyed the room. No sign of a struggle. Nothing out of place. No empty slots announcing items missing. No messages on the desk. If there was a clue in here, it would take the I.D. Tech to find it. I walked gratefully out.

Distant sirens cut through the splat of the rain. I stood, thinking not of Brad Butz lying in the shack but of Liz Goldenstern with her head in the water. She had seen who Butz was talking to and decided to come closer. Because she was angry? Of course. But also because she thought she could handle the situation. And that meant the other person was someone she knew, someone she had reason to believe she could control. Someone with enough at stake in Marina Vista to kill, and enough hatred for Liz to taunt her by leaving her hands on the shore while she drowned.

The rain ran down my neck, sticking the wet collar of my blouse to my skin. From the bay the wind gusted, snapping the faded cloth of the Rainbow Village flags, spreading the thick smell of seaweed over the marina. I scanned the ridge, but nothing moved. Liz Goldenstern had seen Butz's partner. I had never been comfortable with the picture of Brad Butz leaving her to drown so close to the shoreline. But if Liz had called Butz and told him she was coming down here, why would he have called his partner if not for support? Why would the partner have rushed down here, have let Liz know who he or she was, unless he was afraid Butz would cave in and expose him? And unless he was willing to kill Liz? Of the two, it wasn't hard to guess who had done the drowning. But what had happened to alert that partner that I was coming here now to beard Butz? Who would have known I was coming?

Herman Ott, for one.

I walked to Butz's truck and opened the passenger's door. The floor looked like a trash heap. It would take hours to sift through it. But the seat held only a worn magazine—*Runner's World.* The date on the cover was February, two years ago. *Runner's World* was not a publication Brad Butz would save to browse through in his spare moments.

Suspecting what I would find, I turned to the table of contents. The third article was "Sports Complexes Throughout the World." The article I could read later. What it said about sports buildings was inconsequential compared to its presence in Butz's truck.

Anyone could have come across it, but the person most likely to have bought a copy was Greta Tennerud.

Had Greta been Butz's partner? Unless Coleman had come up with evidence, or forced an admission of guilt, Greta Tennerud would have been questioned and released by now. Could she have killed Liz and Brad Butz? She was in good shape. Throwing Liz in the water would have been no problem. She could have planned with Butz to sabotage Marina Vista. Her college degree was in sports management. She would be just the one to see the possibilities in Marina Vista. As an athlete, she would have been in a position to meet sportsmen with money, to cultivate potential backers. And, I thought, with a career that would be sputtering to a close if she didn't win the Bay to Breakers next month, she had to plan for a different future. Managing a waterfront spa would be just what her education had prepared her for. Running it well—and there was no reason to think she wouldn't do that—could lead to bigger things.

But what about the violence of Liz's death? Greta seemed too nice, too easygoing for that level of viciousness. I almost laughed. Easygoing was the first thing to go when life was hard. Ask Howard's drug collars if they found him as easygoing as I did. Ask Nancy and her dog.

Greta Tennerud was no scatterbrain when it came to managing Racer's Edge or planning her training and her future. She said she loved Laurence Mayer. Maybe. Love comes easily when you're twenty-three. How did she feel about the woman he had committed so much to? Did she resent Liz Goldenstern for taking her lover's time, for being the catalyst that caused him to forego a life of wealth and the chance to become a psychological sports guru? Had he stayed in the sports psychology area, there would have been no limit to what he and Greta could have done. Passion, and practicality, would have beckoned Greta to drown Liz. Cunning would have suggested the spot, so near where Liz's husband lived. Had it been she, using Laurence's key, that Aura Summerlight heard at Liz's door? Was she there to remove any evidence connecting her to the shoe theft ring?

Greta had motive, all right, but she wasn't alone in that. Maybe Laurence himself was sick of supporting Liz while he lived in a garage. He was already reneging on his promise not to drive. Then why didn't he cut his ties? No one would have blamed him, not after four years of providing housing, money, and physical help. And if he wanted a more gracious "out," Liz's moving to Marina Vista would have been perfect. And Liz did trust him enough to have him on the board of Marina Vista.

Aura Summerlight? She certainly lived conveniently close to the murder site. But what would she have gained by killing Liz? Liz's flat? If tenancy of a desirable apartment were a motive for murder, Manhattan would be depopulated. But that and the continuation of the shoe theft ring? To Laurence Mayer, neither would merit murder. But Aura Summerlight lived much closer to the edge. Her options were few and her perception of them limited. A nice place to live and enough money for a nest egg would be equivalent to a couple hundred thou in Mayer's world.

But Aura Summerlight, I suspected, would still be at the station. There was ample evidence of the thefts to hold her.

I started toward Rainbow Village. Ian Stuart. How angry was he about Liz's affair with Butz? Had he come to hate Liz as much as Butz? He might have hated her, but he couldn't divorce her, not and keep his green card, too. Had he been serious about wanting the Marina Vista land for a heliport? It was the only remaining spot for one.

But killing Liz wouldn't change that. It would only make his situation worse. He had to have a wife for his green card, unless he could get an employer and the I.N.S. to agree he held a job that no American could handle. But once he did that, once his invention was accepted, he wouldn't need Liz anymore. He told me theirs was a marriage of convenience. What had he promised her for that? Help? Money? Whatever, men had been known to lie. Fanatic as he was to work on his invention, he would have promised Liz anything. Maybe at the time and in the heat of emotion, with the excitement at the prospect of a place to work and the despair over the thought of losing it, he really meant whatever he said to Liz. But later, when he realized what he'd committed himself to, he'd begun to resent that agreement. After all, Liz had lost nothing by marrying him. She wasn't even honoring the bonds of marriage. That he wasn't either wouldn't have come into the equation. In fact, I thought . . . starting to move toward Rainbow Village . . . once his life took on a normal rhythm and the chance to work on his invention no longer seemed a stroke of good fortune, he would think about the money he'd get for his invention and dream about using it to start his own helicopter company. It wouldn't have been surprising if he became infuriated at the thought of Liz getting half, under the California community property laws.

It certainly explained that odd question of why Liz had married him. According to Brad Butz, she had insisted she had good reason for staying in the marriage. Half of his profits would certainly be reason enough. Perhaps Stuart had suggested breaking the agreement, and she—no fool—had refused. Perhaps she had even threatened to confess to the I.N.S. and have him deported. Liz was like Herman Ott in her attachment to agreements made. Once Ian had committed himself she wouldn't have allowed him to renege. She'd had to work too hard to mold her own life to forgive wishy-washiness in others. And if she sensed Laurence Mayer's waning commitment, Stuart's potential money could have been essential.

One of the sirens groaned to a stop. The first car was at the frontage road. The ambulance would be here in a minute.

I was nearly to the Rainbow Village gate when Ian Stuart's pickup truck, with the striated red hot tub catching rain on the back, sped out the gate.

CHAPTER 28

The pickup was going full out. I could only catch a glimpse of a blue wool cap as it flashed by. I ran for my car, hit the siren and the flashers, and jammed the gearstick forward.

The truck was a hundred yards ahead, its lights off. In the thick rain, it almost disappeared. I was tempted to step on the gas and close the distance between us. But the Chief had been on us about high-speed chases. There was nowhere for that truck to go. In a moment it would hang a left toward the city and "escape." In another it would come up against Murakawa at the frontage road. The flashers and siren would alert Murakawa.

Taillights flickered as the truck lurched left. A few seconds later I hit the turn, pulling the wheel and pressing the gas. The car skidded; I held the wheel steady; then the tires caught. I looked ahead. The truck was gone.

It was a moment before I spotted it, pulling in beside Calicopter. I hit the brakes. Now the car skidded for real. Bracing my arms, I turned into the skid, too late. The car slid into the muddy weeds of the center divider and stalled.

Leaving the lights and siren on to signal the back-up units, I jumped out, gun in hand, and ran toward the helicopter barn. The sandy mud tugged on my shoes. I tried to push off with each step, but my feet sunk further into the wet ground, and I had to yank my foot up every time. The rain dragged my hair into my eyes. With my free hand I shoved it back. The helicopter barn was fifty yards away. The hot tub-laden pickup was parked not by the front door but at the side, nearer to the huge sliding rear wall that the helicopters rolled through. Rain splashed through the broken window.

It was too late to count on the back-up. Murakawa would call the dispatcher when the copter took off, and then the dispatcher would notify our own copter and it would fly down here. By that time Ian Stuart's copter would be gone. And on a day like this, with visibility nearly zero, it could go anywhere, south to the Santa Cruz Mountains, east to the Sierras, or to any of the sparsely populated spots in Northern California. Then it would just be a matter of abandoning the copter and hitching a ride.

I forced my legs faster, pulling harder against the gummy mud. My breath caught. When I'd chosen a sport, why couldn't it have been running instead of swimming?

As I rounded the corner of the helicopter barn, the blue and white ship rolled out onto the tarmac. The whir of the rotor blades thundered at me, the blasting wind knocking me back onto my heels. Catching myself, I leaned forward. The maelstrom from the blades slapped my hair against my face. The ship stopped. In a moment it would lift. Forcing my legs faster, I ran for it, lunged through the wall of wind, and grabbed the sides of the door.

Something metal struck my hand knocking my gun loose. It hit the tarmac and bounced. My hand throbbed. Gripping painfully, I caught both sides of the doorway, got my foot on the step and yanked myself up, bracing for another blow.

But that blow didn't come. Instead the ship jerked up. My feet slipped. I clung to the sides of the doorway, frantically feeling for the step. The whirlwind from the blades whipped my hair into my face and eyes; it yanked my rain-heavy jacket away from my arms and slapped the collar of my blouse against my neck. I pulled my head closer in toward the craft. The seat belt lay unbuckled on the passenger seat. Forcing my weakened right hand to hold tighter, I let go with the left and made a grab for the belt. The ship jerked. Something hard hit my shoulder. My feet held. I yanked on the belt and thrust myself forward into the cockpit, landing with my head in his lap. My shoulder hit the control between his knees; the copter bounced, tossing me up in the air. I caught the edge of the dashboard, hung on, and managed to brace my feet inside the door. Despite the wind pouring in through the door slots, I could smell the liquor on his breath. He swatted my wrist with the metal rod, but there wasn't room for a swing. I hung on and pulled my butt under me.

For a moment we stared at each other—he in outrage, me panting too hard to talk. The wool cap was gone. His gray curls stood out, insouciantly mocking the deep, angry lines across his forehead and down beside his mouth. Laurence Mayer's eyes weren't bloodshot, not yet, but they had the blurry look of drink. They looked as they must have when he ran Liz Goldenstern down.

When I caught my breath I yelled, "This is futile, Mayer. Put the ship down!"

His long fingers tightened on the controls. "You forget," he shouted above the roar of the engine and the storm, "I've piloted before. I can handle this ship. You may not fall out now, but there's the whole bay out there waiting for you." His words weren't quite slurred.

"Every police department in the area is watching you, the highway patrol is down there, the county sheriffs. It's all over, Mayer." In the silence, I tried to recall what Ian Stuart had told me. The gearstick between his knees, the cyclic, was for steering. Then the tube to his left would be the collective that raised the helicopter and adjusted the motor. And the foot pedals controlled the tail rudders so the ship didn't spin out when it lifted. Mayer pulled up on the collective, too fast. The craft rose; it weaved to the left. Frantically, he pressed one foot pedal, then the other. I grabbed the sides of my seat and braced my foot against the doorway. The craft shimmied, then eased back upright.

Through the plastic bubble I could see the ground growing dimmer, shrouded in the rain. It was all gray-brown, no blinking red from the pulser lights. I couldn't tell how far we'd flown from the back-up units. I couldn't judge how far up we were. But the drop was plenty far enough to maim us both. The picture of Liz, in the chair, flashed in my mind. Liz with her back to me in the chair, saying, "I'm tired of having to arrange my time so I can have the catheter in or out, so I don't get infected, so I don't die." For a moment the gray closed in from all sides. It wasn't dying I feared.

The ship hovered. With one hand on the cyclic, the other on the collective, and a foot on either of the pedals, Laurence Mayer stared blurry-eyed. I jammed the ends of the seatbelt together.

"What did Liz have on you, Mayer?" I yelled over the wind.

His hands shifted the controls automatically. The ship held its place. The rain beat in through both door slots, but he seemed oblivious to it. He seemed to be considering his options. I was certainly considering mine. The longer I could keep him talking, the better mine were.

"When I hit her, I did more than the decent thing. I didn't stop to think of anything but the horror I had caused her. I was a fool. If I'd only had a lawyer, someone to tell me to keep my damn mouth shut. The insurance would have paid. Maybe I would have spent weekends in jail, but they wouldn't have demanded my life."

"You gave up your flat, your car, your sports practice. You gave her the building; you paid her attendant. When you changed your mind, she wouldn't let you out of it, would she?"

"Bitch. I'm working my tail off all winter, listening to patients, living in a room over the garage, and do you know where she was? She, and her attendant, went to Mexico for two weeks!" Suddenly he laughed. "But those two weeks were the best I've had in years, since the accident. She wasn't there, reminding me every time I looked out my door, every time I walked to the street." He shook his head.

"At first I thought I'd never forget. But I could have. I could have if it hadn't been for her."

"And then Brad Butz and Marina Vista gave you a chance to get even. Brad Butz had been your patient. He told you about the earthquake fissure, didn't he?"

He smiled. "Butz was a fool. Marina Vista was his big chance. I pushed Liz to back him so we could keep control over the construction. Then, after his bid was accepted, he stops in to visit at QuakeChek and decides to go over their maps. He finds the earthquake trace. And he comes running to me—what should he do—tell the city? It took a lot of talking, convincing him we could turn it into a spa, reassuring him that if he kept his mouth shut about his untimely discovery, the trace would be viewed as an act of God, and he'd be a hero for finding it. That and the promise of some fast cash. But he came around."

"And the shoe thefts, were they an added slap? Petty crimes that would lead back to her? A little irony, that people would blame a cripple for stealing running shoes?"

The ship lurched. Automatically he played the foot pedals. Then, as if he'd suddenly realized he was piloting again, he pushed the cyclic forward. The ship accelerated. The rain hit in from the front of the door slots, slapping my face. It slapped his too, but he leaned forward, his eyes sharpened under the film, like the eyes of an arcade player.

"Mayer, put the ship down before you get us killed."

He laughed. "What, and go to jail? *Back* to jail? She's had me in jail for four years. I'm free now, and I'm staying free."

"Mayer, there's no escape."

"There's escape," he yelled. "I'm making my escape. She had me paralyzed. I couldn't move, I couldn't breathe any more."

"You could have left."

"I had a practice here."

"You could have started one somewhere else."

He turned and glared at me. "Don't you hear what I'm

saying? She wouldn't let go. She would have hunted me down. She had a detective. She would have found me. Don't you understand? You can't hang out a shingle and say you'll guide people through their problems when you've got a cripple screaming that you're a drunk. Not when I was fool enough to put it in writing." He pulled the collective and twisted the throttle at the same time. The ship turned to the right, toward the bay. He pushed the cyclic and we moved forward. In another minute we'd be over the deep water, where a falling body would never be noticed, where a dying body could be washed out to sea, where better swimmers than I, under lots better conditions, had drowned.

I grabbed for the collective, but Mayer shoved me back. Reaching down under his seat he came up with the crowbar and swung it at my head. I blocked it, catching the end. His knee hit the collective; the ship dipped to my side, throwing me back, snapping my stomach against the seat belt. My head hung out through the open door, hair whipping in the wind. He wrenched the bar from my hands. The seatbelt bit into my stomach; my legs flailed inside the cockpit.

I kicked at his face. He swung the bar. I grabbed the end and held on. The ship bounced like an amusement park ride. He smacked his free hand into my stomach and shoved me back. I gasped for breath. The belt slipped to my hips. I grabbed for the sides of the door, but my hands slipped in the rain. Pulling on the crowbar, I hung on, panting, my stomach aching with each breath. Making myself breathe deeply, I pulled on the crowbar to hoist myself back in. Mayer let go. I fell back.

He reached for the seat belt. I slammed the crowbar against his arm. He screamed, came at me, pushing under my armpits. The belt slipped to my thighs. The ship lurched. I thought I could see the bay not far below. I hooked my feet under his seat, pulled myself up and smashed the crowbar down on his groin.

He let out a yelp and buckled forward.

I grabbed the doorway and yanked myself in.

The ship was flailing in circles. All around was rain and wind and gray. Below was the inlet. The faded vehicles of Rainbow Village looked like model miniatures. And all of it weaved like the drunken view through Mayer's eyes.

I reached across him for the collective. With more strength than I'd expected, he pushed me away.

"Mayer, pull yourself together. Get this ship down. You're going to get us both killed."

"So what?" he gasped. "If I die, fine." He jammed the collective forward. The ship dropped.

My stomach lurched. The blue-brown of the inlet was coming up. "Mayer," I yelled, "you won't die. You'll crash. It'll snap your spine just like Liz's. Do you want to spend the rest of your life in a wheelchair?"

The color drained from his face.

"Do you want to see your leg muscles waste away?" I yelled. "Do you want to lie in bed every morning and wait till someone comes so you can take a shit?"

He didn't move.

"Do you want to wait for that person to shove a suppository up your ass?"

I saw the terror in his eyes. I had him. It was a terror we shared. When I reached across him for the collective he didn't move. I eased it back. The descent slowed, but the ship waffled. "Work the pedals," I yelled.

Automatically, he played one against the other.

I pressed the collective toward center. The ship steadied some. Then I twisted the throttle and lowered the collective. The ship moved down. Beneath I could see the junk ships in the inlet; I could make out the windows in the patrol cars. I could see a tall guy in a uniform with dark hair blowing— Murakawa, and next to him Howard. And next to him the yellow blob of Herman Ott. I could . . .

Suddenly Mayer yanked up the collective, smacking his

shoulder into my face. The ship jerked up. With all my strength I pushed it down. The engine died.

The ship hovered. Below, I could make out the fear on Howard's face. We floated downward, like a balloon. Soft, cushioned.

The jarring impact of the crash was a shock.

CHAPTER 29

In the distance I could hear a low moan. Beneath the Plexiglas bubble of the helicopter, the blue-brown water came up fast, slapping me, and the wave broke over Cousin John's head as it slammed into the sandbar. I stared out through his eyes. I tried to wiggle his toes, to stretch his fingers. Nothing moved. His body lay leaden. I opened his mouth to scream, but the sound that came out was more like a moan.

"Jill."

I could feel a hand on my arm. My eyes opened. I stared at the strange beige wall that wasn't sand, at Howard, and then my eyes closed.

I don't know how many times I did that, running through that awful dream, waking up to find Howard, or Pereira, or Murakawa—but mostly Howard—and falling back to sleep. When I woke for real a nurse told me it was Monday. I had been in the hospital nearly two days. My whole body ached, every joint, my head, neck, even my feet throbbed. I flexed my fingers and felt the pain. I wiggled my toes, paused, and wiggled them again to feel the pain once more. Tears of relief rolled down my cheeks.

It was late in the morning when I woke again, flexed and wiggled again, sighed again with relief.

Murakawa was sitting in the chair beside my bed. For once his skin looked gray and his eyes had none of their usual sharpness.

"I guess I'll live, huh?" I said.

"Don't worry, Smith, you're tough. I've talked to the doctor. I've seen your x-rays. You didn't even break anything. Most people in a crash like that would have snapped a femur or a tibia or crushed their ilium. But you're fine."

"I don't feel fine," I said, ungraciously. "It hurts every time I breathe."

"Ah, bruised sternum. That's common in an accident like yours, where you didn't have a shoulder harness." Murakawa glanced hungrily at my chart at the foot of the bed. "You've probably got a whiplash, and bruised your abdominal muscles and your transverse colon. And there's always the danger of knee damage in an accident like this. The lateral collateral ligaments could—"

"Enough, Murakawa. I can figure out myself what all I've bruised. But as long as it's not permanent, it's okay. Pain I can stand, admittedly not without complaint, but . . ." I started to shrug, but my neck hurt too much. "How's Laurence Mayer?"

"Not so hot. He did break a humerus and cracked the ribs at T-eight and nine. He's sedated, but he's not too out-of-it to talk. I made sure he knew his rights. He didn't want a lawyer. He just wanted to talk."

I glanced past Murakawa to the window. The fog was just lifting. The room, I noticed, with relief, was private. No snoring roommates like Aura Summerlight had. "Did Mayer admit to the murders?"

"He babbled about everything. He said how clever he was to come up with the scheme to turn Marina Vista into a spa, when all Butz could do was panic. He carried on about the two backers he found, the sports guys with the shady reputations, and how they put up sixty per cent of the funds. Seems the lure of good press from helping the handicapped wasn't so great as the promise of a big return on their invest-ment. He kept saying that they'd take care of him and of Butz, that they knew how to treat friends. He kept telling me what a jerk Ian Stuart was and that when Liz was com-plaining about him, and how his obsession with helicopters made him totally unreliable for anything else, she told him about Stuart's ignition key being stuck in place and Stuart thinking he could protect his truck by locking the door. I must have heard that story five times.

"And Brad Butz, Mayer kept calling him wishy-washy, and a fool, and saying how easy he was to push around. But when he started on Liz Goldenstern, he was really vicious. You'd have thought she maimed him, rather than the other way around. Oh, Mayer admitted killing her—he stood and watched her struggle as she drowned. To hear him tell it, he was perfectly justified because she ruined his life. And Butz, well, according to Mayer, killing him was just a business necessity. He didn't even enjoy that, though he didn't seem like he minded it either. According to him, he was just do-ing what he had to."

"He promised her too much when he hit her, and when she wouldn't let him out of it, he felt more and more abused."

Murakawa nodded. "I've known guys like that. I had a friend whose mechanic took his car for a test drive and totaled it. He felt awful. He promised to find her another car just like hers—it was a sixty-eight Volvo—you can't get them like that anymore. He spent the first week looking all over the area. The second week he was waiting for replies. And after a month, he wouldn't return her phone calls. Of course, that's hardly the same as drowning Liz Golden-stern," Murakawa added awkwardly.

I nodded.

"But you know, Jill, one thing I kept wondering about was Brad Butz. I mean here he was Liz's lover, and they're working together planning for Marina Vista, and all of a sudden he discovers the earthquake fissure. Well, why didn't he tell her, instead of going to Mayer?"

I sighed. "My guess—and I'd stake a lot on this one—is that he didn't want her to think he was worse than malleable, that he was incompetent, too. If he'd told her, she would have said 'Maybe you didn't know about this earthquake trace, but you knew QuakeChek had those maps all along, why didn't you check there sooner? Why did you let me spend all this time on a project that can't be built?' He would have hoped that Mayer, his former shrink, would be more understanding, and would find him a way out, like he had in therapy."

"Well, even if a judge throws out Mayer's confession, we've still got him cold. We got warrants and went through his flat and safe deposit box. We've got a copy of his confession to Liz that he was drunk when he hit her. And we found papers giving him ten percent of Marina Vista as a sort of finder's fee. They're signed by his two backers, who, it seems, put up sixty percent of the Marina Vista money."

"So we're in good shape. What about the shoe thefts? Did he admit to masterminding them?"

He shook his head. "I thought Greta Tennerud was behind those."

I turned halfway onto my side, creating a new line of pain. "I did too, for a while. But the case against her never quite held water. It would have been such an elaborate scheme just to raise the store's profits a few hundred dollars. And there was no assurance the extra sales would have been credited to her. When the victims replaced their shoes, they wouldn't have needed her expertise. They could deal with any sales clerk."

He nodded.

"You know, Paul, I was suspicious of Greta having access to Laurence's keys. But it worked the other way around. It was Laurence who made use of Greta. He waited in the back room of Racer's Edge for Greta to finish work. While he was there there was nothing to stop him picking up the charge card copies from that day—Greta waited until the end of the day to stuff them in the manila envelope. The day's receipts were there, so he could get the name from the credit card and the shoe size from the receipt."

"But why, Jill?" Connie Pereira came up beside Murakawa. She held up a bunch of tulips.

"Thanks."

"Thank me later. Now go on about Mayer and the shoe thefts."

"Because he realized that sooner or later the ring would get broken and the trail would lead back to Aura Summerlight. Aura's a transient. If she'd had an hour's notice, she'd have been gone. It was only because she was overwhelmed by Liz's murder that she didn't spend her four fifty getting her truck in running order and head back to Santa Fe."

"But why would Mayer want to set her up?" Connie asked.

"To undermine Liz, and to set *her* up. He's a bright guy. He knew we'd conclude that Aura didn't orchestrate the thefts. Once we'd passed on her, the trail would have pointed to Liz. Maybe we'd never have gotten proof, but we would have hassled her. And even if we dropped the case for lack of evidence, the stigma would be there. The people on those city boards and committees she dealt with, they'd wonder if she really was a thief."

"But wasn't he afraid Aura Summerlight would have ratted on him? . . . Oh," Murakawa said, as the answer occurred to him. "Who would believe her against him, huh?"

"And if she felt pressured, she would have left. He could have given her money for a plane ticket."

Pereira nodded, knowingly. Looking down at the tulips in her hand, she said, "Let me get these in water." She pulled the rolling bed table around. "Okay if I add them to these daffodils?"

"Sure." I said. "Who brought those? I don't remember anyone with them."

"Jill, your friends have been in and out of here ever since you arrived. It's been nearly two days since the accident. Howard didn't even go home to sleep."

"Are the daffodils from him?"

Connie plucked a note from the styrofoam container.

"Read," I said.

"There's no name. It just says 'from a friend of a friend.' Who's that?"

I smiled. "A secret admirer."

"Come on."

"No," I said. "You see me with unsightly bruises, with my hair matted to my head. Murakawa's been speculating about the prognosis of bones and ligaments I didn't know I had. I'm entitled to a few secrets."

A nurse walked in and planted herself at the foot of the bed. Smiling at Murakawa and Pereira, she said, "So you're back again. I'm glad she's awake this time." To me, she added, "You've got good friends here."

"I know."

"But I'm afraid I'm going to have to throw you two out now. It's time to scrub her down."

"Okay," Pereira said, "but, Jill, make the most of this rest. You've got a lot of paperwork waiting when you get back to the station."

"When do you think that'll be?" I asked, aiming the question at the nurse.

But it was Murakawa who said, "A couple of weeks anyway. Maybe more."

"Inspector Doyle said he'd send someone out to get your statements on both cases. You can believe they'll be here before a couple of weeks!" Pereira added, as they left.

When I woke the next time, the light was on. The sky outside the window was darkening. Howard was sprawled in the chair next to the bed, his eyes half-closed, his chin nearly on his chest.

"Howard, how long have you been here?"

He shrugged. "I don't know. What time is it, five? How many hours is that? But I haven't been here all the time. I had a trap set at University and San Pablo this afternoon. Took me a month and a half to get it set."

I smiled. My cheeks hurt. "And you thought you should be there to snap it, huh?"

"I figured you'd understand."

I smiled again, carefully. "Yeah."

He put his hand over mine. His jaw tightened. "You know, Jill, when that copter come down, I could see you through the glass. I don't ever want to see something like that again."

"I'll try not to do it again. I've run the nightmare about Cousin John diving through the wave and breaking his neck so many times since the crash that it's beginning not to terrify me. Well, not as much as it did."

He squeezed my hand. "You were very lucky. It could have been a lot worse."

"I know. Murakawa laid out the possibilities, graphically." It was not a topic I wanted to pursue. "What's the plant on the floor, the one with flowers?"

As he turned toward the wall, I could see his face relaxing. "The one the size of a Christmas tree? Someone has a lot of faith in your recovery if he thinks you'll be able to lug out something that size." He pushed himself up and walked over to it. "Rhododendron, the tag says. Do you want me to read the card?"

"It can only be from one person, but go ahead, read."

" 'Get well soon. We'll put your bush in the northwest corner of the yard. Don't worry about being bored while you recover. You can help me plan the rest as soon as you get home.' It's signed 'Charles Kepple.' Wait, there's more. 'P.S.—The redwood burls are the right touch.' " Howard turned the card over. " 'I'm thinking of extending the path across the yard. It could end at the rhododendron. I can have the trees hauled over and cut them during the day when the neighbors won't kick up such a fuss and . . .' " Howard grinned. "He ran out of room."

"Oy, and I thought I was sick before. And Murakawa said I'd be home at least a couple weeks."

Howard laughed.

"Howard, I know this man. He won't stop with one path. He'll cover the entire yard in burls."

Howard laughed harder.

"Then he'll think about a deck, maybe two. It's a big yard. Two decks with two or three levels each, with flower boxes and a grape arbor over one, or both. Howard, the chain saw will never be still."

Howard tried to control himself.

"The neighbors will be screaming. The beat officer will be there so often he'll think it's Wally's. Howard, I can't live like that."

His control gave way. A laugh burst out.

"A little lapse of bedside manner, here?" I demanded.

"You're right," he said struggling to control himself. "What can I do for the sick lady?"

"You serious?"

"Of course." He looked serious.

"Okay, its a big favor."

"I'm a big guy. And a nice one!" he added with a grin.

"We'll see how nice. Since you're not using your room at your house now, will you store my stuff there? I don't have much, if you don't count the newspapers and catalogs. And those you can throw out. Or maybe Nancy'd like the *Sporting Dog*. It's not one I'm likely to use."

"Sure. Consider it hauled." But he looked uncomfortable. "What about you?"

"I'm going to call Mr. Kepple, tell him that I'll be convalescing on the beach and that he can keep the burls in my

flat. I guarantee you, by the time you take him this rhododendron, he'll have every inch of my flat filled with burls
and saws and bags and boxes and hoses and mowers and
blowers and . . ."

He held up a hand. "I get the idea. You don't mind, do
you, if I put some of your stuff in the attic?"

"No, but it should all go in your room."

"Not if I have to sleep there."

Before the accident, I might have asked him to explain
that. I might have said that things between him and Nancy
would look better when he got some sleep. But a glimpse of
mortality doesn't always make one a better person. I said,
"The attic's fine."

Howard leaned forward, taking both my hands in his.
"Now that we're through discussing what I'll do for you,
let's talk about what you'll give me if I don't tell anyone
about Herman Ott's daffodils."